AS YOU WISH

BOOK THREE

HOW TO BE THE BEST DAMN FAERY GODMOTHER IN THE WORLD (OR DIE TRYING)

HELEN HARPER

 Created with Vellum

CHAPTER
ONE

I gave the short purple-haired faery in front of me my very best smile. 'So,' I said, 'he's all fixed now then, right? I won't have any more problems with him?'

'He's exactly the same as he was before. I haven't done anything.'

My smile vanished. He'd been in with her for almost an hour. 'Why not?'

She rolled her eyes. 'Don't get your knickers in a twist,' she grumbled. 'You might be a faery godmother but that doesn't mean I have to kowtow to your every demand.'

'I wasn't...' I grimaced and took a deep breath. I needed her on my side. Desperately. 'I didn't mean to make demands. And I'm not trying to take advantage of you. I just want to help this little guy.'

She saw right through me. 'There's nothing wrong with him. He needs to lose some weight so you should stop over-feeding him. Other than that, he's perfectly healthy. There's nothing for me to do.'

Pumpkin waddled over and nudged her hand. She reached down absent-mindedly, allowing the little Jack Russell terrier to give her a delicate lick with his pink tongue. Compared to the looks of hatred and quiet growls I normally received from him, this was effusive enthusiasm indeed.

The animal faery patted his head. 'He's very friendly. I don't know what you're worrying about.'

'He hasn't let me touch him for two weeks!'

'Maybe he doesn't like your shampoo. Try using something different.'

I threw my hands up in frustration. 'He pees on everything.'

She shrugged. 'He's nervous and is merely marking his territory. He'll get over it.'

'I have to request a new magic wand on Monday because he chewed mine last night and left splinters all over the carpet. I'm still picking them out of the soles of my feet.'

'You shouldn't have left it lying around. And perhaps,' she added pointedly, 'you should invest in a vacuum cleaner.'

I sighed. 'He hates me. He blames me for the death of his previous owner, and he spends every minute of every day plotting revenge.'

It was true. His owner, an elderly woman called Rose Blairmont, had been my client. When I'd first met her, she was being hunted down by a crooked politician called Art Adwell because she possessed evidence that he'd employed her to assassinate another Member of Parliament. Adwell had almost succeeded in killing both of us but it was actually an accidental shot from Ethan, the leader of the trolls, that had ended Rose's life.

The only bright side in any of this was that I'd managed to get hold of the evidence needed to put Adwell away. I'd passed it on to a tabloid newspaper and now he was behind bars and awaiting trial. It couldn't have happened to a nicer guy. Tragically, Rose hadn't lived long enough to witness his fall from grace.

Pumpkin lifted his head and blinked at me innocently. The damned creature deserved to win an Oscar for his efforts.

'If things are truly that bad, you could always re-home him.'

Pumpkin chose that moment to let out a tiny, plaintive whine. My eyes narrowed. He knew exactly what he was doing.

The animal faery, who really should have known better, reached into her pocket and pulled out a tasty-looking treat. 'Aw, darling,' she murmured, bending down to scratch his chin and give him the bone-shaped chew.

How was it that she could separate my half-baked lies from the truth in an instant but could let one little dog manipulate her so? Not for the first time, I acknowledged that I could learn a lot from my new companion. If only he'd let me.

'I can't re-home him. His last owner was a client. And her wish was,' I waved my hands in the air in vague explanation, 'this.'

'Ah.' The animal faery squinted upwards and gave me an arch look. 'Just give him time. He'll settle down.'

'That's your advice? Time? What about some helpful animal magic?'

'Pets aren't usually our remit,' she told me gently. 'They have owners to take care of their needs.'

'They're still animals,' I mumbled.

'I'm supposed to be up north dealing with the latest bovine flu epidemic before it gets out of hand, starts to jump species and causes global chaos and a pandemic of obscene proportions.'

My mouth flattened. Well, okay then. I supposed that was slightly more important. Only slightly, though.

The animal faery grinned and patted my arm. 'Don't worry,' she assured me. 'You've got this. Pumpkin is a sweetheart.'

The sweetheart in question gave her another lick then sat back heavily on his chubby haunches. We both watched the faery walk out, leaving us to our unsure fate without a back-ward glance. Once she'd gone, I put my hands on my hips and gave him a glare. 'Nice work,' I said sarcastically.

Pumpkin's lips pulled into the merest suggestion of a snarl. I didn't look away. It was important that he realised who was the real boss in this relationship.

'Don't start blaming me,' I told him. 'She could have helped us. Instead you acted like everything was absolutely fine.'

The little dog sniffed and turned away. I knelt down, reaching out to scratch his ears. Pumpkin jerked backwards like he'd been burned.

Holding my hands up in temporary surrender, I gazed at him. 'I'm doing my best for you,' I whispered. 'But I'm also trying to do my best as a faery godmother. I can't drop every-thing and run around after you 24/7. Life doesn't work like that. I have other commitments, you know.'

Pumpkin looked distinctly unimpressed at my attempt to appeal to his better side. I gave up and clipped on his lead before straightening up and heading for the door. 'Come on then,' I said. 'Let's go home.'

He tossed his head, as if to suggest that had been his plan all along and it was about time I fell into line and did what he wanted. The moment we made it outside, he took off, barrelling forward and almost yanking me off my feet.

Pumpkin might look like a small, overweight lap dog but I swear he has the strength of a Rottweiler. I dug in my heels, calling out to him in my best attempt at Cesar Millan-style dog whispering. It did no good: Pumpkin was a dog on a mission and it appeared that I was only along for the ride.

We whizzed along the street. Pumpkin whizzed; I stumbled and barely managed to keep my footing while resolutely ignoring the disapproving looks of the few other pedestrians out this early on a Saturday. I forced a smile as a nearby bloke with his own perfectly behaved pooch commented, 'Who's taking who out for a walk then?'

In the two weeks since I'd supposedly taken possession of Pumpkin, I'd lost count of how many times I'd heard those words. I was supposed to be a faery godmother; I was supposed to be magical and powerful and in charge of my own fate. In truth, I couldn't even get a pint-sized dog to come to heel.

Instead of turning right at the first crossroads, Pumpkin made a beeline in the opposite direction. I tugged on the lead. 'Wrong way!' I half-screeched.

Pumpkin ignored me in favour of vaulting forward and wrapping himself round a lamppost. Whether this was a deliberate action to get us both tangled up or simply because it smelled good, I couldn't have said.

'Fuck a puck.' I gritted my teeth and started to unwind the lead from the innocent lamppost. 'Why can't you walk in a straight line?'

'Because,' drawled a deep voice from behind me, 'then I wouldn't be able to chew gum at the same time.'

I whipped round, my eyes meeting Jasper's emerald-green gaze. Irritatingly, my cheeks flooded with colour like schoolgirl haphazardly bumping into a crush. That wasn't the case at all. No sirree.

I coughed and tried to compose myself. 'I was under the impression,' I said, 'that multi-tasking was your forte.'

He flashed me an amused grin. 'I'm reliably informed that women are better at that than men.'

'Only because we're forced into it,' I muttered. I looked him up and down. He was dressed more casually than I'd ever seen him in a pair of dark jeans that moulded to this thighs in ways I wanted to think about too much, and a dark grey V-necked T-shirt that displayed just enough tanned skin to make my mouth dry. Friends, I reminded myself. We were friends.

'Friends,' I said aloud without meaning to. Clearly my eloquence was only matched by my ability to appear unflustered.

A brief shadow crossed Jasper's face but it was so fleeting that I might have imagined it. 'Is that a verbal reminder for me or for you?'

'For Pumpkin,' I quickly replied. 'Just so he knows not to attack you.' We both looked down. Pumpkin was more intent on cocking his leg and spraying my foot than in anything Jasper was doing. I jerked away my foot and managed a smile. 'He can be vicious.'

Jasper scratched his chin. 'If you say so.'

We both remained where we were for a moment, staring at each other and not saying anything.

'I'm glad I bumped into you,' Jasper said finally. 'I wanted to speak to you at the office yesterday but I was tied up in meetings all day.'

'Ah' I nodded knowingly. If there was one thing the Office of Faery Godmothers loved it was a good – or bad – meeting. 'And how is the audit going?'

'Only a few more days to go. The draft report is near completion and then I'll leave you all in peace while I collate the final results and write up the last of my recommendations.'

I pretended that was good news and smiled. 'Great! Everyone will be pleased.'

Jasper didn't take his eyes off mine. 'Will you be pleased, Saffron?'

I swallowed. 'It's stressful having the Devil's Advocate around watching your every move and looming over every decision.'

'I've been trying to avoid too much looming.'

It was true. In contrast to the first week of his audit when we'd all been on edge, the atmosphere in the office was now far more relaxed. Jasper made a point of speaking to everyone in the mornings, passing pleasantries and the time of day and going out of his way to make my colleagues feel good. I liked to pretend that he'd softened up as a result of my advice to him but the truth was that deep down he was actually an amiable guy once you got to know him. 'You have,' I conceded. 'I was being unfair.'

He tilted his head. 'Wait a minute,' he said slowly. 'Did … did … did the amazing Saffron Sawyer actually just admit she was wrong?'

'It's been known to happen.' I grinned.

Jasper grinned back. The boyish amusement in his eyes was both out of character and wonderful to see. 'I'm glad.'

'Glad that I'm wrong?'

'Glad that I've not been overly intimidating lately.' His expression grew more intense. 'I take my job seriously, Saffron, and I love what I do. It's not because I enjoy stomping around, scaring people and ordering everyone about. It's because I want all faeries to be the best they can be. Truly. It means a huge amount to me that we're successful. We make positive changes to this world. We're important.'

I looked into his eyes. 'That,' I said softly, 'is music to my ears.' I took in a deep breath. Whoever said that opposites attract was lying through their teeth; in many ways, Jasper and I were like two peas in a pod. 'Anyway, why did you want to speak to me?'

He licked his lips. Was he nervous? 'I thought,' he said, 'it would be good if we touched base. Now that a few weeks have passed and things have settled down, we should take stock. You're likely to be the point of contact for the trolls, so we should discuss what their next steps might be and how we react to them for the best possible outcome.'

'Yup.' Okay then. That made sense. Although the immediate

threat Ethan and his unmerry band of trolls posed had been extinguished after Rose's death, we weren't safe yet. We might have come to a temporary truce, but that didn't change the fact that the trolls still held the Office of Faery Godmothers responsible for almost destroying their entire race because of an old wish gone wrong. It might have happened way before my time but memories were long, especially where near extinction was concerned.

It didn't help that the faery godmothers had also covered up their atrocious deeds. The Director had finally admitted the truth after the trolls' last attack and offered them a formal apology. As a result, Ethan had told me that they would cease their campaign of vengeance for the time being. But the truce wasn't permanent; we still had a lot of work to do to smooth over the ruffled feathers on both sides and avoid a devastating war. There remained a very good chance that the trolls would change their minds and return to their vendetta.

'Should we schedule a meeting for Monday?' I asked. 'I have some new clients to visit but I can probably push them back till later in the day.'

Jasper's mouth twisted. 'I'll be busy with my final inspections. As the trolls are technically unrelated to the audit and we're both so tight for time during the day, why don't we meet for dinner instead? Tonight. Seven o'clock. I'll pick you up.'

'Uh...'

'Unless you have other arrangements, of course. It's Saturday night. Maybe you have a date.' His eyes grew darker.

'No,' I squeaked. 'No date. I can do dinner.'

'Fantastic.' Jasper inclined his head. 'I'll see you then.' He bent over, patted Pumpkin and walked off.

I glanced at the terrier, who had somehow miraculously untangled himself from the lamppost and was sitting quietly by my feet. 'Did you know he was here?' I asked. 'Is that why you led us this way?' Pumpkin ignored me and I sighed. 'Is talking to your dog the first sign of madness?'

An empty crisp packet caught by the wind tumbled past us. Pumpkin lunged for it, barking like it was some kind of unnamed monster. I pulled him away and rolled my eyes. 'Come on. This time we're definitely going home. It might be the weekend, and I might be having dinner with the Devil's Advocate later, but I've still got work to do in the meantime. No rest for the wicked.'

I glanced again at Jasper's broad back. He was already halfway down the street. His head turned and he looked directly at me. I raised my hand in acknowledgement and he doffed an imaginary cap before turning and continuing on his way. Oh my.

~

Surprisingly, Pumpkin curled up in the corner for a nap rather than attempting to gnaw on my furniture or whine from the kitchen for food, allowing me to work in peace for a few hours.

I sat on my squashy sofa, my mug of tea growing cold as I powered my way through several reports and caught up on my paperwork. The clients I'd had over the last fortnight had been remarkably easy to take care of. Once they'd got past their initial shock at the existence of faery godmothers – and that they were lucky enough to be assigned to one – they'd been more than happy to open up their lives and let me help them.

Their wishes had been surprisingly modest. Cynics might imagine that, given half a chance, humans would demand the world on a plate but my experiences so far had proven other-wise. Most people sought happiness more than anything else, and often not for themselves but for those they loved.

I'd had a woman whose sister was a cancer survivor and

who wished for her to get the opportunity to travel the world. I arranged for her to win an open-ended airline ticket, courtesy of a well-meaning travel agency. Then there was the young lad who'd desperately wanted his dad to find love again. Given the single father in question was already eyeing up his next-door neighbour, all it had taken was a few simple magical nudges in the right direction.

My favourite, however, was the middle-aged man I'd dealt with in the middle of the week. He'd recently come to the conclusion that he'd spent too much of life wrapped up in self-involved narcissism and that the best way forward was for him to dedicate his life to making others happy. Frankly, he'd have made an excellent faery godmother. As that was out of the question, I helped him get a job working for the National Lottery. It was now his role to answer the phone to those lucky people who held winning tickets. From now on, he would check their numbers and happily inform them how much money they'd won. Making other people feel good makes you feel good. It's a fact of life.

Unfortunately, it's also a fact of life that completing paper-work of any kind can quickly become soul-sucking and depress-ing. Despite my joy at my recent successes, writing up my reports quickly numbed my brain. That's the reason why, when my doorbell rang, I was groggy and disorientated and stupidly assumed it was Jasper arriving early to pick me up for our dinner. And I'd not even had time to shower and change.

I wasn't the only one who was startled; Pumpkin had leapt to his feet and was alternately barking and growling with all the ferocity of Cerberus at the gates of hell.

'You,' I told him in an appropriately stern voice as I hastily shut him into the bedroom for the Devil's Advocate's own safety, 'need to settle down. Jasper is one of the good guys.'

I paused at the mirror in the hallway. Man. It was worse

than I'd thought. My unruly curls were springing out in all directions like some sort of unkempt yet over-aged Orphan Annie. My skin tone had the pallor of someone who'd spent their entire life inside. I made a vague attempt at smoothing down my hair and pinched my cheeks in a bid to encourage some healthy colour into them. Except now they just looked blotchy. Great. Then I made the mistake of breathing in. I was in dire need of some industrial-strength deodorant. Fuck a puck.

The doorbell rang again, more insistently this time. At that point, I didn't think anything short of a week-long spa would do much to improve my appearance. Besides, Jasper knew what I looked like and he'd still invited me out to dinner in public. I shrugged to myself and wished I didn't feel quite so nervous before grabbing a bottle of air freshener and liberally spraying it around my body.

It's lovely to see you again. I wasn't expecting you so early, I rehearsed in my head. *Can I fetch you a drink while I freshen up before we go out?* I nodded, satisfied, then opened the door with a rueful, but hopefully still welcoming, grin.

'It's lovely to see you ag...' My voice faltered as I registered who was on my doorstep.

'Hi,' grunted the troll, who I'd last seen in the Adventus room in the Office of Faery Godmothers. He'd been with Ethan. And he'd been standing over the dead body of Rose, Pumpkin's old owner.

His companion, a tall female who I didn't recognise, smiled nastily. I could feel waves of simmering magic emanating from her.

I was in trouble. Big trouble.

CHAPTER

TWO

Instinct made me reach for my wand, even though I no longer had one to hand thanks to Pumpkin's sharp teeth and terrible attitude. When I came up short, I did the only other thing I could do and slammed my shoulder against the door to keep my two unwanted guests out of my home.

The female troll thrust out her hand, thwarting my efforts. 'You're coming with us,' she snarled, 'whether you fight us or not.'

My stomach dropped. The wankers were planning to abduct me from my own doorstep. For a moment, I was frozen with fear. Pumpkin's barking had reached hysterical levels and, from the sound of heavy thumping behind me, he was throwing himself against the bedroom door in a bid to escape and help my panicked attempt at defence. His noise provided me with enough of a slap of terrified clarity to react.

'Screw you,' I snarled. Then I reached down inside the pit of my belly and drew on my own natural magic reserves.

Light exploded and both trolls were thrown backwards into the street, flying through the air in a series of involuntary somersaults. Unfortunately, I didn't fare much better. White-hot pain flashed through my veins and arteries and my knees gave way. I collapsed to the floor, my vision blurring.

The agony searing my body dulled my thoughts and I couldn't compute what was happening. I'd thought we were past this kidnapping business; I'd thought that Ethan, the troll leader, had put a temporary stop to his terrorist activities. Clearly I'd been wrong.

I staggered back to my feet, willing myself to stay upright. The burst of magic had sapped most of my energy; without a wand, most faeries find it nigh on impossible to manage any sort of magical intervention. Wandless magic usually results in the need to lie down in a darkened room with a cold compress for several hours. Sadly for me, my would-be abductors were also already getting back up to their feet and approaching for round two.

My hands flailed around blindly, searching for something – anything – that I could use to defend myself. My fingers curled around the canister of air freshener. It wasn't much, but it was all I had. I tightened my grip then, blinking to clear my vision as the two trolls reached my doorway again, I pressed down and sent a jet of Floral Elegance directly into their eyes.

'You godmothering psycho!' the female troll screeched, staggering backwards and throwing up her arm to shield herself.

The man hissed through his teeth and side-stepped. A moment later, I felt the air around me crackle. I tried to dodge this new attack but it was too late. An invisible rope wound its way round my ankles, binding them tightly together. Then it began to coil its way up my legs.

'She doesn't have her wand,' I heard him say as I struggled against the bonds. 'She's all but powerless.'

There was a hawking sound. The female troll spat something phlegmy and green onto the pavement outside and laughed harshly. 'How did those bitching godmothers ever beat us? They're so weak.' She stepped back into my line of sight. 'This was supposed to be easy. You shouldn't have attacked us, sweetheart. You're going to regret it.'

'Melissa, you know what Ethan said.' The male joined her, peering in at me and my continuing efforts to free myself.

'She went for us first.'

He seemed to consider this. 'True,' he said. 'We were only protecting ourselves. We can't be held responsible if the détente collapses.'

'Or,' Melissa added, 'if this bitch dies in the process.'

I barely registered their words through the adrenaline that was pumping through my body and the fight-or-flight instinct that was overwhelming me. 'You tossers,' I croaked. 'You knocked on *my* door. You've done this.'

The female troll rubbed her eyes, which were still red from the air freshener, and grimaced. 'No matter what happens, faery godmothers will always blame someone else. Nothing is ever their fault.'

I clenched my teeth and tried not to rise to the bait. After all, as long as they were talking, they weren't attacking.

Using magic without my wand had cost me and my weakened state put me at an extraordinary disadvantage – but I was still conscious and breathing. That meant I still had a chance. The longer I could delay the trolls' next move, the more opportunity I'd have to round up some vestige of energy so that I could fight them off.

Unfortunately, the two trolls seemed to realise this and abandoned their whining in favour of stepping across my threshold and advancing towards me.

'Get out of my house,' I spat. From behind my bedroom

door, Pumpkin's barking grew more shrill as if to add weight to my words.

'We told you already,' the male said. 'You're coming with us. Boss wants you.' He flicked a look at Melissa, suggesting he was seeking her approval. Ah-ha: she was in charge, then. Understanding the trolls' power dynamic might help me.

I abandoned my vain attempts to break free of the magical shackles and focused on my would-be captors instead, scanning them for some weakness or vulnerability that I might be able to exploit.

Like his superior, the male was tall. He was considerably more muscle bound than her but I suspected that she would find it just as easy to send me flying to the floor as he would. Judging by the tight-fitting clothing they both wore, they were prepared for anything. Physically, I was no match for them. And frankly, even if I'd had a wand, I wasn't convinced that I'd be a magical match either. But there had to be something. I didn't give up that easily.

Melissa reached me first, grabbing my left arm. A moment later, the male took hold of my right arm. They weren't taking any chances. They'd strong arm me out of my own home and into whatever horrors Ethan had planned. Bastard. I'd trusted him when he'd told me he would cease hostilities for the time being. I'd been a naïve fool.

The trolls pulled me forward, dragging me down my hallway. With my feet and legs magically bound, however, the upper half of my body moved with them while my lower half stayed put.

Rather than resist, I let simple physics take over. I keeled over, almost in slow motion, and the carpet rushed up to meet me. The angle of my body, coupled with the narrowness of the hallway, meant that I took Melissa with me and sprawled onto her when we both hit the floor.

The male troll tried to stop us from falling and pulled on my arm to bring me back upright. He was a fraction too slow to stop the momentum and lost his balance. His heavy body fell onto mine, squashing the hapless Melissa even more.

'Finch, you idiot!' she screeched. 'Get off!'

Now I had another name to work with. As any fool faery knows, names have power, not because of magic but because of emotion. Using someone's name allows you to insert yourself into their psyche and it can become a form of subtle domination.

I used my clients' names as often as I could to encourage them to trust me; I'd use the trolls' names now for an entirely different reason. As Finch awkwardly got to his feet, I twisted right. My legs might be tied but my hands and arms were free – and with Melissa beneath me, I had the upper hand, if only for a split second.

I didn't think about it; I couldn't afford to. I sucked in a breath and pressed the base of my right thumb into Melissa's right eyeball, using enough pressure so that I wasn't doing any real harm – yet. But the threat was obvious and she hissed with both shock and fear.

'Finch,' I said aloud, 'walk away now or I will blind Melissa.'

He didn't believe me. His large hand reached for the back of my neck, squeezing hard. I responded by pressing down my thumb. This time Melissa screamed.

'I wasn't bluffing, Finch,' I said calmly, although my heart was thumping so much it felt like it would burst out of my ribcage. 'There goes one eye. Don't worry though, Melissa still has one left. For now. Walk away and she might just get to keep it.' I paused. 'You know it's right, Finch.'

His hand released my neck and I felt him move away. 'I'm not going anywhere,' he said. 'Hurt her again and I'll kill you.'

Yeah. He probably would.

Beneath me, Melissa moaned, tears leaking out of both her eyes and staining her cheeks. I moved my left hand an inch to the side so that my thumb was now hovering over her other eye. 'Can you kill me before I pop her other eyeball?' I asked softly. 'Melissa needs more than magic now. She needs real medical attention. Are you going to get it for her, Finch? Or are you going to worry about me?'

I didn't need to see his face to know he was struck by indecision. Melissa was in no fit state to tell him what to do and he was flailing. I only had to give him one more push.

'I tell you what, Finch, I'll count to five. One, two, three...'

'We'll leave,' he interrupted. 'But she's coming with me.'

I could have fainted with relief. 'I expected nothing less. Get these magic ties off me and she's all yours.'

There was a moment of hesitation then I felt the bonds loosen and vanish. I breathed out and stood up, backing away so that I was beyond Finch's reach. He might still change his mind. From the veins bulging in his neck, it was obvious that he was close to snapping. I had to ensure that didn't happen.

'Take Melissa and get out, Finch.' My whole body was trembling but I couldn't let him see that. A tiny, insistent voice of reason pushed at the back of my mind. 'And,' I said, 'tell your boss that I will meet him tomorrow at midday outside Holy Trinity Church to discuss today's events.'

The troll shot me such a look of vile hatred that I almost flinched. I held my ground, however, and he moved past me. He reached down for Melissa, lifted her up then cradled her against his chest.

She moaned again. 'I can't see. I can't see.'

I swallowed hard. With Melissa still in his arms, Finch walked out. I sprang forward and slammed the door shut behind them, fumbling with the locks before sagging in relief against its reassuringly solid surface.

There was another thump and a loud splintering of wood and Pumpkin burst through the bottom of the bedroom door, quivering wildly. He barked before whipping his head towards mine.

'You timed that well, didn't you?' I said weakly.

A second later my knees gave way and I collapsed.

CHAPTER

THREE

Jasper's face was pale and strained. 'I should have arrived sooner.'

I sighed heavily. 'You got here when you said you would. You couldn't have known what would happen.'

'We need to move you out of here. I don't know how the trolls knew your address but you're clearly not safe.' He turned away, his fists clenching so tightly that his knuckles were white. 'Everything we've worked for up to this point has been for nothing. What the fuck was Ethan thinking? I thought we were getting somewhere.'

'Hopefully he'll show up at the church tomorrow and I'll find out.'

Jasper shook his head. 'You'll do no such thing. I'll meet him myself. I'm not putting you in danger again.'

I felt a sudden rush of warmth at his protective words. Maybe we really were friends. This was my gig, though; I was the one who felt like I'd been betrayed.

'Your presence won't help anything. I'll meet him myself. I'm already the established point of contact between the trolls and the faeries. We need to stick to that. I'll find out what's going on.' My tone was grim but even I detected the edge of hurt to my words. I'd expected better from the troll leader.

I did my best to shake off the feeling. If I made this personal, any naïve hope we might have of avoiding further trouble would be forlorn indeed. In the last month, the trolls had abducted several faery godmothers, set off a suicide bomb and attacked our office. We had to de-escalate matters. There was no choice and, deep down, Jasper knew it as well as I did.

He paced up and down my small living room, his fury still palpable.

'Nothing's changed,' I said. I could be reasonable. I *had* to be reasonable. 'We still need peace between us and the trolls. With luck this … attack will have gained me some sort of leverage. Maybe I can use it to our advantage.'

'And maybe,' he growled, 'Ethan will use the opportunity to meet with you as a chance to finish what he's started.'

'It's a public place. He won't dare try anything.' I thought back over what the trolls had said. It was possible I'd misjudged the situation from the outset. 'Maybe,' I said in a small voice, 'he only sent Melissa and Finch to fetch me and he only wanted to talk. I panicked when I saw them and I might have over-reacted.'

Jasper's eyes narrowed but he didn't argue. Truthfully, I had no clue whether the trolls' intentions had been malicious or whether I'd completely fucked things up for all the faery godmothers.

I was almost certain that I'd not done Melissa's eye any permanent damage. I'd simply used the power of suggestion – not to mention some searing pain – to imply that I'd blinded her right eye. The fact that she'd already been hurting from the air freshener I'd sprayed in her face had helped my cause. But the callous fact that I'd come close to blinding her stunned me.

I stared down at my hands. Would I have popped her eyeball if the situation had called for it and Finch hadn't been manipulated so easily? A tremor of unease ran through me. No, surely not. I wasn't that kind of person. And Melissa would be fine.

In the frightening event that I'd done her some permanent damage, things would go very badly for us. The trolls weren't our friends; far from it. If only I'd had a wand to help me defend myself, I wouldn't have felt so vulnerable and wary and I could have mitigated the outcome somehow.

'You're going to have to teach me,' I said suddenly. 'You're going to have to teach me how to wield magic without a wand. *All* magic.'

Jasper stopped pacing and turned to look at me. 'I'm not sure that's possible,' he said slowly.

'You can do plenty of magic without a wand,' I pointed out. 'Strong magic. You might be the Devil's Advocate but essentially you're still a faery like me.'

'I'm the Devil's Advocate because my magic is so strong. What I can do isn't typical.'

I set my jaw into a resolute line. 'It's typical for the trolls. We need to make it typical for faeries too.'

'Saffron...'

'What's the worst that could happen?'

He paused for a moment, his expression oddly inscrutable. 'I don't want you to be disappointed if you work hard and it turns out you still need a wand for support.'

'The only limits are the ones we place on ourselves.'

Jasper frowned. 'That sounds familiar.'

That was because it was one of Angela's latest motivational posters, which she'd pinned to the noticeboard in the office, but I wasn't about to tell him that.

'What if we all have the same potential as you do but we've

become over-reliant on the tools of our trade to the detriment of our natural skills?' My voice dropped. 'I could have died today because I didn't have a wand. I can still feel the headache from using magic without it. There has to be a better way.'

Jasper put his hands in his pockets. 'The audit puts limits on my time. If we're going to do this, it'll have to be late in the evenings. You'll have to commit to spending a lot of time with me.'

I licked my lips. 'I can manage that.'

His response was soft. 'A *lot* of time, Saffron.'

'That won't be so bad. We're friends.'

Jasper took a step towards me. 'Yes,' he said very deliberately, his gaze still focused on mine. 'We are. But we both know there's something more between us. I don't think we've yet shaken off our ... mutual desire.'

I stared at him. 'Are you asking me if I'm capable of keeping my hands off you?'

His mouth twitched. 'Are you?'

I crossed my arms. 'Of course! I'm a consummate professional! Why? Do you think you're incapable of keeping your hands off *me*?'

'The only limits,' he said, 'are the ones we place on ourselves.'

This time I had no idea what that meant. 'So are we on then?'

Jasper offered me a lazy smile. 'Sure. But don't blame me if it doesn't work.'

'I won't,' I promised.

'Pack a bag. There's a spare room at my place.'

I started. 'Pardon?'

'You can't stay here. It's too dangerous. If we're spending time training together, it makes sense that you bunk up with me until we find a suitable alternative. Friends move in together all the time.' He raised an eyebrow. 'Unless the thought makes you uncomfortable?'

'No!' I squeaked. 'Can I bring Pumpkin?'

'Will he destroy my soft furnishings?'

I nodded. 'Almost definitely.'

Jasper continued to smile. 'Then he can come too. I could do with some redecorating.'

I'D ENVISIONED Jasper's flat as some sort of bachelor pad with marbled white floors, black walls, moody lighting and lots of mirrors. Instead it was surprisingly homely.

Pumpkin wasted no time in darting round, sniffing every nook and cranny suspiciously while I admired the showy artwork. There was an extraordinary painting that looked rather like an original Picasso. I gulped it in before noting the photo frames on the table below.

'Is this your family?' I asked. I eyed the portraits. Unsurprisingly, they were a good-looking bunch.

'Yes.' Jasper picked up one of the frames. 'My mother and father.' He smiled fondly. 'They're both retired and live in the country now. Maybe one day you'll get to meet them.'

My eyes darted to him but he wasn't looking at me. Swallowing, I nodded towards a photo of a young woman. She had dark hair and was laughing, while a much younger version of Jasper tickled her. 'Who's that?' I asked.

His expression immediately closed. 'The bathroom is over there. I'll get you some fresh towels. And the kitchen is that way.'

Oh. Whoever she was, he didn't want to talk about her. Fair enough.

'Great,' I said with an enthusiasm that suggested I was far more of a domestic goddess than was true.

'Her name was Anna,' he said suddenly, taking me by surprise. 'She was my sister. She died thirteen years ago.'

I stared at him. Oh man. 'Jasper, I'm so sorry.'

He smiled slightly. 'She would have liked you.'

I had no idea what to say. I reached out and touched his arm. His hand went to mine. 'I'm sorry,' I repeated lamely.

'It's okay.' His eyes crinkled at me and he straightened his shoulders. 'Anyway, I've not finished the grand tour. Follow me. Fortunately, the spare room is already made up,' he said, opening a varnished door.

I peered inside. Pale blue walls, splashes of bright colour from some cheerful modern art and comfy-looking cushions, not to mention a pristine white coverlet adorning the large bed. I blinked.

'It's very ... nice.'

'You don't like it?'

'Quite the opposite,' I said honestly. 'I was expecting something darker and more ominous.'

'Blood dripping from the walls, you mean?' He grinned. 'I have to keep up appearances. The door to the real torture chamber is hidden in my bedroom. I'll show it to you later if you're good.'

I laughed but it was an effort; I really was still feeling rather ill.

'Why don't you make yourself at home?' Jasper suggested, missing nothing. 'You can have a hot shower and I'll sort out something for us to eat.'

'You cook too?'

His smile stretched. 'I'm quite the catch, aren't I?'

I bit my lip and looked away. Yeah. He was. I came very close to telling him in no uncertain terms that we shouldn't be friends at all before grabbing him and pulling him towards me. Except things were complicated enough as they were, and I'd promised the exact opposite. And, given what he'd revealed about his sister, it would hardly be appropriate.

'Thanks for all this, Jasper,' I said quietly.

Something glinted in his green eyes. 'It's what friends are for.'

I crashed out almost immediately after dinner, with even Pumpkin's combined efforts at snoring and taking over most of the bed not managing to wake me up. Right before I drifted off, I'd felt the small dog nose up to my face; he checked on me before cuddling up in a tight ball in the crook of my arm. I slept so deeply, however, that I couldn't be entirely sure I'd not dreamt the whole thing.

I'd not been sleeping well recently, so waking up feeling genuinely refreshed was not only unusual but rather wonderful. In fact I felt so well rested that the sensation of comfort and total relaxation continued right up until Jasper and I strolled into the lobby of the Office of Faery Godmothers. He was holding Pumpkin's lead, which spoke volumes that I hadn't stopped to consider.

Mrs Jardine's eyebrows rose as she watched us enter. From the delighted amusement in her expression, not to mention her surprise, she'd obviously leapt to a very wrong conclusion about our togetherness.

'Good morning, Miranda,' Jasper smiled.

She smirked. 'Good morning, Devil's Advocate.'

'Morning, Mrs Jardine,' I mumbled.

'Saffron,' she chided, 'I've told you already that you may call me Miranda.' Her smile grew. 'You're looking tired,' she said. 'Did you have a late night?'

Jasper moved an inch or two closer to me. What was that about? Did he want her to get the wrong idea? 'No,' I said, hastily. 'It was a very early night, in fact.'

Mrs Jardine's mirth only grew. 'Of course it was,' she said. Then she winked. Unbelievable. I'd not thought that the faery receptionist was capable of such a thing. Still, at least she was discreet enough not to tell the entire office that we'd walked in together. If she'd been Delilah, the gossip would have spread through the entire building before we made it to the office floor.

'Oh my goodness,' Delilah's voice exclaimed behind us. 'How lovely to see you both together this morning!'

I raised my eyes heavenward and turned to greet her. 'Hi, Delilah.'

'Hi!' she trilled. She was giddy with excitement.

I knew Delilah well enough by now; she possessed an innate understanding of body language that would tell her nothing material had changed between Jasper and me. I also knew that she loved gossip more than anything else. Whether that gossip was true or not was immaterial. The last thing I wanted was for my colleagues to think that I received preferential treatment because I was sleeping with the Devil's Advocate. I wanted them to think that I received preferential treatment because I deserved it for being the best.

'Two trolls paid an unexpected and unwelcome visit to my house yesterday,' I said loudly. 'The Devil's Advocate has allowed me to stay with him until the matter is resolved.'

'Fantastic,' she beamed. Then she paused. 'Wait.' Alarm lit her expression. 'Trolls went to your house? To the place where you live?' Her voice rose. 'Your home?'

Fuck a puck. I should be trying to ease faery godmother fears about Ethan and his cronies, not stoking the fires of terror, hatred and panic. At least until I had absolute confirmation that they'd turned on us again.

'It was probably a misunderstanding on their part,' Jasper said smoothly, stepping in to cover my blurted mistake with a sidelong look of warning in my direction.

I waved a hand. 'Indeed. I'm meeting with Ethan later today to resolve the matter.' I hoped.

Jasper draped an arm over my shoulders. 'Besides, who wouldn't want to have Saffron Sawyer as their house guest?' he said. His words were innocuous but his tone was laden with meaning.

Before I could say anything else, he steered me towards the lift. Once the door had closed and we started to rise upwards, I rounded on him. 'You realise that's going to spread round this office like wildfire? Everyone will think we're shagging each other's brains out!'

He regarded me mildly. 'Is that really so distressing?'

'It's not true! It's not ... not ... professional either!'

He shrugged. 'I had to say something. You know as well as I do that we can't afford the other faery godmothers being afraid of the trolls. We're trying to dampen down fears and emotions, not make matters worse. Whether the trolls deserve it or not,' he added darkly.

I twisted my hands together. 'I've had to work really hard to get the people in this office to respect me. I don't want them to think I'm sleeping my way to the top.'

Jasper relaxed slightly. 'So you're not ashamed of me?'

'You're the Devil's Advocate. Why on earth would I be ashamed of you?' I asked blankly, staring at him. It didn't happen very often but occasionally I got a hint that Jasper was far more vulnerable than he let on.

I reached out and touched his arm. 'You're quite the catch,

remember? I'm proud that you're my friend. I'd be even prouder if there really was more between us.'

His gaze seared me with sudden intensity. 'Is that so?' he murmured.

'Jasper, I...'

I didn't get the chance to finish. The lift doors opened to reveal the Director waiting for us. 'The two of you, into my office now,' she commanded. 'And leave the damned dog out here.' She stalked off, clearly expecting us to follow.

I wrinkled my nose. Pumpkin and I had been enjoying the Director's good graces for the last few weeks. Admittedly, nice as it was to be treated kindly it was mostly so that she could pretend that the office hadn't almost been destroyed by Ethan and his trolls. Unfortunately, it appeared that the forgiving time was now well and truly over. It was never going to last but I'd been hoping I'd have a few more weeks.

If Jasper was unhappy at being ordered around, he didn't show it. He strode forward with a confidence that belied what he'd just said to me in the lift. I had no choice but to trail after him, hastily passing Pumpkin off to a reluctant Billy along the way.

When I reached the Director's office, she indicated to me to close the door. I did as she asked and sat down in front of her desk with Jasper by my side.

'Well?' she snapped. 'Have there been any further developments? Have the trolls made any further approaches?'

I glanced at Jasper. He must have already informed her about what had happened yesterday. That was fast. I reminded myself that he was doing his job. 'No,' I said aloud. 'Hopefully, Ethan will meet me at Holy Trinity today and I can find out what he really wanted.'

'And if he attacks you again?' she enquired. 'What then? I told you both that I believed war with the trolls was inevitable and I see nothing here to disavow me of that belief. That public apology I was forced to make was a complete waste of time. I knew it would be.' Her bitterness was palpable. 'Our office was weakened for no reason whatsoever.'

Taken aback by her vehemence, I chose my next words carefully. 'It's possible,' I hedged, 'that yesterday Ethan just wanted to meet me and I over-reacted to his, uh, friends on my doorstep.'

The Director snorted in derision and looked at Jasper. 'I understood from you that there was a death threat against Saffron.' Her eyes hardened. 'Nobody threatens my faery godmothers and gets away with it.'

'I might have jumped to conclusions when the trolls appeared,' I told her hastily. 'Let's not jump to conclusions now.' It was, I reflected, considerably easier to be rational and calm when I didn't feel like my life was in danger and I was safely ensconced in the godmother office, even if the anger in the Director's eyes was enough to make me quake in my boots. 'I'll see what Ethan has to say for himself first.'

'And how,' she sniffed, 'will you be able to trust anything he says?'

Good question. 'I think,' I said cautiously, 'that he's a fairly honourable person.'

'I wouldn't call terrorist activity honourable.'

I winced.

The Director passed a hand over her eyes. 'Devil's Advocate, you'll stay in the vicinity in case this meeting goes wrong?'

Jasper nodded. 'You can count on it.' He reached across and squeezed my hand and I shivered briefly at his touch.

'Will this delay the completion of the audit?' the Director asked.

'I shouldn't think so. Not if we can smooth things over with Ethan.'

The Director muttered something inaudible under her breath. 'Very well.' She turned towards me. 'I expect you back here directly afterwards, whether you're in one piece or not. You might enjoy playing hero, Saffron, but your actions have far-reaching consequences for us all. Don't fuck this up.'

It was good to know that I inspired such high levels of confidence. 'I'll do my best,' I said aloud.

The Director glared. 'Do better than that.'

CHAPTER
FOUR

Billy was waiting at my desk with Pumpkin at his feet. Both of them were acting suspiciously quiet and calm.

I approached warily. 'Thanks for looking after my dog, Billy,' I said. I bent down to give Pumpkin a scratch behind his ears and, true to form, he jumped backwards and out of my reach.

Billy grunted. 'That slobbery beast shouldn't be allowed in here.'

Was it really only two weeks ago that Pumpkin and I had both been fêted as the heroes of the office? 'I can't leave him on his own. He's a whirlwind of destruction when he's not supervised.'

'He's not the only one.' Billy folded his arms and glared at me. 'I can't believe you need another replacement wand. They don't grow on trees, you know.'

'They're made of wood.'

His glare intensified. 'You know what I mean. The rules state quite clearly that any faery godmother who loses her wand not only has to meet the cost of the replacement but is to be given a formal warning. You've barely been here a month and you've lost two.'

'Technically,' I said, 'I didn't lose the last one. I know where it is.' I coughed. 'Or at least I know where it was. There's not much left of it now.'

Billy sniffed. 'My dog ate my wand is a terrible excuse.'

'It's not an excuse!' I protested.

Billy tutted. 'Come with me. You have to sign for your new one. But if you lose this one too, then I can't be responsible for the consequences.'

I threw a mock salute. He screwed up his face. 'A simple thank you will suffice. Gestures of a military bent are considered to be in poor taste. In fact, in the rule book you'll see that…'

'I get it,' I said. 'You don't have to spell it out.'

I followed Billy to his store room, leaving Pumpkin where he was. As soon as the door closed behind us, the bald faery's face broke into a wide grin. 'Is Delilah right? You're shagging the Devil's Advocate? Come on. Tell me all the gory details!'

'First of all,' I hissed, 'I'm not. Second of all, there has to be a rule against office gossip. I can't believe there isn't one.'

His grin didn't alter. 'Actually, there's not. Despite the layers upon layers of rules, no one has ever been against either good- or bad-natured tittle-tattle. It's the lifeblood of any office. And if you're annoyed because I called you out for losing your wand, you know that I have to treat you the same as everyone else. It's for your own good. The others all loved you for a hot minute, but that will quickly turn to jealousy if you continue to get special treatment.'

'I don't think I've had any special treatment whatsoever.'

He gave me a long look and started to tick off his fingers. 'You're shacking up with the Devil's Advocate. You get to bring your dog into work. You're the only faery godmother who talks to the trolls. You're in and out of the Director's office like a yo-yo.'

'You know that last part isn't actually a good thing, don't you?'

'It doesn't matter.' Billy was surprisingly earnest. 'Faery godmothers are fickle and very jealous. I've worked here for long enough. I should know.'

'You're saying the better I am at my job, the more people will hate me.'

He shrugged. 'It's the way it is. Things might be better here than they were before, but we're still not a real team.'

'The audit is almost finished. When Jasper finishes his report...'

Billy held up his hands. 'There you go. You call him Jasper. Even the Director doesn't do that. When he's around, she minds her Ps and Qs in a manner I've never seen before. You, on the other hand, turn into a giggly mess.'

'What?' I frowned. 'I do not! I'm never giggly!'

'Whenever he steps out of that office, your eyes track his every move. You're worse than Pumpkin when someone's eating a ham sandwich.'

'I...'

'And what's worse,' Billy continued, 'is that he does the same to you when he thinks you're not looking.'

He did? My tongue glued to the top of my mouth and I stared at my friend. Unfortunately, however, his diatribe wasn't over.

'You know that his report isn't going to be pretty,' he said. 'You know what's wrong with this place and how much it needs to change.' He leaned in. 'You also know that people *hate* change. Do you really think the Director will be happy to implement those changes? She's ruled this fiefdom for years without any sort of interference. The Devil's Advocate will tell her what to do, then walk out that door and never come back. You will still be here. If you're tight with him, you'll end up being blamed for his recommendations. Especially,' he added, 'if you continue to be so successful.'

I frowned unhappily. 'I'm sure that whatever Jasper recommends will be good for this place. And I'm not going to fail at my job deliberately just so that I have more mates in the office.'

'I'm not suggesting that you do any such thing. I'm merely pointing out your current situation. Don't shoot the messenger.'

I sighed. He was right. I wouldn't change anything about myself because of Billy's words, but I couldn't deny the truth of them. But I still had time before the audit was completed. If I played my cards wisely and went on a charm offensive before the goodwill ran out, I'd be doing my future self a favour.

I ran down my mental checklist. Avert war with trolls. Again. Avoid falling over the Devil's Advocate and melting into a lust puddle whenever I saw him – but also find out if Billy was right and he watched me when I wasn't looking. Ingratiate myself with my colleagues before they turned on me. Learn how to use magic without a wand, unlike almost every other faery in the whole world. I nodded to myself. I could manage all that.

Billy handed me a new wand. 'Look after this one,' he said. 'You have a new list of clients waiting for you. You will need that wand if you're going to help them and grant their wishes.'

Oh yeah. I stared at the wand. I mustn't forget that I had to do my normal job as well.

~

WITH ONLY A FEW hours to go before my meeting with Ethan, I trotted back to my desk, brand new wand in hand. Bearing

Billy's words in mind, I made a point of smiling and saying hello to everyone I passed. Fortunately, most people still smiled back. Operation Nice Faery was underway.

I grabbed the pile of folders with the details of my new clients and sat down in my chair, ready to start on the first one without further delay. There was a loud creaking sound and the chair gave way. Both it and I fell to the floor with a loud clatter just as Alicia was passing. I let out a pained 'oomph'.

Alicia raised a delicately manicured eyebrow. 'Have you been putting on weight recently, Saffron?' she enquired. 'You should eat more salad and fewer fish-finger sandwiches.' She smoothed her hands down the front of her body to emphasise her own natural slimness.

I bit back the caustic comment on the tip of my tongue and smiled sweetly. 'Alas, Alicia, if I only ate salad I wouldn't be this healthy or this voluptuous. It takes work to maintain these curves.'

'It takes reinforced seating requirements too, apparently,' she said. 'I can give you the name of my personal trainer if you want.' She looked me up and down. 'He's a miracle worker.'

'I'm too busy performing miracles for others to worry about miracles for myself.'

She raised her shoulders in an elegant shrug, as if to suggest that it was no concern of hers if I chose to remain as I was. 'Don't say I didn't offer.' She glided off, leaving me sprawled on the floor.

Pumpkin ambled up. He opened his mouth and dropped something onto my lap. I ignored the drool coating the object and picked it up to examine it. It was part of the chair leg. No wonder the dratted thing had fallen apart when I sat on it – the dog had probably chewed it off. 'Great,' I said sarcastically. 'Thanks, Pumpkin.'

The corner of his mouth lifted up slightly in a semblance of a snarl then he dipped his head and took the plastic oblong back to a corner underneath the desk where he gnawed on it enthusiastically.

I gave up and pushed the broken chair out of the way before picking up my strewn folders and sitting cross-legged on the floor. If you can't beat 'em, I decided, join 'em.

Scanning the scanty details in the first file, I made a few notes. Eric Maker. Thirty-two years old. Two children. Long-term partner called Kelly. I turned the paper over. He'd moved recently and was now living in Ipswich. He'd made his wish, whatever it was, while blowing out candles on his birthday cake. So far so normal. I smiled to myself. He was definitely about to get a lucky break.

I checked my watch and decided to forego further research on Mr Maker. The fastest way to learn what his heart desired was to visit him. The personal touch was always best. I glanced at Pumpkin. I had no choice but to take him with me. Now that he had a taste for chairs, there wouldn't be a single one in the office that was safe.

I got to my feet and coaxed him out. 'You can leave the chair leg behind,' I told him. 'It'll still be here when we get back.'

Pumpkin glared at me and held onto it, his jaws clamped tightly round it.

I shrugged. I wouldn't start a tug of war that I couldn't win. 'Or keep it,' I said. 'Your choice.'

Delilah popped her head over the partition and grinned at me. 'Right then, you. Let's hear all about what's going on with you and the Devil's Advocate.'

I waved at her. 'Got to visit a client! I'll talk to you later though. I promise.'

She waggled her fingers at me. 'I want to hear all the dirty details, Saffron. You know you can trust me with your secrets.'

Yeah, yeah. I wondered sometimes if Delilah believed her

own hype. A sieve had fewer leaks. 'You betcha,' I said. I grinned at her and left for the Metafora room as fast as my little legs would carry me. Even Pumpkin seemed surprised by my sudden spurt of speed.

I wasn't the only faery heading for the magical transportation room. I gestured to Figgy, letting her go in front of me. 'Aw, Saffron,' she said. 'You're so nice.'

'Yes.' I nodded vigorously. 'I am nice. Thank you, Figgy. You're nice too.'

She beamed at me before disappearing inside. I checked my watch again and tapped my foot. I didn't have much time before meeting Ethan, but I wanted to get started with Eric Maker while I had the chance.

The Metafora room buzzed, indicating it was free to enter. Out of the corner of my eye, I saw Rupert heading towards me. Nope: there were limits to my ability to remain polite and I'd just about reached them.

I stepped hastily into the small sparkly room, dragging Pumpkin with me. I had the better part of an hour to get a decent first impression of Eric before I had to get back to leave for Holy Trinity Church. It was time to get ready to weave some magic.

FIVE

The beauty of the Metafora room is that it automatically transports any faery godmother directly to their client, no matter where they happen to be. It is clever enough to deposit us outside any buildings rather than directly inside. After all, no one wants to find themselves magically appearing in a toilet cubicle at the same time as their client is carrying out their, uh, ablutions. We don't need to know *everything* about the people we're helping.

On this occasion, I found myself standing in what appeared to be an industrial estate. I wheeled round slowly, taking a look before returning my gaze to the building in front of me.

The file I'd read on Eric Maker hadn't deigned to tell me what he did for a living but, judging from the building in front of me, he was a mechanic. And a busy one at that. The place was packed with cars. Some were obviously the worse for wear, with alarming-looking dents and crumpled bonnets. Others were better maintained and probably just booked in for their annual MOTs.

I squinted inside, trying to locate which one of the grubby, blue-overall clad workers might be my guy. Quite a few of them were smeared with grease and oil, so it wasn't easy to tell their ages or to see their features clearly. Eric's file had included a photo but the garage was so busy that I couldn't spot him from where I was standing. I had a tongue in my head, though. I'd wander in, grab the nearest person and ask.

Pumpkin, still miraculously holding the plastic chair leg in his mouth, trotted next to me. 'Be good,' I told him in a low tone, 'and don't show me up.'

I glanced round, my gaze falling on a young lad not more than twenty years old. I walked up and tapped him on his shoulder. 'Excuse me,' I said. 'I'm looking for Eric Maker. Can you point him out to me?'

The bloke, who was younger than I'd realised, suddenly looked petrified. Perhaps he was the shy and retiring kind.

'Who—' He cleared his throat. 'Who is that?'

I frowned. 'He works here. Mid-thirties, brown hair, brown eyes. It's very important that I speak to him.'

The young man gave me a helpless shrug. 'I don't know who he is but I can find out. What do you want him for?'

I tapped the side of my nose and winked. 'I could tell you,' I said, 'but then I'd have to kill you.'

He blanched and swallowed. I stared at him. I was obviously joking – he realised that, right?

A far older and far burlier man with blond hair and a range of tattoos, including a rather alarming one stretching up his neck and curling round his jawline, walked up and clapped his colleague on the shoulder. 'I'll deal with this,' he said in a distinctly East End accent. 'Who are you and what do you want?'

Hmmm. Customer service around here left a lot to be desired. Then again, maybe this garage was so busy that they could afford to turn people away. I smiled, as if none of this was a problem in the slightest, and repeated my question. 'I'm looking for Eric Maker. I just want to talk to him. Can you help?'

'You didn't answer my first question,' the man grunted. His beady-eyed stare made me feel surprisingly uncomfortable. 'Who are you?'

'I'm Saffron Sawyer.'

He gave me the once over, his eyes slipping up and down my body. It wasn't a lascivious leer; truthfully, I had the impression that he'd rather slam his fist into my face for daring to step onto his hallowed garage ground. I was beginning to think that I'd made a terrible mistake in introducing myself. Watching from a safe distance and learning the lay of the land would have been a safer option.

'There's no one called Eric here.' He started to turn away. 'You've got the wrong place.'

I stood my ground. 'I'm not here to cause any trouble.'

'It doesn't matter why you're here,' he said. 'There still isn't an Eric.'

Except there was. I had no idea why the man was lying, but the Metafora magic wouldn't have brought me here unless my client was inside. 'Look,' I said, 'I only want to talk to him.'

The tattooed man rounded on me. 'Listen, lady.' His voice rose further. 'You can stay here all fucking day, if you want. It won't change the fact that there's no bleedin' Eric here.'

There was a clatter of metal hitting the ground from behind a dark-green sedan. I glanced round, catching a glimpse of a fallen wrench before looking up at the face of its clumsy owner. For one instant, the brown eyes of a dark-haired man met mine, panic flaring in their depths. Then his shoulders sagged in apparent resignation and he walked towards us.

The burly tattooed bloke frowned at me. 'You with the police?' he asked.

I shrugged. It was as good a reason as any to be here, and

better than telling the man that I was a faery godmother. 'Yes.' I smiled. 'I'm with the police.'

At least three of the mechanics working to my right froze. As Eric Maker reached us, his brow knitted with anxiety. The youngest-looking mechanic took off, dropping his tools and sprinting out of the garage as fast as his legs would carry him.

Pumpkin, who'd apparently decided this was some sort of fun game designed for his benefit, belted forward with such force that his lead yanked out of my hand. Barking loudly, he pelted after the poor guy.

I swore under my breath. Damned dog. 'I'll be right back,' I muttered.

The other mechanics stopped what they were doing to watch. I ducked and dove, veering my way round cars, bits of metal and machinery that did goodness knew what. A few voices called out, yelling at their mate to run harder. It's just as well I have a reasonably thick skin otherwise I could end up with a serious complex.

I turned the corner in time to see the young bloke scrabbling at a door handle and Pumpkin leaping up and grabbing hold of his trousers. There was the sound of tearing fabric but, thankfully, no sign of any real damage to his flesh.

'Pumpkin!' I bellowed. 'Get your arse back here!'

The dog didn't pay me the slightest bit of attention; neither did the man. He wrenched open the door, revealing the boundary of the industrial estate and the fields beyond. Then he threw himself outside, speeding up again to get away from Pumpkin's sharp teeth. Naturally, Pumpkin went after him.

The last thing my shoes were designed for was running. I hissed to myself as I stumbled and then slid on an oil patch. I wouldn't get anywhere like this. Skidding to a halt, I pulled out my new wand and wasted several precious seconds magicking up a pair of decent trainers to replace my daft pumps. Now I had a half a hope.

I dashed after dog and man again. This was definitely not what I'd signed up for when I got out of bed that morning.

Now able to run reasonably unencumbered, I picked up speed. Once I'd zipped through the door and out the back of the garage, I spotted the mechanic vaulting over a fence and into a wheat field. Despite my curiosity as to his reasons for running, sprinting after him would only panic him further. He might do something foolish. If he ended up splattered onto a car windshield, I'd have no one to blame but myself. And Pumpkin – I would definitely blame Pumpkin.

The dratted dog, who was too short to leap the fence, had found a gap in the bottom and was squeezing himself through it.

'Pumpkin! Come!' I paused. 'Now!'

He gave no indication that he'd even heard me. Still moving, I pointed my wand at the dog, flicking magic towards him. Sadly for both of us, I was a fraction too late and missed. Pumpkin's hind legs gave one last push and he was already disappearing into the tall sheaves by the time the magic reached him.

I came to a halt, pushing my hair back and wiping the sheen of sweat off my brow. Great. Just great.

'Thought you weren't going to cause any trouble,' said a voice behind me.

I glanced round at the burly bloke. 'Sorry. My dog is an idiot.'

He gave me a long look that contained more than an edge of derision. 'You're not with the police. No copper brings a mutt like that with them on a job.'

I sighed. 'Alright, I'm not with the police. I'll head back to your garage, chat to Eric for a few minutes and then I'll be out of your hair.'

I'd have to hope that Pumpkin gave up on his chase and the young man on the run escaped without injury.

The big man snorted. 'Except there still isn't anyone called Eric here and you've already caused enough problems at it is.' His eyes hardened and I caught a sense of violent menace emanating from him. 'So get the fuck off my property.'

~

IF I'D HAD any sense, I'd have abandoned Pumpkin to his fate. I had better things to do than tear around the English country-side chasing a dog that despised me. It had been Rose's wish that I look after him, however, and I always did the best by my clients. Even if they were dead.

By the time I finally grabbed hold of the dog, at the base of an old oak tree that the young mechanic had scrambled up in a desperate bid to escape, I was in an extraordinarily grumpy mood.

'I'm sorry,' I called up through the leaves after I'd scolded Pumpkin and wrapped the lead round my hand so that he couldn't escape again. The poor kid had obviously assumed that, since I'd announced myself as police, I was after him. A part of me wondered what he was guilty of and why his boss hadn't remarked on his sprint for freedom. At least neither of them would remember any of this once I'd gone. Although the young mechanic would be mightily confused to find himself up a tree.

'Sausage factory,' I told Pumpkin as I dragged him away. 'That's where you're going.'

The dog wagged his tail.

I glared. 'Not to *eat* sausages, I might add.'

He bounced up and licked my hand. I blinked. That was almost the first time since Rose's death that he'd shown me any sort of affection. He tilted his head, his ears flopping to one side. Then he leapt up and licked me again. How cute. How heart meltingly…

My eyes narrowed. 'Manipulative,' I said aloud. I sighed, checked my watch then grimaced. Fuck a puck.

Holding Pumpkin's lead as tightly as I could, I allowed the Metafora magic to transport us back to the office. We'd barely made it through the door when Jasper stomped towards me. 'Where have you been? It's midday already!'

I screwed up my face in an attempt at an apology. 'I'll explain later.' I jerked my head backwards. 'I'll head out to the church ASAP using the Metafora room. If you can keep your distance while I speak to Ethan, hopefully this will get sorted out in a jiffy.'

Jasper clicked his tongue. 'We don't have time for that.' He took my elbow in a steely grip. 'I thought something had happened to you,' he muttered. 'I was worried.'

'I…' I didn't get the chance to finish my sentence. Something very strange was happening to my body. I felt light-headed and somewhat queasy, and my insides felt like they were being turned inside out. It wasn't entirely unpleasant but it was definitely weird.

A whoosh of cold air seemed to travel through me and my heart skipped a beat. I gasped aloud and clutched my chest, staggering slightly as the marbled floor underneath my feet slipped and slid into something very different.

I stared at the grey cobblestones, unable to understand what had happened. Various human passers-by wandered past us, oblivious to the fact that we had materialised right in front of their noses. Pumpkin whined, his nostrils flaring as he tried to work out the abrupt change in scents. At least I wasn't the only one who was completely freaked out.

'It takes a bit of getting used to at first,' Jasper said. He released my elbow and my body wavered.

'What the hell was that?' I croaked.

'I don't have to use the Metafora room's magic to transport myself,' he told me kindly, as I did my very best not to keel over like a sack of potatoes. 'You know that.'

'Why hasn't anyone noticed that we appeared out of nowhere? We're not invisible right now.'

'It's an integral part of the magical process. Essentially, it's the same memory magic that protects every faery when they're out working. It's just more ... fleeting, shall we say.'

Huh. I poked myself. I still felt ... odd. 'I didn't know you could take people with you. Why did we walk to the office this morning? Why didn't we travel this way?' I suddenly grinned. 'This is much more efficient!'

'It takes a lot of magical energy. I only use it when I have to.'

I peered at him. Actually, now that he mentioned it, his skin did have an unusual flushed tinge. 'You're definitely going to have to add it to the list of things to teach me.'

Jasper offered me a brief, rueful smile, implying that he had no faith whatsoever that I'd be able to pick up this particular trick but he didn't want to shatter my dreams. He still didn't realise how determined I could be when I wanted to achieve something.

He nodded to the right. 'Holy Trinity Church is just round that corner.' He drew in a breath. 'If Ethan tries anything...'

'He won't,' I declared, sounding a lot more confident than I felt.

'If he does,' Jasper repeated, 'use your wand to defend yourself and shout. I'll be by your side in a breath.' His face darkened. 'He won't get the chance to do anything. I promise you that, Saffron.'

'It'll be fine.'

'Maybe I should come with you…'

'The presence of the Devil's Advocate will only inflame matters. Don't worry,' I reassured him. 'If I feel even slightly uneasy, I'll holler.'

Jasper dropped his head so that his face was close to mine. 'Remember that you're my friend,' he said, putting heavy emphasis on the last word. 'I don't allow my friends to get hurt.'

I shivered even though it was a warm day. Then I pushed myself up onto my tiptoes and kissed his cheek, pausing for a second too long but unable to pull myself away.

Jasper's eyes met mine, his emerald irises darkening. 'Saffron,' he said, his voice a rasp.

I swallowed then I brushed my lips against his cheek again. 'Once more for luck,' I whispered. It was too tempting to forget about the trolls and stay here with him. I swallowed and gave myself a mental slap. We were supposed to be friends. I had to remember that. 'I'd better go before Ethan gets too annoyed.' Or before I did something that might embarrass us both.

I stepped back, tugging on Pumpkin's lead. 'This won't take long,' I promised.

'You get five minutes. Then I'm coming after you, no matter what.'

There was something deliciously ominous about that. I nodded agreement before turning on my heel. It was time to find out what the leader of the trolls had to say for himself.

At first glance, Colchester's Holy Trinity Church doesn't look particularly impressive. It's positioned awkwardly in the centre of the town, right next to a road, and architecturally it appears almost rustic. However, it's the only Saxon building still standing in the town, having been there for nigh on a thousand years, and the rough-looking stonework includes re-purposed Roman bricks. On a sunny day, the terracotta roof tiles and reassuringly solid tower provide a stunning focal point against blue skies and the vivid green leaves of nearby trees.

The weather today was grey and gloomy and the irritation etched on Ethan's face as he leaned against the wall next to the arched doorway detracted somewhat from the ancient building's grandeur. Still, I was glad that he'd chosen to appear – and that enough tourists were milling around to help guarantee my safety.

The troll leader didn't move a muscle as I walked up the narrow pathway. When I came to a halt a metre away from him, however, he spoke. 'Is this some sort of power play?' he enquired. 'Invite me to a rendezvous and then arrive late? Because I don't have time for uppity faery godmother games.'

Okay. He was pissed off. Then again, so was I. 'My punctuality – or lack thereof – is as a result of matters outside my control,' I said, with more than a touch of uncharacteristic primness. 'I'm not playing a game here. Not when lives are at stake.'

A muscle jerked in Ethan's jaw but otherwise he remained preternaturally still. 'Did you have to bring the dog?'

Pumpkin was quivering at my feet, not with fear but with rage. His growls were growing in intensity with every second that passed. It was nice to not be the focus of the dog's antipathy for a change. I reminded myself that the object of this meeting was to calm matters down, not cause more friction, and hushed him. For once, Pumpkin did as he was told though he continued to snarl silently at the troll. I couldn't blame him – and, frankly, neither could Ethan.

'Where I go, he goes,' I said with more drama than was necessary. And then, because I couldn't help myself despite the precarious nature of this meeting, I added, 'After all, his original owner is dead. You shot her.'

Ethan pushed himself off the church wall, his features darkening. 'I've not forgotten.' He glared. 'And I've not covered up what I did. I'm not a faery godmother. I admit my mistakes.'

I folded my hands together to stop my fists from clenching. 'My office issued an apology to your kind.'

'Decades after the fact.'

We glowered at each other. I counted to ten then drew in a deep breath. 'Now that's out of the way, let's talk about why we're both here.'

'Indeed,' he said without smiling. 'Let's do that. You attacked my trolls and almost blinded one of them.'

Relief washed through me. Melissa was alright after all and

she wasn't permanently blind. It was a small success but an important one. 'Your trolls came to my door and tried to kidnap me.'

Ethan's pupils flared. 'They did no such thing. They were sent to your door to bring you to me for a meeting. It was an entirely cordial affair.'

'It didn't feel very cordial at the time,' I shot back. 'It felt like they were trying to attack me on my own doorstep.'

Conflicting emotions flitted across the troll's face. 'It is possible,' he said grudgingly, 'that they didn't explain themselves very clearly and that I should have given you some warning first.'

'A phone call would have been nice.' I sniffed and looked away. I like to think that I'm mature enough to admit my mistakes too. 'It's possible that I over-reacted to the sight of them – it was unexpected. I could have handled it better and I'm truly sorry I hurt Melissa.' I paused. A little over-sharing wouldn't hurt. 'I was scared.'

For the briefest moment, Ethan seemed to soften. 'In aiding your own kind, you have also helped our cause, Saffron. Regardless of what eventually happens between the trolls and the faery godmothers, I give you my word that you will not be harmed by us. Not now. Not ever.'

I wasn't sure that was a promise he'd be able to keep but I appreciated the sentiment and what it cost him to make it. 'If you want to talk to me,' I said, 'call in advance to set up a meeting. There won't be anything so urgent that it requires trolls turning up unannounced at my home.'

'Sadly, that is where you are wrong.' He watched me carefully. 'There is a very urgent matter to discuss. It's why I wanted to meet with you yesterday. Someone in the Office of Faery Godmothers has fucked up badly, and it could have implications for all of us.'

I stared at him. 'You're exaggerating.' He had to be. He'd spent so long hiding in the shadows with the rest of the trolls that he was skittish and jumpy and altogether paranoid. Except that Ethan didn't strike me as that kind of person at all.

He laughed humourlessly. 'Oh,' he said, 'you'll wish I was exaggerating when you hear what I have to say.'

'Go on then.'

'There is a human somewhere – I can't work out where or who – but there is a human in this country,' he said, 'who has possession of a wand.'

My brow furrowed. 'A magic wand?'

Ethan's dark solemnity increased. 'Yes. I've seen photos of it online. And it's not just a magic wand. This wand definitely belonged to a faery godmother.'

I stepped back and scratched my head. I didn't get it. 'So?'

He looked at me as if I were crazy. 'So? How can you not see what a disaster this is?'

'Faery wands only work for faeries,' I said slowly. 'You must know that. There's no chance that some humans will run amok because they have a wand to wave around. It doesn't work like that. As far as your human is concerned, all they have is a stick.'

Ethan didn't relax; if anything, he looked more annoyed. 'This human knows exactly what they have. They know it's a wand and they're trying to find out more about it. They also know,' he said deliberately, 'that it belongs to a faery godmother.'

I shook my head. 'That's not possible. There are stringent safeguarding measures in place. Memory magic means that the humans we come into contact with don't remember anything about us. It's probably just some daft internet prank.'

'It is not a prank,' he bit out. 'And can you honestly guarantee that there are no humans anywhere in this country who know that faery godmothers exist?'

Uh... I paled. Vincent knew. The ex-drug dealing human knew about faery godmothers because I'd messed up the memory magic when I first met him. But he didn't have a damned magic wand in his possession...

Then my stomach flipped. Oh, wait. Yes, he did. I'd left my wand in Vincent's house when I was dragged there by Art Adwell, the creepy politican who'd been after Rose. I'd been forced to escape at short notice and leave my wand behind. Fuck a puck. Maybe Vincent had it.

'You see?' Ethan said softly, reading my expression. 'You've just thought of someone. I bet there's more than one human out there who knows about your kind. What happens if they tell the world?'

I tried to scoff. 'No one will believe that faery godmothers exist.'

He folded his arms. 'There are plenty of people who believe in Bigfoot, the Loch Ness Monster, ghosts, aliens in Area 51, crop circles, faked moon landings, Atlantis, Eldorado, El Chupacabra...' His voice trailed off. 'Need I go on?'

'Some of those things are actually true,' I argued. 'And the world hasn't imploded because a small group of humans happen to believe in them.'

'They don't have any evidence.' His expression soured further. 'A magic wand is evidence. And if the humans realise faery godmothers are real, they'll realise trolls are real too. We'll end up in cages being gawked at, or being used for our magical powers. We'll be enslaved by humanity until the end of time.'

'That's ridiculous. It'll never happen.'

Ethan's response was quiet but determined. 'Are you really willing to bet everything on that supposition? Tell your faery godmother friends what's happened and get this fixed before those words come back to haunt you.' He paused. 'If you don't, we'll have no choice but to take drastic action.' He raised his head and looked over my shoulder. 'Your chaperone is here,' he said. 'I don't imagine that this news will be a favourable addition to his audit of your office.'

Fuck a puck. I turned and followed his gaze then waved frantically at Jasper, who was striding towards us with dark intent.

'We're fine!' I called. 'We're all fine here! I'll be back with you in a second!' I swung back to the troll. 'Don't tell him. I'll sort this out. There is nothing to worry about. Honestly. By the end of today, I'll have dealt with it. Just,' I licked my lips, 'just send me what information you already have.'

'Email?'

Email would leave a trail. 'No. Courier. Use a delivery faery if you have to.'

Ethan's eyes held mine. 'I'll expect a call by tomorrow morning at the latest. You have my number?'

'Include it with the other information.' My mind whirred. I'd bloody throttle Vincent if this was him. It *had* to be him. The self-serving wanker. 'This won't be a problem for you, Ethan. It won't be a problem for anyone.'

'It had better not be. I've put a lot on the line with my people by trusting you, Saffron. I don't want to tell them I made a mistake.'

'You haven't,' I promised. 'You've really not.'

He inclined his head. 'Don't let me down.' He put his hands in his pockets and walked away, disappearing round the corner of the church and out of view.

Jasper wasted no time in marching up to me. He scanned my face. 'What happened?' he demanded. 'Are you alright?'

'I'm absolutely fine,' I said, dissembling as best as I could. I spread out my arms. 'Hale and hearty and untouched by trolls.'

Jasper grunted. 'So what did he want?'

I bit my lip. 'We discussed what went wrong yesterday. I

had indeed jumped to conclusions, while his trolls weren't clear about their intentions. We've resolved the issue and I'm confident that it won't happen again. All's well that ends well.'

Jasper tapped his foot. 'So what *were* their intentions?'

'Mmm?'

'What were the trolls' intentions? Why did they go to your house?'

If I told him, there would be no going back; the genie would be out of the bottle. As Ethan had pointed out, we were in the final stages of the audit. Revealing the news about the wand could colour the results of Jasper's report. It would be far better, I decided, to sort out this problem on my own. Then, when I did tell him the truth, I'd show him that I'd already solved the issue so there was nothing to worry about. It wouldn't be a lie exactly. It would simply be a ... delay.

I squashed down my guilt. I'd wait and see what Vincent had to say before mentioning anything concrete. If it turned out that I couldn't resolve this mess on my own, I'd tell Jasper everything this evening. Faery godmother's honour.

'Well,' I hedged, 'it turns out that Ethan is something of a conspiracy theorist. He mentioned the Loch Ness Monster. And Atlantis.' I shrugged. 'I promised him that I'd look into his concerns.'

Jasper looked thoroughly confused. 'He's worried about the Loch Ness Monster?'

I waved a hand. 'Amongst other things. Anyhow, I'm hungry. Now that everything's resolved, I could do with some lunch. My treat. There's a great café round the corner.'

Jasper raised his eyebrows. 'You're offering to buy me lunch?'

'Sure.'

'Like we're on a date?'

Uh... 'If you like,' I squeaked.

His face broke into a sudden smile. 'Hold that thought. If you're sure that Ethan is out of the way for now, I'd better get back to the office and tell the Director what's happened. And I still have a lot to do before the end of the week.' He leant forward, allowing to me catch a heavenly whiff of his deep cinnamon scent. 'Make it dinner instead and you've got a deal.'

Mutely, I nodded agreement.

'Oh, and Saffron?' Jasper added, reaching for my hand and trailing his index finger along the length of my palm. 'Once we've finished eating, and enjoyed a decadent dessert and a bottle of wine or two...'

I stared at him. 'Yes?'

He let go. 'Then you'll tell me what's going on and what Ethan really said.'

Fuck a puck. My eyes dropped. 'Okay,' I mumbled.

SEVEN

As much as I'd have enjoyed the experience of Jasper's magic transporting me back to the office, I let him go ahead, telling him that I'd forego the delights of the canteen in favour of picking up a sandwich and strolling back on my feet.

If he was suspicious, he didn't say anything. He already knew that I was withholding information so I suppose he didn't need to labour the point.

I waited until he'd gone, then twisted round and made a beeline for Vincent's quiet street. Now that it was afternoon, the untrustworthy bastard had to be out of bed.

At least Pumpkin appeared happy. It didn't take the little dog long to work out which direction we were heading in. By the time we got to Vincent's door, he was apoplectic with excitement. I rang the doorbell and waited patiently as Pumpkin danced around my feet in doggy ecstasy.

If I'd been expecting Vincent to appear sullen or look unhappily surprised at my visit, I was mistaken. When he opened the door, he was not only fully clothed and cleanly shaven but also grinning widely. 'Saffron Sawyer! And darling Pumpkin! How lovely to see you both!'

I raised an eyebrow at his effusive welcome but didn't comment. 'Hi Vincent,' I said. 'May we come in?'

'Of course, of course!' He stepped back. 'How are things?' He smirked. 'Granted any tasty wishes lately?'

I wrinkled my nose and walked inside, heading for his living room – and the last place where I'd seen my poor wand. He'd tidied up since my previous visit. Any evidence that Art Adwell and his goons had been here had been sorted out. There was even a small vase sitting on the coffee table with some flowers in it.

Vincent caught me looking at them and gave me a sheepish smile. 'I might not have known Rose for long but she had an extraordinary impact on my life. You should see my little garden out the back. I've been taking her advice and pottering away.' He waggled his fingers at me. 'Green thumb!' he crowed. 'That's me!'

From the dirt under his fingernails, Vincent was more brown thumbed than green. Maybe it was a good thing that he'd found himself a hobby, but it wasn't quite good enough.

While Pumpkin leapt up onto a nearby chair and settled down for a quick nap, I got right to the point. 'Where is my wand?'

Vincent flushed. Ah ha. 'Oh, Saffy,' he said. 'Has your own crazy memory magic started to affect you?' He tutted in dismay. 'I'm so sorry.'

My eyes narrowed. Vincent coughed and pointed at my midriff. I glanced down, noting my replacement wand tucked into my belt, and frowned. 'Not that one!' I snapped. 'I mean the one that I left here.'

He tilted his head. 'You left a magic wand here?' He looked

around as if half expecting the damned thing to materialise out of thin air. 'Where?'

I gritted my teeth. 'When you escaped on your motorbike with Rose, Art Adwell's goons knocked me out and brought me back here. I managed to get out but I left behind my wand. It must be here somewhere.'

Vincent frowned blankly. 'I didn't find anything. I definitely haven't seen a wand. I'd have told you if I had.'

I folded my arms. 'What do you want?'

'Huh?'

'What do you want in return for my wand?' I wouldn't grant him a full wish but, if it kept Ethan quiet, I'd come up with some sort of bribe that would keep Vincent off my back.

A crafty light crossed his face, arousing all my suspicions. 'Teeth,' he said suddenly. 'I'd like some new teeth. Dentists terrify me. If you give me a bright, shiny white smile and I don't have to undergo hour upon hour of painful, expensive treatment, I will find your wand for you.' He opened his mouth wide, displaying his crooked yellow molars. 'Gimme that Simon Cowell smile, Saffron Sawyer!'

My shoulders sank and I dropped down onto the sofa. 'You don't have it then. You don't have my wand.'

'I didn't say that I did. But give me my teeth and I will find it.' He beamed. 'Almost definitely. I'm great at finding things. In fact, I reckon your wand is probably wedged under one of the sofa cushions as we speak.'

I sprang up and whirled round, pulling out my replacement wand and twirling it. All of the cushions immediately rose into the air. Pumpkin yelped, his eyes wide as he was included in the levitation process. I scanned the now cushionless sofa and chair with desperate optimism. Vincent let out a crow of delight and, for a second, my heart leapt.

'Fifty pence!' He scooped up the silver coin. 'Brilliant!'

I pointed at the squashed brown splodge in one corner. 'What's that?' I asked dubiously.

He glanced down. 'Jaffa Cake, I think.' He reached forward, grabbed it then crammed it into his mouth. 'Yesh,' he said through a mouthful of stale horror. 'Definitely Jaffa Cake.'

I was too disappointed to be disgusted. I twirled my wand again, returning the cushions to their original position. Pumpkin glared at me as he landed back on the chair with a soft oomph. 'Sorry,' I muttered. 'I was desperate.'

Vincent swallowed the last of the biscuit. 'Can you make me float too?'

I sat back down and covered my face with my hands. 'No.'

'Aw, Saff.' He sat down next to me and put his arm around my shoulders. 'It can't be that big a deal. The wand will turn up. I can still look for it.'

I appreciated his buoyant attitude but I knew deep down that it was misplaced. 'If it's not here,' I said, light-headed and nauseous, 'then Art Adwell has it.'

I felt Vincent's body stiffen at my mention of the murderous politician but he kept his tone light. 'He's in jail. Even if he does have your old wand, he can't do anything with it. Besides, he won't remember meeting you or that it's a magical object capable of granting amazing wishes. Right?'

I didn't answer.

'Right, Saffron?'

I licked my lips nervously and dropped my hands. 'In theory.'

'Oh no.' Vincent pulled his arm away and looked at me. 'What did you do?'

I didn't meet his eyes. 'You remember I gave Rose a cup of tea with gingko biloba in it so that the memory magic would stop affecting her and I could help her properly? It was against the rules but I had to do something to get her to trust me. She was in deep trouble and it was my job to find out what was going on. It was too hard when she kept forgetting that I existed, so I came up with a solution that I thought would help all of us.'

'Yeah, I remember.' He frowned. 'So?'

I picked at the threads of a nearby cushion. 'Art Adwell drank some of the gingko biloba tea when he was here.'

Vincent stared. 'He did what?'

'He threw it all up again almost immediately afterwards! I didn't think it would be a problem. I was sure that it wasn't in his system long enough to work against the memory magic.'

'And now?'

'Now,' I said in a small voice, 'I think I could have been wrong. He might remember me and what happened between us. I told him I was a faery godmother. I used magic in front of him.'

'Your actions also put him in prison and made him the most hated man in the country,' Vincent added helpfully.

I pushed back a loose curl, tucking it behind my ear. 'He might not know that part was because of me.'

Vincent made a face. 'Just because he's a politician, doesn't make him stupid.'

True. Unfortunately, I had no one to blame for this mess except myself. 'No one will believe him,' I said, as much to myself as to Vincent. 'No matter what he says, no one will actually believe that faery godmothers are real. Art Adwell has no credibility and no future. Everything will be fine.'

'Sure.' Vincent nodded, before giving me an arch grin and a cheesy thumbs up. 'Can I still get some new teeth, though?'

I flicked my wand. 'There you go.'

He frowned at the tube of toothpaste that now sat next to the vase of flowers on his coffee table. I shrugged. 'Four out of five dentists approve it. And more than one tooth faery has told me that you won't get better minty freshness anywhere else.'

'You're lying about the last part, aren't you?'

'Yeah. But if you don't want it...'

Vincent's hand snapped out and took the toothpaste. 'Beggars can't be choosers – though I reckon I deserve better than this. I do everything I can to help you whenever you need it. Memory magic doesn't work on me and I've kept my mouth shut about what you really are.'

'You've told everyone you know,' I said flatly.

'Alright,' he conceded. 'I might have done that. But they don't believe me. Everyone's convinced it's a joke. So you're right. Adwell won't cause any real problems no matter what he says.'

'Yup.' I got to my feet. 'Come on, Pumpkin. We should vamoose.'

Vincent looked disappointed. 'You're leaving already?'

'I'm supposed to be at work. I've got loads of new clients to deal with.' I paused and thought about Eric Maker. 'Actually, maybe you can still help. Can you think of any reason why, in the same small business, there would be one person who wouldn't want to use their real name, another who runs away at high speed because they think the police are after them, and a boss who cares about neither of them?'

'Saffron, babe, I can think of loads of reasons. Most of them involving serious criminal action.'

I sighed. 'Yeah. That's what I thought.'

ETHAN HAD STAYED true to his word. By the time I got back to the office with Pumpkin in tow, there was a small neat package waiting for me on my desk.

I eyed it warily, thinking about the last time the trolls had sent a package to this office that had contained the severed bloody digits of several unlucky faery godmothers. I hoped this parcel wouldn't end up causing the same level of chaos. Frankly, I was tempted to toss it directly into the bin and pretend I'd never seen it, but I was no ostrich and I wasn't going to bury my head in the sand. No one ever made it to the top without first making a few mistakes along the way.

'I'm not perfect,' I said aloud.

Angela, walking past with a pile of folders in her arms, flicked me a glance. 'We know, Saffron. Believe me, we know. In fact, a rather clever man called Stanley J. Randall once said that the closest anyone ever comes to perfection is when they fill out a job application form. As a senior manager in HR, I can confirm that is very true.' She sniffed. 'Personally, I'm an advocate for lie-detector tests prior to interviews.'

'Water-boarding too, I imagine.'

She snapped her fingers. 'What a great idea. That would definitely weed out a lot of time wasters and lazy layabouts.' The worrying part was that there was a good chance she wasn't joking.

Angela smiled. 'Don't forget that it's our first Team Building Tuesday tomorrow!' she chirped before continuing on her way.

I grimaced. After the success of Rainbow Friday, an idea which Angela had stolen from me, she was now instituting more initiatives. I supposed anything would be better than today's version of Messed-Up Monday.

I ripped open the package and gazed at the memory stick that fell onto my desk. It'll be fine, I told myself. Ethan was just over-reacting.

I gingerly tested my chair, sitting down only when I was absolutely sure that it would hold my weight, then plugged the memory stick into my computer and waited as it whirred into life. Pumpkin gazed up at me from the floor.

'Don't chew this chair,' I commanded.

He continued to stare at me.

'And stop silently judging me. The man's already in prison.'

Pumpkin didn't twitch.

I glowered. 'I'm going to deal with it. Alright?' I leaned back and looked around. 'You didn't hear it from me,' I told him, 'but I'm pretty sure there are some left-over sandwiches in some of those desks behind me. It might be worth checking them out.'

The small dog flicked the end of his tail, either in acknowledgement of my words or dismissal of my existence. Then he picked himself up and trotted off, his head bowed as he snuffled around looking for discarded titbits. I breathed out and returned my attention to the computer.

A single folder, unhelpfully marked Apocalypse Now, appeared on my screen. I clicked on it then opened up the first document. It appeared to be a series of screen shots from an online forum. I frowned and leaned in to read them, making a note of the website address so I could check it out later.

The discussion was centred around an anonymous blogpost. As far as I could tell, the blogger had stated categorically that 'fairy godmothers' existed, using the spelling humans applied in children's stories. The forum mostly involved a range of comments suggesting that the author of the blog seek medical help. I started to relax. My suspicions were accurate. No one would take such an allegation seriously. No human, anyway.

I skipped to the next document, gasping aloud when a photo of the exact wand which Art Adwell had taken from me filled my screen, with a caption of a web address below. Fuck a puck. That confirmed two things, neither of which filled me with any sort of joy. First of all, whether he was behind bars and awaiting trial or not, Adwell was definitely the slimy bastard behind the faery godmother rumours. Secondly, his memory was clearly unimpeded by any sort of magic. Whether he'd vomited it up or not, the gingko biloba had done what it was designed for and made him immune to the memory magic's effects – and that was entirely down to me.

Not for the first time that day, nausea rose from the pit of my belly. I already knew that Art Adwell was dangerous; the risk he posed had just increased tenfold.

I told myself it was okay. He was locked up. He couldn't cause any real harm – although I was distinctly unimpressed that he appeared to have unimpeded access to the internet. It didn't matter. Even if he had my old wand with him in his cell, which seemed unlikely, he couldn't use it. His words were already being dismissed as those of a complete crank.

I opened up a browser, carefully typing in the address for Adwell's blog. There were several entries, each one ranting about the evil presence of 'fairy godmother fuckers' who were messing with the 'fabric of British society'. Each post was accompanied by photos of my wand, taken from different angles. There was even a video. I held my breath and clicked on it. A clip of a hand gripping the wand began to play, with a disembodied and obviously disguised voice in the background.

'I've tried various methods to get it to work with no success so far,' the voice said, whipping the wand from side to side and then spinning it like some sort of majorette. 'I know this might be hard to believe but there is incredible power wrapped up in this thing. All I have to do is to find out how to unlock it and...'

'Wotcha doing?'

I scrambled, fumbling with the mouse as I hastily closed the webpage. I spun round in my chair and snapped at Rupert, who was standing directly behind my desk. For some reason, he'd decided that today was the day to start growing a wispy beard. It didn't suit him in the slightest but, from the way he was stroking it, he was extremely proud of his efforts so far.

'I'm working,' I snapped. 'What else would I be doing?'

'Watching porn,' he answered. 'Obviously.' He pointed at my screen.

I glanced back round, realising that an uninvited pop-up was now being displayed. A man and a woman, in a position that didn't just appear uncomfortable but also looked physically impossible, flashed back at me. I cursed and shut it down.

'Don't let Billy catch you doing that,' Rupert told me. 'Apparently it's against the rules to watch healthy interactions between two consenting adults when you're in the office.'

Imagine that. I crossed my arms over my chest. 'What do you want, Rupert?'

He gave me a lopsided smile and tilted his head in a move that I supposed was designed to make him look sweet and harmless. 'I wanted to tell you that I understand, Saffron.'

I gazed blankly back at him. 'Understand what?'

His smile grew. It was definitely on the wrong side of smarmy. 'Why you've been playing so hard to get. You're taking one for the team and working on the Devil's Advocate so that he gives us a good report card. Your dedication to your job is impressive.' His tongue darted out, wetting his lips. 'Don't worry. I won't hold it against you. I'm not the jealous type. I'm patient, too. I can wait until you're done with him.'

Don't slap him. Don't slap him. Don't slap him.

'Rupert,' I began.

'I mean,' he continued, 'it can't be easy for you. He doesn't have much of a sense of humour, does he? And he's not very ... attractive.'

Clearly Rupert didn't see what I saw. 'Actually,' I said, 'I find him sinfully sexy.'

Delilah, whose head had been bent over her work, whipped round in our direction.

Rupert's nose wrinkled. 'Really?'

'But unfortunately,' I said, 'the Devil's Advocate and I are merely friends. The reason I've not gone out with you, Rupert, is because I don't like you.'

He chuckled. 'If you say so, Saffron.' He winked. 'We both know the truth though. I've seen your eyes drift over in my direction when you think I'm not looking.'

'Your desk is right in front of the kitchen. And the coffee machine.'

'Sure.' He leaned forward. 'You're thinking about me right now, aren't you?'

'Rupert,' I sighed, 'I'm *talking* to you right now.' I couldn't deal with this deluded crap. Trying to complain about him was pointless because he held favoured status on account of his well-connected family. He wasn't trusted enough to deal with clients so he did admin instead in the Adventus room. Rupert still counted as a faery godmother, though. More's the pity.

I paused. 'Actually,' I said slowly, 'I *have* been thinking about you.'

'I knew it!'

'Yeah.' I nodded with a serious expression on my face. 'I've been thinking that it's impressive that you don't care that you're called a faery godmother even though technically you're a godfather.'

He blinked. 'We're supposed to use gender-appropriate terms,' he said. 'But no one actually does. It's not a big deal.'

'You see?' I gestured to Delilah to encourage her to agree with me. Her eyes shone and she bobbed her head with fervent delight. 'You don't mind that you're not considered important enough to be labelled with the correct job title. We use faery godmother for everyone because women are nurturing and caring and powerful. And men are,' I shrugged, 'not usually like that. It's impressive that you can put your own identity aside and be counted with us girls.'

Two high spots of colour appeared on Rupert's cheeks. 'Men are powerful. And caring.'

'Of course they are,' I soothed. 'But you know what our mantra is.' I repeated the chant with which we started every morning. 'We are faery godmothers.'

Delilah joined in. 'We are faery godmothers!'

From the other side of the room, Figgy banged her desk. 'We are faery godmothers!' she called out.

I smiled.

Rupert took a step back. 'Huh,' he said. He scratched at skin underneath his beard. 'Huh.'

'Anyway,' I jerked my thumb back at my computer. 'I ought to get back to work.'

'Yeah.' Rupert sniffed. 'Me too.'

Me too indeed. I swivelled round, catching Delilah's raised eyebrows. Maybe today wasn't going to be a chaotic failure after all.

EIGHT

I allowed myself thirty minutes to look through the rest of the links and files that Ethan had sent over. As far as I could tell, they were just more of the same.

It was smart that Adwell was concealing his identity because the more he babbled on about magic, the more of a lunatic he sounded. If the tabloids noticed what he was up to, he'd be the laughing stock of the country. Since his past actions had come to light, he was already considered to be the most despicable man alive and he was roundly derided from Perth to Penzance.

Once I got over my initial dismay at the revelation that he both remembered me and had my wand in his corrupt, sweaty hands, I started to relax. Knowledge was power – but that didn't mean Art Adwell was anything other than completely powerless.

A plan of action to keep Ethan happy was already forming in my head. Honestly, there was little else to worry about. I decided that I'd come clean to Jasper that evening after dinner and take my licks from there. Job done.

Feeling considerably more buoyant, I skipped happily to the

canteen for a quick snack to fuel me for the rest of the day. The only other people present were Alicia and Figgy, giggling in the corner, their heads bent towards each other. I grabbed a banana and a pre-wrapped sandwich and sat down some distance away. Figgy, however, glanced up and beckoned me over. 'Saffron! Come and join us!'

Alicia made a point of rolling her eyes and pouting, but she didn't argue.

Shrugging, and hoping I wasn't going to regret it, I ambled over. 'Hey.'

Figgy patted the chair next to her. 'Pull up a pew.'

'Yeah,' Alicia drawled. 'Join us. We're just discussing the state of the economy.'

I raised an eyebrow. Figgy giggled. 'Don't be daft. I don't watch the news or pay attention to any of that stuff. It's far too depressing.'

I sat down and smiled at her. Most of Figgy's life, at least as far as I could tell, involved trailing after Alicia, smiling at her jokes and enjoying rainbows and glitter.

I unpeeled my banana and took a bite. Both women started giggling again. Wondering if I was the butt of their joke, I took another bite and swallowed.

Figgy motioned towards the banana and wiped her eyes. 'It's my latest client,' she explained. 'He calls himself Pistol Pete.'

Alicia nodded, mirth in her eyes. 'By day he's an accountant and by night...'

'...he's a male stripper,' Figgy finished. 'He's actually very talented. He does this thing involving a fruit bowl where he starts with a grape and...'

I held up my hands. 'I don't need to know the details.'

'I didn't take you for a prude,' Alicia commented.

'I'm eating.' And I didn't think that smirking over our clients' proclivities was helpful. To each their own, after all.

'His dream is to take his show worldwide,' Figgy said. 'And to appear in the Royal Variety Performance.'

'Which obviously isn't going to happen,' Alicia added. 'Can you imagine the look on the Queen's face?'

Ah. Quite the conundrum. Some wishes could not be fulfilled.

'He's very specific about what he wants.' Figgy took a sip of her drink. 'I'm not convinced there's anything I can do to help him.' Her expression was earnest. 'What do you think, Saffron?'

I considered for a moment. 'Is his bottom line to perform or to rub shoulders with royalty?'

Figgy's brow creased. 'Good question.' She tapped her long, perfectly manicured fingernail on the table top. 'I'll have to investigate further. Thanks, Saffron!'

I wasn't quite sure what I'd done but I nodded anyway. 'You're welcome.'

Alicia nudged Figgy. For a moment, the other faery looked confused then something flashed in her eyes. She leaned over and delved into her bag, taking out a pristine white envelope. 'Here,' she said, handing it to me.

I glanced down at it. My name was written on the front of the envelope in beautifully, looping calligraphy.

'It wasn't my idea,' Alicia sniffed. 'This is all on Figs.'

Figgy shrugged awkwardly. 'I'm having a party in a couple of weeks. Everyone who's anyone is going to be there. It'd be great if you could make it.' She offered me a shy but wholly genuine smile. 'Please?'

Well, this was unexpected. A stirring warmth flitted through me. Billy was wrong, I decided; I was making friends, not enemies – and I couldn't have been happier about it.

'I'll be there,' I promised.

She beamed. 'Wonderful.'

~

I FINISHED EATING and headed back upstairs to the Metafora room, noting that Rupert had cornered Billy and was gesticulating wildly at him. I pressed my lips together and pretended not to see. It was time for me to pay Eric Maker a second visit. Hopefully, this time I'd be more successful.

From the gentle snores in the far corner of the room, Pumpkin was otherwise engaged. It was probably just as well – I'd done enough running around after him today. We could both do with the break.

I reached forward and opened the Metafora door but I'd not even stepped inside when there was the sound of skittering paws. A moment later, Pumpkin barrelled towards me, throwing himself into the little room and landing beside my feet. He looked up at me with an expression of deep reproach.

'I thought you were sleeping.'

He growled softly, in case I was in any doubt about his displeasure.

'You're supposed to let sleeping dogs lie.'

He contorted himself, lifting up one leg so that he could lick his balls.

'Maybe,' I said thoughtfully, averting my eyes, 'that saying should be sleeping dogs are lying.' It was possible that Pumpkin didn't want me to leave him behind. Perhaps he did actually enjoy my company. 'Where I go, you go. Happy now?'

He wasted no time, jumped back to his feet and allowed me to clip on his lead. Feeling somewhat emboldened, I went in for a stroke. His spine stiffened. Apparently that was still a step too far for him.

Fortunately at that moment the Metafora magic took hold

and the familiar whoosh of power transported us, negating any further chance at affection.

'I'm still the boss,' I told Pumpkin as the sparkly Metafora walls gave way to a narrow street filled with terraced houses. The curious part of me was disappointed; I'd been hoping to visit the unfriendly garage again. 'I'm the pack leader.'

'Miaow.'

I jumped and stared at the dog. 'Did you just…'

A large ginger cat jumped down from a nearby wall and walked slowly towards us. 'Miaow.'

Pumpkin leapt behind me with astonishing speed. Apparently if anyone was going to be clawed to death, it would be me.

'Tiddles!' A woman came scurrying out of the nearest house, lunged in the cat's direction and scooped it into her arms. 'You're not supposed to be outside,' she scolded. She glanced up and saw me watching. 'He's an indoor cat,' she explained with a rueful smile.

I wasn't sure that anyone had explained that to Tiddles. Given Pumpkin's ability to run rings around me, however, I wasn't in a position to comment. I checked the number of the house the woman had come out of and offered her my best smile. 'It's Kelly, right?'

Her smile faltered. 'I'm sorry. Do I know you?'

I knew from his file that Eric and Kelly had two kids. 'I'm from the school.' That would be a better lie than saying that I was from the police. After this morning, I'd decided that I would be more likely to gain Eric's trust if I told him I was involved with his children rather than the long arm of the law.

'I was hoping to catch you and your partner.'

Her expression dropped. 'Oh no,' she said. 'What's Laura done now?'

Excellent. 'It's best if we discuss it inside.'

Her shoulders slumped. 'Okay. Come on in, then.'

Pumpkin and I followed her in, squeezing in past a collection of bikes leaning against the wall in the hallway. Kelly led us into a small living room which looked clean but untidy because of the piles of car magazines and toys scattered about.

'Would you like a cup of tea?' she asked, dropping Tiddles.

'That would be lovely,' I said, as Pumpkin scooted underneath my legs.

Tiddles sent him a baleful look and offered a half-hearted hiss before wandering out, no doubt in search of another escape route.

'I'll call Mark then I'll pop the kettle on. He's home from work early today.' She sent me an anxious look as she went towards the kitchen.

I smiled benignly and sat down. Who the hell was Mark?

A moment later, Eric Maker ambled into the room. He'd cleaned off the oil and grease from the garage and was now wearing jeans and a T-shirt instead of grubby blue overalls.

'Hi. I'm Saffron Sawyer. I'm here from the school.'

'Mark Smith,' he grunted, taking my hand and squeezing it slightly. There wasn't the faintest flicker of recognition in his eyes. At least I'd not been completely abandoned by the memory magic.

Despite being annoyed that his file hadn't included details of his false name, I continued to smile. 'So you're home from work early today?' I asked.

'Yeah. I'm a mechanic but the boss sent us home.'

Interesting. That had to be the burly, blond-haired fellow's doing. 'Lucky for me, then,' I said. 'I'm pleased I've got this chance to talk to you.'

He gave me a hard look. 'What's happened with Laura?'

'It's best if we wait for Kelly to join us,' I said, hoping for an opportunity to question 'Mark' on his own.

He sat down next to me on the narrow sofa, picked up one

of the car magazines and flicked through to the middle pages, his eyes fixing blankly on it. 'Okay,' he said. He held the magazine up in front of his face. He seemed to be making some sort of point beyond just creating a barrier between us, but I couldn't quite work out what that point was.

'So you must like cars,' I said. It wasn't much of a conversation starter but I had to try something. 'I see there's an article in there about the new Tesla engine. Are you a fan of super cars?'

He snapped the magazine closed and put it down. 'Who isn't?' he answered shortly. Then his gaze dropped to Pumpkin and he seemed to soften.

Kelly chose that moment to bustle back in, china mugs clinking on the tray as she laid it down in front of us. 'Shall I play mother?'

'Please. No sugar for me.'

She poured the tea then perched on the edge of a chair. I felt bad about the ruse I'd used to gain entrance. She was clearly worried about her daughter, even if Eric/Mark didn't appear particularly bothered. But the deception was only temporary and neither of them would remember me after I left.

With that thought in mind, I took a sip of my tea and leaned forward. 'Laura has been finding it difficult to settle in class,' I said.

Kelly bit her lip. 'Her dyslexia,' she began, as Eric/Mark stiffened.

I waved a hand. 'It's not that,' I said. Interestingly, he seemed to relax more than Kelly did. 'But I was wondering if there'd been some trouble at home lately. Children do pick up on stress.'

Kelly's eyes flew to her partner's. 'No,' she said quickly. 'No trouble. Why? What's happened?'

I hesitated, implying that it was something delicate. 'Well,' I said, 'the thing is that she seems a bit confused. She told the teacher that her father was called Mark but she told her friends that he was called Eric. Normally, we wouldn't make an issue out of this sort of thing – so many families these days are blended. But she also had some trouble with her surname and—'

Eric/Mark got to his feet. 'We'll speak to her about it. Thank you for your time. I'll show you to the door.'

I stayed where I was. 'It would be helpful if you could give me some indication as to why she's confused. If it's a child-protection issue, it's important we know about it.'

'It's not,' he said. 'There is no issue.'

'We only want the best for her.'

He reached down and took the mug out of my hands. 'It's time for you to leave.'

I looked at Kelly; her head had dropped and she was refusing to meet my eyes. Considering how welcoming she'd been initially, she was very quiet now.

I got to my feet. Pumpkin sprang up, obviously relieved at leaving Tiddles' abode. Eric/Mark ushered both of us out.

It was only when I was stepping outside that I made my move. 'Well,' I chirped, 'thank you for time anyway, Mr Maker. It's been a pleasure.'

For a moment he didn't say anything and I wasn't sure that he'd heard me, then he grabbed my arm and manhandled me out of the house and round the corner. He slammed me against the wall of his garden shed where we were out of sight of any pesky neighbours. 'Who are you really?' he hissed. 'How do you know that name?'

I examined his face. It didn't look like he was being driven by anger. Far from it – the expression in his eyes was terrified. 'Are you in the witness protection programme?' I asked.

He raised his fist as if to hit me. I cringed out of instinct rather than anything else and my hand moved down to my wand. If need be, I was perfectly willing to use magic against my client to protect myself. I wouldn't be able to help him if I ended up in hospital. I didn't particularly want him to end up in hospital either, of course. I'd have to be careful.

Before I could pull out my wand, he seemed to realise what he was doing and dropped his arm. 'Just get out of here,' he muttered. He released me and spun away without a backward glance. A second later, I heard his front door slam. Okay then.

Pumpkin tugged on his lead, keen to get away from the place. I suppose I should have been glad that he'd not tried to bite Eric Maker. Or Tiddles.

'Don't worry, Pumpkin,' I said aloud. 'There's more than one way to skin a cat.'

I walked to the end of the street then I doubled back and returned to the same front door. Pumpkin whined but I ignored him and rang the doorbell.

'Yes?' Eric opened the front door and peered out. There wasn't the remotest trace of suspicion on his face. Go memory magic.

'Hi there! Mark Smith?'

'Yeah?'

'I'm here from Scotland Yard.' I held up my hand, using a touch of weak glamour to suggest that I was holding up a badge. 'We have some concerns about your new identity so I'm here to touch base with you.'

Tiddles wandered down the staircase, sat on the bottom stair and glared at Pumpkin. I tightened my hold on my dog's lead, just in case.

Eric stared at me, his face turning pale. 'My identity?'

'Yes.' I glanced round making a show of checking that no one was close enough to overhear. 'You're really Eric Maker, right?'

His nostrils flared and he stepped back. 'I did my time.

You've got no right coming back here and harassing me. I'm allowed to change my name if I want to. I filled in all the paperwork. It was done properly.' He started to close the door. 'So fuck off!' he called out before slamming it shut in my face.

I tapped my foot. Hmm. Not witness protection then. He'd been in prison, though; had he changed his name in order to make a fresh start?

I pursed my lips. Then I made the same little walk as before as I thought about where to go next with my enquiries, before ending right back on Kelly and Eric's doorstep. Third time lucky.

This time it was Kelly who answered. Just as she opened the door, I heard Eric call out, 'Kells? Why did you make three cups of tea?'

She frowned. 'Going crazy!' she yelled back. She smiled at me. 'Sorry about that. If you're selling something, I don't want it. I'm sorry but we're broke.'

'Don't worry.' I beamed and stuck out my hand.

Tiddles was still on the bottom stair. This time his hackles were raised and his tail was swinging from side to side in a display of extreme unhappiness. His owners might not remember me but I had my doubts about the ginger beast. Cats were indeed canny creatures. Pumpkin whimpered quietly and cowered.

'My name is Saffron Sawyer. I'm ... Mark's new probation officer. Is he in?'

Kelly's face fell. 'I'll go and get him.'

I counted to three before he came storming through, his face red. 'I'm not on probation any more!' he yelled. 'How did you get this address? Did the police give it to you?'

'Of course,' I replied smoothly, not missing a beat. 'Where else would I have got it from? There's nothing to worry about.

I'm updating our records. If you're down on our list in error, I'll get it sorted and we won't bother you again.'

He snorted derisively. 'I've heard that one before.' He screwed up his face. 'Once a crim always a crim, right?'

'Certainly not, Mr Maker. We believe wholeheartedly in rehabilitation.'

This time even the tips of his ears flushed with rage. 'It's Smith. Mark Smith. As you fucking well know.'

I did know. And now that I had an inkling about his background, it would be easier for me to do a focused search back in the office to learn the details. First, though, I wanted to hear more from the man himself. There's nothing like getting your information directly from the horse's mouth – especially if Eric Maker's wish related to his altered identity.

If he wanted to be called Mark Smith, that was his prerogative. I wanted to be called the best faery godmother in the world. Maybe if I was determined enough, one day I would be.

I made a show of frowning. 'Obviously there are some problems with our paperwork,' I said. 'I can come in now and get the correct information from you so this doesn't happen again, or I can leave it for now and get some uniforms to pop round later.'

If there's one thing I've learned when dealing with obstructive clients, it's that giving them the illusion of choice works wonders. People like to feel that they are in control. Of course, there wasn't actually any choice for Mark Smith to make. The last thing he would want was the police showing up on his doorstep. This was a nice neighbourhood and he'd changed his name for a reason. He obviously wanted to keep his past, whatever it involved, as quiet as possible. It wasn't just in the Office of Faery Godmothers that gossips abounded.

He sighed heavily, making no secret of his irritation, but in the end he gave in. 'Very well,' he muttered. 'But this is the last time I'm doing this.'

I smiled. 'I completely understand.'

Mark Smith might have conceded to the inevitable but Tiddles, alas, had other ideas. The cat had clearly decided that enough was enough and I could see his hind legs bunching up as he prepared to launch himself at Pumpkin. The last thing I needed was a fur fight.

'Do you mind if I leave my dog in your garden?' I asked quickly. 'I don't want to upset your cat by bringing him inside.'

Mark blinked and looked down, noticing Pumpkin for the first time. Tiddles took full advantage of the moment and leapt forward, claws extended. My hand dropped to my wand, tweaking it enough to cause the cat to freeze in mid-air before landing a full foot away, as if he'd merely misjudged the jump.

'Tiddles!' Mark scolded. He shooed the cat out of the way then bent down and gave Pumpkin a scratch. 'I'm sorry, doggy.'

I stared down. Unbelievable: Pumpkin would let this complete stranger with a criminal record pet him, but not me. I shook my head. Bloody mutt.

'The garden's fine. He can have a play around there. Some of the kids' toys are out so they'll keep him occupied.' For the first time, Mark's voice was warm.

'I'll take him round.' I tugged Pumpkin away, aware that I was feeling more than a twinge of jealousy at his warmth towards my client. I closed the garden gate carefully so that he wouldn't escape before I returned to my quarry.

Mark grudgingly led me inside. I elected to sit in a different spot this time; maybe a different seating arrangement would provide different results. I did, however, reach for the same mug of tea that I'd been drinking earlier, ignoring my host's frown as I did so. Normally I wouldn't have been so uncouth but it was a damned good cuppa.

'So,' I said, magicking up a notebook and chewed-up pen to give myself an appropriate air of officialdom on a budget.

'You've changed your name from Eric Maker to Mark Smith. That's by deed poll, correct?' I sneaked a look at him and noted his nod.

'I've been through all this before,' he said. 'I passed on the paperwork to your office and to the police when I moved here.'

'Uh-huh. And that was when exactly?'

He glanced upwards, recalling the date. 'Last year. Mid-August.'

'I see. What was your previous address?'

He folded his arms. 'You must have this on record.'

'It's purely for confirmation purposes, Mr Smith.'

'38 Bolston Road, Manchester.'

I scribbled it down. 'Thank you. Now the reasons for changing your name were...' I looked at him expectantly and waited.

'Personal. It's not against the law, so you can't tell me off. I was still on probation when I changed it and I told the police.' He gave me a pointed look. 'I'm not on probation now, no matter what your records tell you.'

I waited again.

Mark sighed; the weight of the silence between us was annoying him. 'Fine,' he snapped. 'It doesn't take a genius to work out why I changed it. I wanted a new life, one where everyone doesn't know what I used to be. It's not easy getting a fresh start. People don't believe you can change.' His tone was sour. 'I can see it in your face. If I hadn't been banged up, you wouldn't be looking at me like that.'

I was surprised. I wasn't aware that I was looking at him strangely. In fact, I wasn't aware there was anything about his criminal record that made me feel differently about him.

Mark laughed sharply. 'Don't deny it. I'm not completely stupid.'

I opened my mouth to defend myself but then I thought

about how I'd chosen a different seat this time so that I wasn't sitting directly next to him. Maybe he was right. That revelation troubled me.

'I'm sorry,' I said, being honest with him for the first time. 'It wasn't conscious.'

His mouth flattened and he looked away. 'It often isn't.'

'Your employers, ' I said suddenly. 'Do they...'

'Yes.' There was a defiant tilt to his chin. 'They know. New name or not, I had to tell them I've been inside. Your lot don't make it easy to start again. I applied to dozens of places before I even got an interview.' His mouth turned down. 'That's what happens. You do your time and you think you've paid your debt to society but it's not over. It's never over.'

Ah ha. I allowed myself a tiny, secret smile. 'Do you wish that it was over? Do you wish that you could start afresh?'

'Sometimes.' His expression shadowed. 'Sometimes I think I should be allowed to move on and never have to think about it again. Then sometimes I think that it's good that I can't.' He gave an awkward shrug. 'It's like I tell the kids, you learn from your mistakes but you shouldn't ever forget them. Otherwise you might slide back into your old ways and make the same mistakes again. Besides, I got my family back. I moved away from the old place. I got a new job. It took a while and it was hard, but I did it.'

I should have known it wouldn't be that easy to work out what Mark Smith wished for. However, I was already feeling much better about my new client. I'd definitely made the right call by speaking to him rather than simply reading the facts on a computer screen. Cold, hard facts don't allow for nuance – and people are all about nuance.

'What did you do that landed you in prison?' I asked, before I could stop myself. 'I mean,' I amended, 'I have the details but I'd like to hear it from you.'

He rubbed his fist without realising. 'I got into a fight. The other guy almost didn't make it.' His eyes took on a distant sheen. 'I only threw one punch but it landed badly. I'll pay for that punch for the rest of my life.' He paused. 'And so will he.'

'He shouldn't have provoked you.' Both Mark and I jumped. Kelly had walked back into the room, her face filled with a fierce protectiveness. 'It wasn't your fault, Eric.'

'It was,' he said quietly, without correcting her use of his old name. 'It was all my fault.'

NINE

When I got back outside after saying my farewells, I was shivering. I should have been happy that I'd uncovered so much information about my client, especially considering what he'd done with his life. Instead I felt depressed. It didn't seem that there were any winners where Mark Smith was concerned, even if he was doing everything he could to turn over a new leaf and move on with his life.

Sighing, I started to invoke the Metafora magic to return me to the office. Then I caught sight of a slit-eyed Tiddles glaring at me from the bathroom window on the first floor. Fuck a puck. I'd forgotten about Pumpkin.

Hastily cancelling the transportation magic, I darted for Mark Smith's garden gate. The look Pumpkin gave me when I opened it told me that he knew exactly what I'd just done and he was clearly offended. He turned his back on me and headed for a clump of weeds, picked something colourful out from amongst the greenery and lay down to chew on it.

I hissed. 'Pumpkin! For goodness' sake, that's not ours! Stop that!'

He ignored me, tearing off a chunk and spitting it out before continuing. I gritted my teeth and stalked over. It looked like he'd got hold of a kid's book. For all I knew, it was Mark and Kelly's kids' favourite book. 'Give me that,' I ordered in my sternest voice.

Pumpkin gnawed harder. I cursed again and reached down, hooking one finger under his collar and using my other hand to retrieve whatever he was destroying so methodically. He was very reluctant to give it up; the more I tugged, the more determined Pumpkin seemed to hang on it.

'This is not a game! Yes, I'm sorry I almost forgot you. You can chew on my stuff in revenge. That's fine. Please don't chew someone else's stuff!' I wrestled the book from him. It was all but destroyed, saliva dripping from the torn corners. I sighed. 'Look at what you've done.'

I was certain that dogs were supposed to look guilty when you told them off but my recriminations only seemed to make Pumpkin look prouder. I pulled out my wand and gave it a wave, returning the book to its former glory. 'This,' I scolded, 'is not what magic is supposed to be used for. It's supposed to be used to help people, not to fix our own fuck-ups.'

Pumpkin didn't appear in the slightest bit bothered. I tutted loudly and glanced at the book. *Learn To Read With Fantastic Phonics.* If Pumpkin had his way, it would be more like *Learn To Read With Disgusting Drool.* There was a picture of a cartoon cat on the cover. I rolled my eyes. 'You really don't like cats, do you?'

If he could have shrugged with disdain, I'm sure he would have. I made a face and put the book down on the wooden bench. Enough already. It was getting dark and I had a date with the Devil's Advocate. Sort of.

I called upon the Metafora magic once again and headed back.

I'D NEVER THOUGHT of commuting as a particularly joyous part of my day. Faery godmothers or not, we couldn't use Metafora magic to take ourselves home as it was considered an unnecessary waste. Instead, the journey home from the office was a necessary tedium that involved sitting on a smelly bus or trudging through drizzle with a bag over my head to stop my hair from turning into unmanageable frizz.

Usually I didn't even make it home on the first attempt. Typically, I'd be waylaid in the Stagger Inn and have a pint or two with Harry, my rainbow faery friend. Not today, though. Today I was enjoying myself so much, I realised I was deliberately slowing my steps to draw out the journey. Jasper adjusted his own stride accordingly.

'It's safe now,' I said, wondering if he genuinely wanted me as his house guest when he had so much work to do. 'I'm sure I can go home. Don't forget I've got Pumpkin to guard me.'

'We shouldn't take unnecessary risks,' he told me in a perfunctory fashion. 'Let's give it a day or two first until we're sure that things have settled down.' He glanced at Pumpkin trotting beside us. 'And anyway, I'm not sure you have the most effective guard dog.' He placed a hand on my elbow and steered me to his other side. 'Let me walk on the outside of the pavement.'

'Are you too bedazzled by the shop-window displays to want to be close to them?' I asked. I pointed at a fetching mannequin wearing a pink tutu with diamante sparkles on the bodice. It was about as far from Jasper's style as it was possible to get – he was usually wedded to black. 'Is that outfit calling to you?' I altered my voice. '"Buy me, Jasper. Buy me." You always wanted to be a dancer and now's your chance.'

'Actually,' he returned, 'I'm an excellent dancer.' Given his poise, I had no trouble believing that. I also quite liked the idea of him in a tutu. And very little else. I mentally slapped myself. My imagination was leading me down dangerous avenues.

A slow smile crossed Jasper's face, as if he knew exactly what I was thinking. He paused. 'One day I'll prove it to you.'

I smiled back. 'I always fancied being able to foxtrot.'

'I was thinking more along the lines of a tango. Hot, sweaty, sultry...' He turned and gave me a long look of green-eyed intensity. Suddenly, the only person being bedazzled was me. I swallowed. Then Jasper winked, broke the spell and glanced away.

'One minute it seems like you're flirting, the next you're joking around,' I muttered. 'I can't work you out.'

Jasper didn't answer immediately. When he finally spoke, his voice was low. 'You can work me out, Saffron. I'm beginning to think you're too afraid to.'

'I...' Before I could complete my sentence, a bus trundled past, its heavy wheels hitting a dirty puddle. A cascade of sludgy water sprayed upwards. Jasper flicked out a hand, halting its approach and shielding us both.

'That,' he said, 'is why a gentleman should always walk on the outside of his partner.'

'So he can use magic to stop them both from being covered in street slime?'

He smiled faintly. 'So he can protect his lady,' he corrected gently.

I shifted uncomfortably. Part of me desperately wanted to continue down this conversational avenue and part of me was indeed too terrified of the outcome. Jasper was right; in this, at least, I was a complete scaredy-cat. I could face down trolls and evil politicians, and stand up to office politics and setbacks without a second thought – yet I couldn't face another knock back from the man by my side. He was the one who'd told me he wanted to be friends. Hadn't he?

I bit my lip and opted for a safer topic. 'I couldn't have stopped that puddle without either my wand or a migraine,' I pointed out. 'You said you'd teach me how to use magic on my own.'

Jasper rubbed his chin. 'I have to admit,' he said, 'I was hoping you'd forgotten about that.'

'Why?' I teased. 'Are you worried about a little competition?'

He chuckled. In that instant, I knew that he genuinely didn't expect me ever to use magic properly without a wand. It wasn't that he didn't believe in me or thought that I wasn't capable, and I was certain that he would try his hardest to teach me; he was simply convinced that the task was insurmountable. All of a sudden, my resolve hardened. Impossible wasn't a word in my vocabulary. I'd learn to wield magic just like he did – better, even. If Jasper could do it, so could I.

In case the steely glint in my eye wasn't enough, I straightened my shoulders and cracked my knuckles to show I meant business. 'Come on, then. There's no time like the present. It's a good twenty-minute walk back to your place and, as we've already established, I'm perfectly capable of multi-tasking.'

'Alright.' He nodded. 'I'm not sure I'll be the best teacher in the world but I'll give it my all. But please don't expect too much.' He paused, clearly thinking about how to begin. 'Inside you,' he said finally, 'there is a barrier. All faeries have it. There's a well of magic trapped inside you that needs a wand to draw it out. The wand acts as a conduit between you,' he pointed at my chest, 'and the outside world. What you have to do is find a way to access that conduit without the need for the wand.'

Fascinated, I gazed at him – and narrowly avoided smacking into a lamp post which someone had inconveniently placed in my path. So much for multi-tasking. 'How did you do it?' I asked. 'How did you first access that conduit?'

He waved a dismissive hand, his eyes shifting away. 'It was an unconscious thing. It's not something I can explain.'

I sensed that there was more to that story than he was letting on but, given that he clearly didn't want to talk about it, I was prepared to let it go for now. Besides, he'd already provided me with another avenue to explore. 'Everyone?' I prodded. 'How many other faeries can use magic without wands?'

'Five,' he answered, without missing a beat. 'Well, four, I suppose. The fifth one is a tooth faery who's over a hundred. She doesn't get out much any more.'

'Who are the others?'

Jasper ticked off his fingers. 'Miseko Awahashi – she's one of the Yosei, the Japanese equivalent of our faeries. Humbert Holstead in Germany. He's your Director's counterpart. Jack Flanagan, a leprechaun who's based in Ireland. And Carlos Sanchez in Columbia.'

'And you,' I said quietly. 'You're the only one in this country?'

'If you don't include the trolls,' Jasper answered.

I grimaced. How could I forget? Faeries might require wands to perform effective magic and not end up ill as a result, but trolls could blink and cause utter devastation. I was exaggerating but it was almost true. 'Could trolls do magic like that before we almost wiped them out?' I asked. 'Without a wand, I mean?'

Jasper was slow to answer. 'I don't think so.'

I noted the dark shadow that flitted across his face and filed away that little detail. 'Well,' I said, changing the subject for now, 'theory is all very well. Let's focus on some real practice.'

'We'll have to start slowly,' Jasper cautioned. 'The last thing we need is for you to collapse on top of Pumpkin in broad daylight.'

At the sound of his name, the small dog squinted upwards. Jasper smiled at him and Pumpkin nudged his leg gently in response. I smiled too. Pumpkin turned to me and bared his teeth. I looked away.

'Right,' I said, rubbing my palms together and pretending I wasn't bothered, 'where do we start?'

'Hmm. I suppose we need to find a way to break down the barrier inside you that holds in your magic. Small steps.' He frowned then pointed ahead. 'Can you see that tree? The oak on the corner?'

'Yep.'

'There's a pigeon on one of the branches. Try to send out a tiny burst of magic to jiggle the tree and make the pigeon fly away.'

It sounded easy enough. I squinted at the tree and prepared, steeling my stomach for what was to come. Jasper placed a hand on my arm, his skin searing into mine. 'Remember,' he cautioned, 'if you were using your wand, you'd require little more than a tweak. Don't overdo it. We're aiming for a breath, not a roar.'

I licked my lips and concentrated. He was right; moving a single branch shouldn't take much effort. I bunched my hands into fists. I could do this. Of course I could.

Initially, nothing happened. The branch didn't budge and the magic within me remained dormant. I pushed a little harder.

'Careful,' Jasper said. 'We know you can blast out magic and end up almost comatose afterwards. Aim for finesse.'

I gritted my teeth. I was all about finesse; finesse was my middle name. If you wanted finesse, all you had to do was call for Saffron Sawyer and...

There was a loud crack. Pumpkin jumped, whining in surprise. The tree gave a creaking groan and split down the centre. The pigeon squawked and flapped its wings in alarm while various passers-by stopped and stared as the trunk crashed down. One driver was forced to slam on her brakes, swerving desperately to avoid her windshield being smashed by the heavy branches.

Unfortunately, I didn't see any of this happen. I was already on my knees on the cold hard pavement, choking up bile and trying not to pass out.

Jasper crouched beside me. 'Are you alright, Saffron?'

I moaned. He helped me up, brushing away tendrils of my hair that were now plastered with sweat. 'You were trying too hard.' He put an arm around me. 'This is a bad idea.'

I tried to bring my breathing back under control. 'No, it's not,' I gasped.

He ran a hand through his inky-black hair. 'It'll never work. I shouldn't have encouraged you.'

'It's just a bit harder than I thought it would be.' Oddly, using a tiny bit of magic without my wand was harder than using a gigantic burst. I staggered slightly before shaking myself. I wasn't about to give up. I'd barely begun.

Something wet and sticky splattered down onto my head then trickled down the side of my face. 'What the...?' I glanced upwards in time to see the pigeon from the tree wheeling round above me. 'It's just as well that I never got a job as an animal faery,' I muttered. 'They all hate me. Every single one of them.'

Jasper pulled out a pristine white handkerchief and gently wiped away the white gunk. Somehow he always managed to have a handkerchief ready to pull out at a moment's notice.

'You knew that was going to happen, didn't you?' I asked.

He gave me a sympathetic look. 'I didn't know the bird

would take its revenge on you. I had a fair inkling about the rest, though.'

I wrinkled my nose. There was a very nasty taste in my mouth. 'I'm not giving up,' I told him. 'I don't give up.'

'I had a fair inkling you were going to say that, too.' He smiled slightly. 'Using magic like I do is not all it's cracked up to be, you know. There's nothing wrong with depending on a wand.'

'You're the most powerful faery in the country,' I pointed out. 'And that's because you don't use a wand.'

A shadow crossed his face. 'It can be surprisingly isolating,' he said, so quietly that I almost didn't hear him. Then he seemed to realise that he might have given away more than he wanted to share about himself and he cleared his throat. 'And I'm far from omnipotent.' He sighed. 'But I do love my job. There have been times when I'm not sure I'd have survived without my work.' He shrugged. 'It gives me purpose.'

The man was a frustrating mix of honesty and half-truths but I couldn't help feeling that he was starting to let me see the real person behind the Devil's Advocate's mask.

'I know exactly what you mean,' I said. 'I feel the same way about being a faery godmother.' We exchanged a look of perfect understanding. Then I grinned. 'But let's wait until tomorrow before we try any more experiments.'

'Saffron...'

'Please?'

Jasper grimaced. 'Okay. Remember not to expect too much. And don't try too hard.'

If my legs hadn't been quite so wobbly, I'd have demanded that we try again right away. 'Fine,' I said. 'Although I have to tell you that I feel great.' I flexed my fingers. 'I'm only agreeing to wait until tomorrow because I don't want to miss out on dinner.'

Jasper's eyes suddenly gleamed. 'Dinner with *me*, you mean.'

I bit my lip. 'Yeah,' I said. If I could be brave enough to risk public collapse and loud vomiting, I could be brave enough to be honest with Jasper. 'I don't want to miss dinner with you.'

CHAPTER
TEN

I wasn't nervous. Not even a teeny tiny bit. The faint tremor to my hands was the result of not eating for a while and low blood sugar. It was nothing to do with being scared of having a meal. I had meals every day. Just because this meal was in an intimate corner of a candlelit restaurant with a freshly shaven Jasper smelling of cinnamon right in front of me didn't mean anything. Nope. Not a thing.

'I hope Pumpkin doesn't destroy too much of your flat while we're out,' I said.

'I gave him a bone to chew while you were in the shower. He's happy enough.'

'It's just that you have some very nice things and…'

Jasper reached across and took my hands. I flinched at the heat of his touch. His face darkened. He released my hands and leaned back. 'Don't worry about Pumpkin. He'll be fine.'

Uh-huh. I nodded, although I was certain that when we got back to Jasper's flat we'd be confronted with a trail of devastation that a force-ten hurricane would be proud of.

A shadow fell between us. I glanced up at the waiter who bowed briefly and laid a silver platter on the table. 'A dozen oysters,' he announced, 'fresh from the ocean this morning and with the compliments of the chef.' He bowed once more and backed away.

I looked at the platter. I'd always been of the opinion that oysters were more like salty snot than real food. Given the choice between a fish-finger sandwich for a quid at the staff canteen or some artfully arranged oysters at a swanky restaurant for a small fortune, I knew exactly what I'd prefer.

Jasper scooped one up. 'You know, of course,' he said, in a low murmur, 'that oysters are an aphrodisiac.'

'So they say,' I muttered.

He seemed amused. 'Casanova ate fifty of them for breakfast every morning.'

'From what I recall from school, Casanova also died miserable and alone.' I eyed him as he tipped the oyster into his mouth. 'Are you likening yourself to Casanova? Are you a decadent womaniser, Jasper?'

He swallowed the oyster and met my eyes. 'No,' he said. 'And no. It might surprise you to learn that that I'm quite the opposite. I don't find intimate relationships very easy. For some reason, my job always gets in the way.'

I dropped my gaze. 'We have a lot in common.'

'Yes.' He sounded amused. 'I suppose we do.' He picked up an oyster and held it out to me. 'Go on,' he urged. 'Try one.' Yuck. Then Jasper continued, the tenor of his voice changing to something far huskier. 'Who knows where it might lead?'

My heart skipped a beat. 'Isn't this supposed to be a working dinner?'

'You know what they say about all work and no play.' His face remained serious but there was a hint of a darker emotion flickering in his eyes. 'Maybe it's time that we both stopped letting our jobs get in the way.'

This time I was surprised. 'Did the Devil's Advocate just advocate for less work?'

'Yes.' He placed the oyster on my plate. 'Give it a shot.'

I licked my lips. 'Are you trying to press an aphrodisiac on me for a reason, Jasper?'

He didn't answer.

I drew a deep breath, pushed the oyster to one side and leaned across the table. This time I was the one who took his hands. He stiffened but didn't say anything. 'So,' I said carefully, 'this friends thing.'

He raised an eyebrow.

'I'm, uh, not sure it's working out.'

Jasper's expression didn't change. He picked up his glass of wine, raised it to his lips and took a small sip before placing it down on the table again. 'What makes you say that?'

I gritted my teeth. He certainly wasn't making this easy. He was going to make me say it out loud. Fine: I'd burn my bridges and then deal with the consequences. What else was new?

I cleared my throat. 'Because you were right earlier,' I told him. 'I *have* worked you out. You don't want to be friends either.'

His green eyes held mine, pinning me into place. 'Honestly, Saffron,' he told me, 'I never wanted to be friends with you.'

What? I glared at him. 'Yes, you did.'

'No.' He gave his head a tiny shake. 'That was all you. I was trying to respect your wishes.' A frown marred his forehead. 'It's not been easy. I've been trying to drop hints for weeks that I'm amenable to a different kind of relationship.' The look in his eyes intensified but I thought I registered a hint of anxiety in those emerald depths. 'More than amenable,' he added quietly.

'Wait a minute. *You're* the one who said you only wanted to be friends. You came to the Stagger Inn and told me that weeks ago.'

'No, I didn't. I went to the Stagger Inn to see you and lay my soul bare. You're the one who jumped in and suggested we should just be friends.'

'That's not how it happened at all.' I pulled my hands away.

'Yes, it is.'

'No, it isn't.'

'Yes, it is.'

'No, it...' He raised his eyes heavenward. 'Fuck this,' he said under his breath. He pushed the oyster platter to one side and leaned across the table, cupped my face with his long fingers and gazed at me. 'Do you want to be my friend, Saffron?'

I stared at him. 'No,' I squeaked.

He nodded once. 'Good,' he said. His lips descended on mine.

He tasted better than I remembered. It wasn't just the spicy cinnamon that pervaded his mouth, his skin, his touch. Jasper's kiss tasted like fire. His heat pushed its way into my body and caused flames to flicker from my toes to the pit of my belly and up to my head, which swam with prickles of dizzy delight.

I reached across for him, pulling him closer and knocking over my glass of wine in the process. I didn't care. Nothing mattered other than this. My heart was beating against my ribcage in painful thuds and I felt girlishly breathless. If this was what a single oyster did for Jasper, I thought vaguely, I'd feed them to him by the bucket.

Jasper pulled away and I gasped. Why was he stopping?

'Fuck dinner,' he said. 'Let's get out of here.'

Good call. I nodded, suddenly aware of the other diners. Hot sweaty sex on top of a plate of oysters in front of a restaurant filled with people probably wasn't a good idea. At least one of us was thinking straight.

I drew in a ragged breath. 'Now,' I whispered. 'Let's go now.'

A shadow fell between us. 'Can we have the bill, please?' I asked, without taking my eyes from Jasper's.

'I think you have me confused with someone else,' Ethan said.

I froze. Fuck a puck. What was *he* doing here? Why now?

Jasper sprang up, lithe as a cat. He grabbed Ethan by the collar and spun him round before slamming him against the nearest wall. The pretty paintings hanging next to us shuddered – and so did the wide-eyed people at the next table. 'Are you following us?' he snarled in Ethan's face.

Ethan didn't look even mildly perturbed. 'I have people watching her,' he said. 'Why? Am I interrupting something?'

Jasper let out a low guttural hiss, released Ethan and backed away. But the threat of violence hadn't gone and the air still crackled with unspent emotion.

Ethan smoothed down his jacket. 'I was under the impression, Devil's Advocate, that you were key in negotiating peace between our two kinds.'

Jasper's jaw tensed. 'You know that to be true,' he ground out. 'But there is a time and place for discussions and, believe me, this is not it.'

Ethan looked at me. 'Unfortunately, there is no choice in the matter. I presume you informed him of the details of our earlier discussion?'

I swallowed. No, I'd been going to get to them. Truthfully, with everything else that had happened since this morning, I'd put the matter of Art Adwell to one side. His machinations hadn't seemed like that big a deal.

'I know who's behind the rumours about faery godmothers,' I admitted. 'I'm sorry. I should have got in touch with you sooner. There's no reason to worry about them. The human in question is out of the way and can't do anything. He's already been discredited. I'm planning to visit him, retrieve the wand and solve the problem.'

Jasper's eyes narrowed. 'What wand?'

Ethan continued to look at me. 'You didn't tell him. I wonder why?'

'Saffron,' Jasper began, 'what's going on?'

'I was planning to speak to you about it after dinner,' I said helplessly. 'You knew that.'

He folded his arms. 'Speak to me about what?'

'It's not that big of a deal.'

Ethan glared. 'It is. And in the last hour, it just got a whole lot bigger.'

I turned to him. 'What do you mean?'

He turned his head, noting the other diners, including two couples not far from us who had taken out their phones and were filming the action. Great. That was just what we needed.

Ethan snapped his fingers and the people gasped, dropping their phones in shock as plumes of smoke drifted up from both devices. 'This is not the place to discuss it,' he said shortly. 'Come with me.' He glanced at Jasper. 'Unless you really are looking for a fight?'

The only answer was a clenching of Jasper's jaw. Unfortunately, I couldn't work out right now whether the impending fight was going to be with Ethan or with me.

THE IMPLIED THREAT of violence still emanating from Jasper's large frame was enough to make the maître'd blanch with fear so I hastily pulled out my purse and paid the bill. It was the least I could do. It didn't seem to make Jasper's mood any better; if anything, his dark glower deepened.

'Ethan's a worry wart,' I said under my breath, ignoring the sharp look the troll leader gave me. 'This isn't the problem that he thinks it is. But I *was* going to tell you about it. I wasn't trying to hide anything. I wanted to clean up the mess first. And then I got ... distracted.'

Jasper gave me a terse nod of acknowledgement. 'Is there any chance this is some sort of ruse?' he bit out.

I blinked. 'Ruse?'

'Do you think Ethan is spinning a tale to put us on the back foot and lead us into some sort of troll ambush?'

I swallowed. 'No.'

Jasper's shoulders tightened. 'Have your wand ready in case.'

I didn't pull it out – that would only enflame an already tense situation and I could still grab it in a second if need be. I reminded myself that Jasper had been poisoned by the trolls and then abducted. He could have died. For all his attempts to broker a peaceful resolution and prevent the faery godmothers from escalating the problems, it made sense that he would still be on edge when they approached us. Yesterday's shenanigans proved that they put me on edge as well. But at least I was now fairly sure that his ire was directed at Ethan – although I wasn't sure that was a good thing.

Ethan moved in front of us, clearly tired of our muttered chat. 'I can assure you,' he said, 'that it is not my intention to cause further confrontation between our races. Not at this particular moment in time, anyway. Neither of you are in any danger, and this isn't about what has happened in the past. It's about what might happen in the future.'

The men stared at each other. I couldn't have said for sure whether Jasper believed the ring of honesty in Ethan's words, or their combined glares were enough to settle the matter; either way, Jasper relaxed a little. 'Fine,' he said. 'Let's go.'

'I have a car parked out front. We can talk in there.'

As we followed Ethan out of the restaurant, a blast of cool night air made me shiver. Jasper didn't miss a beat; he simply shrugged off his jacket and placed it round my shoulders. I inhaled his lingering scent, its familiarity helping me to remain calm. Unfortunately, that sensation didn't last long.

Ethan's car was indeed sitting outside, a gleaming black beast of a thing that appeared like something a Mafia boss would drive. Just in case that wasn't intimidating enough, when the driver's door opened and a figure stepped out, my heart sank.

Melissa. She was wearing an eye patch; that didn't stop her from sending me shots of pure hatred with her good eye. 'Ready for round two, faery?' she snapped.

'Melissa,' Ethan warned. 'Enough.'

I jerked up my chin. 'I'm game if you are,' I said aloud.

'Saffron.'

I glanced at Jasper. 'I know, I know.' I mimed zipping my mouth closed. Melissa pursed her lips and looked away. Actually, our little confrontation had relaxed me slightly. If she'd appeared with a smile and a friendly wave, it would have been obvious that there was more to this impromptu meeting than I'd thought. Her inability to play nice made me trust her intentions – and Ethan's.

She opened the back door before standing to the side to allow us to get in the vehicle. Jasper put an arm out, blocked my path and ducked down to check the interior of the car.

'Your boyfriend is very suspicious,' Ethan said. 'Perhaps I should have gone with my first instinct and contacted the Director personally, rather than going through you. I'd hoped that you would take my earlier warning seriously.'

'I did,' I said quietly. 'After speaking to you, I went to investigate further.'

'I know.' At my look, Ethan shrugged. 'I did say that I had

people watching you.' He clicked his fingers and Melissa abandoned her position, walking round to the back of the car and opening the boot.

I stiffened. 'Jasper.'

He pulled his head out of the car. 'What?'

I swallowed and pointed. Jasper straightened and both of us watched as Melissa hauled out the trussed-up figure. I hissed and started forward but he put a hand on my arm in warning. It didn't matter. I was about one inch away from blasting Ethan with every ounce of magic available to me. He'd be nothing more than a pile of cinders by the time I was done with him. Screw the consequences.

There was a purple bruise underneath Vincent's eye and his hands and ankles were tied with rope. The only reason he remained upright was because Melissa was supporting him. Other than that, he didn't appear to have been harmed, although there was a gag stuffed in his mouth.

When his gaze landed on me, Vincent's eyes rolled upwards in an exaggerated display of irritation. I breathed out in relief. Stay calm, Saffron, I told myself. Don't make matters any worse than they already are.

'He's not the one you're looking for,' I said quietly.

'But he is human,' Ethan replied. 'And he knows about faeries.'

'It's a long story. He's not a threat.'

Jasper crossed his arms. His earlier fury had been replaced by a look of intense boredom, which worried me far more. 'At some point,' he said, 'one of you will explain exactly what's going on.'

Ethan gestured to the car. 'Step into my lair,' he said, 'and you can find out.'

ELEVEN

Melissa returned to her position in the front of the car and closed the screen between the seats to allow us privacy. There was more than enough room in the back for all of us to sit comfortably. Not that anyone looked comfortable apart from Vincent, who leaned back and did his best to stretch out his legs, no mean feat given his bindings.

'Mmmf. Mmmf. Mmmm.' He paused and looked at me. 'Mmmmmmmmf!'

Unsurprisingly, I had a good idea what that was supposed to mean. I didn't take it personally.

'We gagged him because he talks a lot,' Ethan said. 'He's incredibly annoying. Even for a human.'

Vincent's eyes took on a sheen of pride and he tossed his head in acknowledgement.

Jasper steepled his fingers and gazed hard-eyed at Ethan. 'Why don't you explain to me exactly what's going on?'

Ethan permitted himself a smile. 'Saffron? Bring the Devil's Advocate up to date, why don't you?'

I sighed. Okay then. It was better coming from me than

coming from him. 'The reason Ethan wanted to meet so desperately is because he's concerned that a human has obtained a wand that formerly belonged to a faery godmother.'

Jasper's expression didn't change and nothing about his body language betrayed his thoughts. 'I see,' he said slowly.

'Keep going, Saffron,' Ethan said. 'I wouldn't want you to miss any of the details.'

I gave him the fakest smile I could muster. 'This human individual,' I continued, 'has been using the internet to advertise the wand and its provenance in an apparent bid to uncover more information.'

There was a beat of silence while Jasper absorbed this. 'So,' he said finally, 'if I understand you correctly, there is another human out there who knows that faery godmothers exist and he has a wand that he knows is magical. This human is actively trying to find out more and broadcasting our secrets in the process.'

I shifted, causing the leather underneath me to creak. 'Pretty much.'

Jasper's mouth tightened and he turned to Vincent. 'What is it that you want? Money? You have to know that no one will believe your stories, regardless of how true they are.' He glanced at me. 'I assume it's one of your wands he's taken?'

I opened my mouth to answer. Vincent took a more physical approach, thrashing his bound arms and legs, his eyes writhing wildly in their sockets. 'Mmmmf! Mmmmf!'

'It's not him,' I said quietly. 'He's not the person responsible.'

Ethan reached across and pulled away Vincent's gag. Vincent stuck his tongue out like a child turning up their nose at broccoli and started his tirade. 'I ain't done nothing! You think that because I've done bad things in the past I'm a bad person? I don't have her wand. I never had her wand! So get this shit off of me and let me out of here before I go mad and turn the lot of you fucking faeries inside out!'

A detached part of me noted that he'd made a return to his old, acquired accent. Perhaps he thought it made him sound more threatening. Or perhaps it was because he felt threatened.

'It's not Vincent,' I repeated. 'I spoke to him this afternoon and I'm satisfied that he had nothing to do with either my missing wand or the internet posts.'

'See?' he yelled. 'See, you faery fucker?'

'I'm not a faery,' Ethan replied. 'Although I do agree that they're fuckers.' He leaned forward and returned the gag to its original position. 'Now be quiet or I'll use magic to shut you up permanently.'

'Mmmmf!'

Ethan raised his hands. Vincent flinched before finally gesturing reluctant compliance, though he managed another glare at me first. I was on a roll; by the time this week was over, the entire world would probably despise me. I seemed to be having that effect on people.

'There really isn't any need to worry,' I said, twisting my hands in my lap. 'When I realised it wasn't Vincent who was responsible, I worked out who the real culprit was. It's just one man – one man who is currently serving at Her Majesty's plea-sure. He's in no position to cause any damage and no one will ever believe him. You're getting your knickers in a twist over nothing, Ethan.'

Jasper placed a hand on Ethan's arm. This certainly wasn't the time for a bromance. 'Saffron,' he said, 'who has the wand?'

I looked away. 'Art Adwell.'

Ethan's brow creased into a frown. 'I've heard of him. Isn't that...?'

'The politician,' Jasper finished grimly. 'The politician who was trying to kill your previous client. Pumpkin's old owner.'

Ethan started. 'The old woman I shot?'

'Yes.'

He stared at me. 'And is it *your* wand that he has in his possession?'

I nodded reluctantly. 'He took it from me after his goons knocked me out. They dragged me to Vincent's house and Adwell questioned me. I told him that I was a faery godmother.'

Genuine alarm lit Jasper's eyes. 'He would be bound by memory magic. You could tell him anything and he wouldn't remember it. He wouldn't know that the wand is from a faery godmother unless he has magic of his own or,' he grimaced, 'the memory magic has failed.'

'He doesn't have magic,' I whispered.

'Pardon?'

'Art Adwell doesn't have magic. He's human.' I gestured helplessly towards Ethan to reiterate that there was no cause for alarm. 'So he can't use the wand, no matter what he remembers.'

Ethan leaned forward, making a leap of logic that was wholly wrong but for which I couldn't blame him. 'If the memory magic is failing, then all faeries need to cease operations immediately. It's too dangerous to continue otherwise. And I'm not saying that because I'm a troll. It's imperative that the existence of magic is kept secret. It's bad enough that this idiot here knows about it. Can you imagine the consequences if there were more like him?'

Vincent glared but at least he stayed quiet.

'The memory magic isn't failing,' I said. 'It just didn't work with Adwell, that's all.'

'Saffron,' Jasper said, staring at me, 'do you know why it didn't work?'

I twisted my hands together. 'Uh, he might have drunk some of the gingko biloba concoction I made for Rose.'

'What?'

'Adwell threw it back up again almost immediately! I didn't mention it to anyone before because I didn't think it was worth mentioning. It couldn't have been in his system for more than a few seconds.' My shoulders dropped. 'But I guess those seconds were enough for it to work against the memory magic.'

'And you faeries wonder why we have problems with godmothers.' Ethan shook his head. 'I thought you were one of the better ones, Saffron. I couldn't have been more wrong.'

I threw up my hands. 'I fucked up, alright? I admit I fucked up. I'll visit Adwell and sort this out. He's in prison. He's not going anywhere. I'll find out where he's hidden the damned wand and get it back. All anyone is going to think is that he's a stark raving madman.'

'A stark raving *rich* madman,' Ethan said.

'What do you mean?'

The troll reached inside his coat pocket and drew out a folded piece of paper. 'Here's the real reason for tonight's interruption,' he told us grimly. 'You keep saying there's no need to worry about this man because he'll never be believed. Well, there's a million reasons.'

Jasper took the paper, opened it up and scanned it. With his mouth pressed into a flat line, he passed it to me.

It was a printout from the internet. The address looked to be the same blog that Adwell had used earlier to post his rantings. I quickly read through it, feeling worse and worse by the second. 'He's offering a million pounds to anyone who can help him unlock the magic contained in the wand,' I said dully. 'That's a lot of money.'

'Indeed,' Ethan said.

Desperately, I clung to whatever I could think of. 'It won't make a difference. It's a faery godmother's wand so it will only work for another faery godmother. Even if another faery saw the blog and decided to try and get the money, they can't do anything. And no faery godmother would help that slimy bastard.'

'You have a far higher opinion of your colleagues than I do,' Ethan murmured. 'I bet there's more than one godmother who would think about it when there's a million pounds on the table.'

'I know you have good reason to think ill of us, Ethan,' I said, 'but we take our jobs seriously. All of us take our jobs seriously. Nobody would jeopardise the office by dealing with Art Adwell.'

'Would you bet a million pounds on that?' he asked.

Jasper straightened. 'I'm the Devil's Advocate,' he said without a trace of false modesty. 'You know what I'm capable of. I will ensure this matter is dealt with. You won't have anything to worry about.'

Ethan didn't relax. Neither did he smile. 'I certainly hope not. Because if the truth about faery godmothers is revealed to the world, then it will only be a matter of time before the existence of trolls is also broadcast. We've spent decades hiding ourselves away. We're not prepared to do so again.' He looked at me. 'And certainly not because of one faery godmother's fuck up. As trolls, we've been down this road before.'

'It will be dealt with.' I stared down at the piece of paper, my hands tightening around its edges and crumpling it. 'This man will be dealt with.'

'Seventy-two hours,' he said. 'I will allow you seventy-two hours to deal with it in your own way before we take control. Our methods tend to involve more of the bloody, bludgeoning approach but they are effective. You might not appreciate the resulting fall out, of course.'

'We'll sort it out ourselves,' Jasper promised.

Ethan nodded; whether he believed that we would or not, only he knew. He jerked his thumb towards Vincent. 'This one must also be dealt with. He knows too much. We can dispose of him quietly. I know how you faeries like to pretend not to get your hands dirty.'

Vincent's eyes widened. 'Mmmmmf!'

Fuck a puck. 'He's no danger,' I said. 'I'll vouch for him. I give you my word that he won't cause any problems.'

Ethan smiled faintly. 'Forgive me for saying so, Saffron, but your word doesn't count for a great deal at the moment. We can't take any chances. Don't worry, he won't feel much pain. We'll make it quick.'

Vincent started to shake his head violently from side to side, then he lunged for the passenger door, trying to use his elbow to open it. He bashed his shoulder against it and succeeded in doing little more than hurting himself. Jasper flicked out a hand and Vincent's body stiffened before falling still.

'No!' I cried out.

'I didn't kill him, Saffron,' Jasper said irritably. He looked at Ethan. 'There is another way. We can ensure his loyalty.'

Ethan tilted his head. 'Such a thing has not been done for generations,' he said.

'No,' Jasper agreed. 'But it can be done.'

I frowned. 'What?'

'It might not go well.' Ethan raised his eyebrows. 'Both might suffer.'

My voice rose. 'What are you talking about?'

'But you agree?' Jasper pressed. 'It's enough for you?'

Ethan pursed his lips. 'It's enough.'

I exploded. 'I'm still fucking here! Just because I created a bit of a mess doesn't mean you have to treat me like I'm invisible. What are you talking about?'

'I can use magic to bind Vincent to you,' Jasper explained. 'He will be unable to go against your explicit orders. It was a technique used long ago by faeries who required servants and didn't want to worry about their loyalty. It won't hurt him.' He paused. 'It does mean, however, that you are responsible for his welfare. And the nature of the binding means that any pain dealt to him will be absorbed by you instead.'

'If someone breaks his nose,' Ethan offered helpfully, 'you are the one who will require treatment.'

I stared at them both. 'You've got to be kidding me.'

Ethan was unconcerned by my horror. 'There had to be some sort of payoff for the humans who were bound and this was it. It was the main reason why the practice was discontinued. Your enemies merely had to target your human servants in order to physically hurt you. Of course, if you don't want to leave yourself open to that sort of vulnerability, we can stick with the original plan.'

'No,' I said hastily. I glanced at Jasper. I was glad that he hadn't offered to take on Vincent like this instead of me. I'd created this mess; I had to deal with the consequences. I knew when I was beaten. 'Bind us. It's my fault Vincent is in this situation.'

Jasper gave Ethan a hard look. 'No one else is to know. No one outside this car can know about the binding unless Saffron agrees.'

'That is no problem. But the human also has to agree to it for the magic to work,' Ethan said.

Jasper nodded and twisted his hand, releasing Vincent from his frozen state. He groaned, jerking himself upright. 'That wasn't funny,' he spat. 'How would you like to be turned into a damned doll?'

'Did you hear the conversation?' Jasper asked.

'Yeah.' Vincent's lip curled. 'I heard.'

'You understand that it's either this or...'

'I understand.' He glared at me. 'I'm not doing your fucking laundry. I won't be your skivvy.'

I drew in a deep breath. 'That's not what this is about. I won't make you do anything. It's only to ensure your silence in such a way that Ethan here is happy.'

'Ethan who was trying to kill you all a few weeks ago?'

'It's complicated, Vincent.'

He folded his arms. 'It always is.' He ran a hand through his lank hair. 'Fine. Do it. I agree.' He rolled his eyes. 'Whatever. It was the worst day of my damned life when I met you.'

Unfortunately, I wasn't in a position to disagree with him. 'I'm sorry,' I said. He huffed and looked away.

'Are you sure about this, Saffron?' Jasper asked. 'Is this what you want?'

'There's no other choice.'

Vincent pouted. It didn't suit him. 'I'm glad that I'm such a delightful prospect,' he muttered. 'First you accuse me of thieving, then I'm kidnapped, and now I'm being forced into slavery. Great.'

'I'm happy to go with the alternative,' Ethan butted in.

Vincent looked at Jasper. 'Do it. Do your stupid magic thing.'

Jasper nodded then his brow furrowed with concentration. He raised his hands, his fingers dancing through the air. I watched, fascinated despite myself. The complexity of this sort of magic was beyond my capabilities, even with a powerful wand in my possession.

At first I didn't feel anything and I wasn't convinced that it was working. Then there was a whoosh of air that rippled my curls and made Vincent's shirt billow. Something tugged at my skin; it felt like a thousand tiny hooks had planted themselves up and down my body and now someone was pulling at them.

'Ouch!' Vincent rubbed at his arms. 'That fucking hurts.'

He was right. I gasped aloud – was my entire skin about to be ripped off? It certainly felt like it. I squeezed my eyes shut while Vincent moaned. My heartbeat thumped in my eardrums, sounding oddly out of kilter. Then I realised that it wasn't my heart that I was hearing: it was Vincent's. It grew louder and louder. At the exact moment when I thought that I couldn't take it any more, a giant wallop slammed into my chest and my body shuddered. Everything went quiet.

I breathed out; it was over.

I opened one eye and peeked. Vincent looked as disturbed as I felt. He raised a finger and poked at himself, almost as if he were checking that he was still there.

'Damn,' he said. 'Hot damn.'

'Saffron?' Jasper prompted.

I opened my other eye. 'I'm fine,' I said.

'Good. Make the command.'

I averted my gaze from Vincent. I was effectively taking away his free will; even though it was for a good cause, it didn't feel right. 'Vincent,' I mumbled, 'you can't tell anyone about magic or faery godmothers ever again.'

Vincent's lip curled. 'As you wish,' he said sourly. Then he turned his head to the car window, drew back and smashed his forehead into the glass.

Pain exploded through my skull. I yelled. Jasper's arm shot out to Vincent to stop him doing it again. He didn't have to, though; Vincent had made his point. He sniffed. 'I feel better now.'

Ethan leaned forward, his eyes flicking from Vincent to me and back again. Eventually he nodded. 'I am satisfied,' he said aloud. 'But if anything happens to Saffron, then...' He made a slitting motion across his throat with his finger and pointed at Vincent.

Jasper's expression was dark. 'Nothing will happen to Saffron.'

Ethan raised his eyebrows. 'We shall see.' He held up three fingers in warning. 'Three days,' he reminded us. 'Seventy-two hours. Make good on your mess.'

CHAPTER

TWELVE

I won't admit to being a control freak but I know deep down that the label fits me perfectly. It was part of the reason why the events of that last hour had made me feel so small. That and the fact that the chaos was all my fault. Recent events had slipped away from me, with Jasper and Ethan taking control. I hated that.

'I created this situation,' I said, as much to myself as to Jasper or Vincent. I rubbed my forehead, which was still throbbing from Vincent's little test. 'Accidentally or otherwise, it's my responsibility to clear it up. And I still don't think that Art Adwell is going to achieve anything, regardless of what money he offers.'

'Vincent,' Jasper asked, 'what would you be prepared to do for a million pounds?'

Vincent grinned. 'Whatever you want me to, darling.'

I rolled my eyes. 'There's no faery godmother on this planet who would compromise their position for something as mundane as money. We are faery godmothers,' I said primly. 'We're better than that.'

'If you say so,' Jasper replied. 'But believing something in theory is very different to doing something in practice. You can believe you wouldn't cannibalise an already dead faery under any circumstances. But unless you're starving, you don't actually know what you'd do in that situation.'

'I'll cannibalise a faery for a million pounds,' Vincent interjected cheerfully.

I glared at him. He wasn't helping. 'You're suddenly Mr Happy Pants,' I sniped.

He shrugged. 'I'll admit I wasn't particularly thrilled at the idea of being your slave to begin with but, now that I've had some time to think about it, I've decided that it might not be all bad.' He grinned some more, opening his mouth wide and displaying his yellow teeth. Then, in case I hadn't quite got the hint, he pointed at his incisors. 'There have to be some perks, right? A wish a day will keep the trolls away!' he trilled.

I passed a hand over my forehead. It would be far easier to pretend that he wasn't there. I turned to Jasper. His jacket was still round my shoulders. Its warmth was comforting, but I continued to feel cold inside. 'Are we alright?' I asked quietly. 'You and me, I mean?'

'You should have told me about all of this earlier.'

I couldn't disagree with that. 'Yes.'

'You've created the perfect storm.'

I couldn't disagree with that either. 'Yes.'

He heaved a sigh. 'Your intentions were honourable.'

I bit my lip. 'Yes.'

'But incredibly misguided.'

Fuck a puck. 'Yes.'

Jasper hesitated. 'My job as Devil's Advocate,' he said finally, 'doesn't just involve audits. I'm also responsible for dealing with faeries who break our laws.'

Here we go. Misery clutched at me. By giving Rose gingko biloba, I'd broken faery law. I'd known I wasn't supposed to but I'd done it anyway. It had been for a good cause; I'd needed her to remember who I was so that I could get her to trust me. It had seemed like the right thing to do at the time. But it was still wrong. The fact that Art Adwell had taken some of the gingko biloba massively compounded the situation.

'Last year,' Jasper continued, 'I was tasked with investigating the untimely death of a luck faery.'

'A what faery?' Vincent interrupted.

'A luck faery. Someone who ensures the supply of four-leaf clovers, casting spells on houses by hanging horseshoes, that kind of thing.'

'Ohhhh.' Vincent nodded wisely. 'I thought you said something else.' He nudged me. 'What I heard sounded much more fun. Instead of luck faery, I thought you said a fu—'

I elbowed him sharply back. Good grief. I was quite possible about to end up in faery jail and Vincent was trying to crack crude jokes that would make even Rupert blush.

'Anyway,' Jasper said, eyes narrowed, 'my investigation uncovered that the *luck* faery in question had been in a long-standing vendetta with a tooth faery. Both of them were romantically involved with the same man. Rather than abandon him as a two-timing cheat, they'd been engaged in a series of one-upmanship situations where each would make the other's life as unpleasant as possible. They blamed each other for the problem. When this particular luck faery was found at the bottom of a staircase with her neck broken, it seemed likely that either her love rival or her love interest was responsible.'

I swallowed, unsure where he was going with this. 'That makes sense.'

'I brought them both in for questioning. The tooth faery had nothing good to say. Dead or not, she still hated the luck faery for stealing her boyfriend. That's how she saw it anyway. She denied killing her rival but admitted that they'd been arguing that afternoon and she was probably the last person to see her alive. She had no alibi and I was convinced that she was the culprit. I charged her with murder.'

'It was the guy, right? He pinned the blame on his missus. He set up his missus for killing his missus,' Vincent said.

Jasper shook his head. 'No. What I'd failed to notice was that there was a loose step. Three days after the tooth faery was formally arrested, another person fell down the very same staircase. They didn't break their neck – but they did break both legs and their collarbone. I went back and looked at how the luck faery had fallen. Because of the circumstances, I'd assumed that she'd been killed. When I examined the evidence again, it became clear that it was a tragic accident. I'd jumped to conclusions and I didn't see the whole picture. I almost sent a faery to prison for life because I'd been too blinkered to look beyond the obvious. If that second faery hadn't also fallen, I'd never have gone back and checked.' His expression grew grimmer. 'It's not the worst move I've ever made but it's close.'

Vincent scratched his head. 'So?'

'So,' I said, answering for Jasper with my heart in my mouth, 'we all make mistakes. We all fuck up.'

Jasper reached for my hand and squeezed it. 'We're not perfect, no matter how hard we try to be. What you did was wrong, Saffron. There will be considerable fallout that I might not be able to mitigate. But it was a mistake and we can still fix it. I doubt Mr Adwell has got far with his attempt at bribery. We'll deal with this.'

I gave him a small smile. He was being far kinder than was necessary. 'Thank you for that.'

'It might have escaped your notice,' Vincent said loudly, 'but *I'm* perfect.'

'In that case,' I told him, feeling slightly better about myself, 'you don't need to change a thing about yourself.'

'Nope!'

'Especially not your teeth.'

He frowned. 'Wait a minute...'

I breathed in and stood up straight. Everything would be fine. I just knew it. With Jasper by my side, I wouldn't permit it to be anything but fine.

THINGS WERE MOST DEFINITELY NOT fine. In fact, my first reaction to the sight that greeted us when we walked back into Jasper's flat twenty minutes later was utter horror.

'Mate,' Vincent breathed, 'do you know that you've been burgled?'

The devastation was all but total. Jasper's immaculate leather sofa had been ripped to shreds and a trail of stuffing led across the floor, like the intestines of some over-fed animal. A shelf had crashed down and there were books spilled and broken glass wherever I looked.

'Stay here,' Jasper ordered, striding forward with his hands raised.

I already had my wand out. If the bastard who did this was still here, I'd have him. He'd be mincemeat. I'd squash him so flat that he'd wish he'd been run over by a steamroller instead. I'd...

Pumpkin ran out from underneath a sofa cushion, one of his legs entangled in a long strip of leather. In his mouth was a hard-backed book, although half of its pages seemed to be missing. He pelted past Jasper, came to a skidding halt about a foot away from me then dropped the book and sat down, licking his lips and looking proud.

'That's a first edition,' Jasper said faintly.

Vincent gaped. 'Did that dog do all of this?'

I stared round. It certainly looked like it. Fuck a puck. 'Uh,' I said nervously, 'sorry, Jasper.'

He exhaled. 'I can't say you didn't warn me.'

'Bad dog,' I scolded.

Pumpkin just yawned.

Vincent ambled forward, picking up the strewn cushions and depositing them back on the remains of the sofa. Then he jumped on top of it and stretched out. 'Any chance of a drink?' he called out. 'Something cold and alcoholic would be lovely.'

'Don't you have a home to go to?' Jasper growled.

'It's not safe there,' Vincent objected. 'Those nasty trolls might come back. Besides, someone has to stay here and keep poor Pumpkin company while you go off and sort out Adwell. That dog must have been terribly lonely to have caused such chaos when you were out.'

I checked my watch. 'Poor' Pumpkin hadn't been alone for more than a few hours. I sighed. 'At least clean this place up in the meantime.'

Vincent sprang back up again. 'Yes ma'am!' He scurried to the kitchen. 'Where do you keep your cleaning stuff, Devil?'

'Devil's Advocate,' Jasper bit out. 'Not Devil.'

Vincent didn't seem to hear him. There was the sound of various cupboards banging. I raised a questioning eyebrow. 'This isn't because of that binding thing, is it? Did I just order Vincent to do my bidding?'

Jasper shrugged. 'It's not an entirely bad thing if you did.'

Hmmm. I still felt guilty. 'Vincent,' I called out, 'you don't have do this. You don't have to clean up. I'll sort it out.'

Vincent reappeared with bright-yellow rubber gloves on his hands. 'But, ma'am,' he said, 'you ordered me to do it.'

Oh no. I winced. Then Vincent winked. 'Don't worry,' he said. 'I've got it. I quite like cleaning. Cleanliness is next to godliness.'

I blinked. Okay then. 'He's right about one thing,' I said to Jasper. 'The sooner I get to Adwell and stop his idiotic plans, the better.' I liked the idea of contacting Ethan in a few hours and telling him that I didn't need three days to sort everything out.

'This isn't just on you,' Jasper said, doing his best to avert his eyes from the devastation surrounding him. 'I promised Ethan as well.'

Even better. I gave him a bright smile. 'There's no time like the present. Adwell's in Belmarsh Prison. If you can transport us there and do your invisible thing, we can find him, speak to him straightaway and put a stop to all of this.'

'It takes a lot of effort to use magic for that kind of transportation. If I'm going to cast an invisibility spell as well, I'll be all but tapped out.'

I swished my wand in the air. 'I have this. And maybe soon I'll have my old wand back too. Art Adwell doesn't stand a chance.'

We exchanged looks of grim determination. From the floor, Pumpkin added in a plaintive whine.

'No chance,' I told him. 'You're not coming.'

The dog's head dropped mournfully – though I was certain I detected a cheeky glint in his eye.

'And,' I added, 'no more destruction. You're not even going to think about chewing on anything else.' I put my hands on my hips. 'I mean it.'

Jasper looked down. 'Will that work?' he asked.

I didn't want to tell an outright lie. 'Mmm.'

'It's as well we're not friends any longer, Saffron,' he

murmured. 'Otherwise I'd have to seriously rethink our relationship.' He gave me a searching stare and my heart skipped a beat. Taking a chance, I leaned across and brushed my lips against his. He smiled down at me. 'Ready to go?' he asked.

I nodded. Ready. Between the two of us, Art Adwell wasn't going to know what had hit him.

CHAPTER
THIRTEEN

This time I was more prepared for the sensation of being transported by Jasper's magic. What I wasn't prepared for was the prison. When the oily rolling of my stomach ceased and I looked around my new surroundings, dropping my tight hold on Jasper's arm as I did so, my earlier confidence deserted me.

It wasn't the drab beige walls or the harsh strip lighting that did it. It wasn't the pervading smell of bleach or the hallway stretching in front of us with its many steel cell doors. It wasn't the desperate singing from one of the inmates who clearly couldn't sleep, or the yells from his neighbours to shut up. What got to me was the aura of desolation and abandonment that clung to everything. I'd spent plenty of time around police stations and cells in the past but I'd never been inside the walls of an actual prison before.

Shivering, and wishing that my chest didn't feel so tight with the encroaching terror of claustrophobia, I glanced at Jasper. When I couldn't see him, I started to panic.

'Saffron,' he whispered, 'are you alright?'

Invisible, I reminded myself; for our own protection, we

were both invisible. It was all very well relying on memory magic to ensure our presence here was forgotten but we couldn't risk being spotted by any prison guards. Magic or no magic, this was still a high-security prison.

I took a deep, shuddering breath. 'I'm fine.' Then, 'Are you okay? Do you still have enough energy to continue?'

I could hear the smile in his voice. 'You're worried about me. That's not a sentiment I usually arouse in people.'

My heart rate was thankfully returning to normal. 'To be fair,' I whispered back, 'it's not what you usually arouse in me, either.'

I felt his hand reach out for me. 'We'll have to work on that later. I look forward to arousing other ... emotions.'

I licked my lips. Further down the hallway, a uniformed figure appeared – a prison guard doing the rounds. Darn it. I nudged Jasper and moved to the side so that the guard had a clear path. Invisible or not, our bodies remained solid. It wouldn't do to collide with the guard.

I could still feel the walls encroaching on me, penetrating my subconscious. The sensation of being trapped wouldn't go away. I needed to distract myself.

Jasper shuffled closer to me, the heat of his body pressing against mine. I put my hand out. Was that a bicep? I let my fingers trail down it, enjoying his sharp intake of breath. I moved my fingers. Mmm. Man chest.

The guard was pausing at every cell to peer inside. I kept an eye on his approach, while my fingers danced lightly across Jasper's body. When the guard was merely metres away, Jasper's hand covered mine. I could feel his heart pounding. There was something satisfying about knowing that I affected him in the same way that he affected me. Unless, of course, Jasper was feeling the same weight of claustrophobia as me.

There was a clank as the guard reached the cell nearest to

us and slid open the viewing pane to peer inside. I remained as still as possible, watching as he gave a satisfied nod and closed it again. Whistling, he turned and strode past us. He was older than I'd have expected, with a kindly face. I hoped that matched his personality. Whether the inmates of Belmarsh Prison deserved to be there or not, seeing the place with my own eyes made me fully appreciate the term 'stir crazy'. There was little kindness to be found in our surroundings.

The guard walked past, oblivious to our presence. I breathed out, just as his steps faltered and he came to a stop. He turned round, frowning, his eyes scanning the seemingly empty hallway. Then he pursed his lips and continued, his footsteps echoing eerily.

Once the guard had disappeared, Jasper pushed himself away from the wall. 'That was closer than I liked,' he said.

Tell me about it. The sooner we found Adwell and did what was necessary, the sooner we could get out of here. And much as the distraction of Jasper's body both delighted and astounded me, I couldn't wait to get out of this place.

'Let's go,' I said. 'This is the right wing. We simply have to find Adwell's cell.'

'Any ideas?' he asked.

My fingers fumbled for my wand. Adept movements while invisible were harder than I'd expected. I drew it out clumsily and gave it a wave. Almost instantly, I felt the magic tugging me forward. 'This way,' I whispered. 'Follow me.'

I allowed the magic to lead us past cell after cell; they were so dizzying in their uniformity that I started to feel light-headed. The sounds coming from some of them didn't help. Although the guard's rounds had halted the out-of-tune singer's attempts at keeping the rest of his block awake, not everyone was sleeping. Some men were snoring loudly. Some were quietly chatting to their bunkmates. One or two were whimpering.

The magic's pull grew stronger, drawing us forward like a magnet until we were directly outside one of the cell doors. I leaned towards the cold metal, listening for any sounds of life. There was nothing to be heard. Swallowing hard, I raised myself on tiptoe and slid back the viewer so I could check inside.

There were two beds, although only one appeared to be occupied. The lump in the right-hand bed didn't move. I squinted, trying to ascertain if this was our quarry. Unsure, I twisted my wand slightly, causing a gentle flicker of light to illuminate the slumbering body more clearly. When I finally saw the man's face, I pulled back.

'It's him,' I said quietly. 'And he's alone.' I set my mouth into a thin line. 'I've dealt with Adwell before. There's no point in giving him another face or voice to remember. I'll take care of things from here.'

I could sense that Jasper wanted to argue. After all, he'd come this far. Fortunately, he understood my logic. 'Do you know how you'll play this?' he asked.

Grim anticipation shuddered through me. 'Oh yes.' I nodded. 'He deserves what's about to happen.'

'You know you can't hurt him, Saffron.'

'I won't touch him,' I said simply. 'Watch and learn.'

I flicked my wand again, using a tiny jet of magic to unlock the door. There was a faint click but Adwell didn't react. I didn't hesitate any longer before pushing open the cell door and stepping inside. First on my agenda was to find my accursed wand.

I left Adwell where he was for now. On the far wall, underneath the barred window, there was a wide shelf with a stool beneath it – the shelf presumably doubled as a desk. I tiptoed over and started to examine the objects strewn on top of it. I didn't know how he'd managed it but I was certain that Adwell had smuggled the wand in with him. He wouldn't have wanted to leave such a potentially valuable – and useful – object behind when he was brought here.

There were three books stacked up and I tilted my head to read the titles. *The Man in the Iron Mask* by Alexandre Dumas. I nearly snorted aloud at the thought of Art Adwell comparing himself to the hero of that story; he was certainly no unfairly imprisoned prince. *Grimm's Fairy Tales*: I supposed that was his attempt at research into faery godmothers. It wouldn't get him very far. The last book was along similar lines and was entitled *Wiccapedia*. Boom-boom.

I picked up each book in turn and leafed through them on the off-chance that anything useful fell out. Adwell had underlined several sections but he was obviously floundering. I smiled. A million pounds or not, he was going nowhere, either literally or figuratively.

I'd been right all along. In fact, I reckoned that before long Adwell would start to doubt his own memory if he was left to his own devices. His recollections of me and what I'd achieved would fade into obscurity in his mind, just as he would fade into obscurity in mine.

Abandoning the books, I turned my attention to the rest of the desk. There was a pile of unappetising looking instant noodles and a grubby kettle. A pair of grey socks were drying on the stool. Oh, how the mighty had fallen. Any sympathy I might have felt for the other inmates certainly didn't extend to Adwell. He deserved everything he got.

Towards the back of the desk, there was an empty yoghurt pot. Perched inside were two pencils and a biro. I examined each implement. There was no wand. Not in view, anyway.

Sucking on my bottom lip, I tried to think. There had to be some little corner where contraband was hidden. I knelt down, checking the underside of the desk. For a brief moment, my heart leapt. There! Then I realised it wasn't my old wand that was taped to the corner, it was just a damned mobile phone. I glared at the offending object before yanking it out, dropping it onto the floor and smashing my heel into it. I had no doubt that Adwell would smuggle in a replacement before too long but at least this would delay his efforts at communicating his million-pound reward to the outside world.

The sound of the phone's destruction jolted Adwell awake. He sat up straight in his bed, blinking furiously and whipping his head round in alarm. He couldn't see me. He could, however, see both his smashed phone and the open cell door.

Go on, I urged silently. Make a run for it. Spin those spindly legs and try to get out of here. He'd be noticed and caught within seconds – and no doubt thrown into a more secure cell as punishment. The sort where the only communication he'd be allowed to make would be secret messages he could write to himself with alphabetti spaghetti.

Alas, he wasn't that daft. He twisted round, pushing his spine against the wall so that he couldn't be attacked from behind and, in a voice that was more imperious than scared, called out, 'Who's there?'

I grinned. Swishing my wand in the direction of Adwell's stack of books, I made the copy of *Grimm's Fairy Tales* flip open, turning the pages until I found a suitable illustration. Eyes wide, Adwell stretched out and grabbed the book, staring down at the open page and the horribly stylised image of a snarling boar. Let him make of that what he could.

The ex-politician closed the book with a snap. He didn't appear scared; if anything, he seemed delighted. A slow smile of nasty glee spread across his face.

'I knew it,' he said. 'I knew you wouldn't be able to resist coming. You might as well show yourself, Ms Sawyer. I already know exactly what you look like.'

I didn't move.

Adwell's glittering eyes scanned the tiny room. 'Come out, come out wherever you are!' he chanted. 'If you want that money, you're going to have to let me see you.' He rubbed his palms together. 'Let the negotiations begin.'

Art Adwell was more naïve than I'd given him credit for. I might not have spent much time in his company but he could surely have worked out that I wasn't the type to take a bribe. Maybe he assumed everyone was for sale. I wasn't a grubby politician or an assassin for hire, however; I was a faery godmother. Our principles were pristine.

'Are you shy?' Adwell asked. 'Are you nervous that I'll be angry because you put me in this godforsaken place?'

I was getting bored. If I let him continue like this, he'd keep going all night. I waved my wand again, this time drawing a far greater burst of magic. This wasn't the sort of spell that faery godmothers would normally create – but I hadn't always been a faery godmother. Hopefully Jasper would have the sense to keep out of the way and remain in the corridor.

The conjuration that appeared was one of my better ones. I beamed with pride as the shadowy corner of the cell gave way to something completely different.

There was a loud, huffing snort. Adwell stopped talking and his jaw dropped open. A moment later, the hunched figure of a snarling beast stepped forward. Its eyes glowed red, piercing through the gloom, and its vast muscled body rippled with black fur.

I flicked my wand once more and the monster took another step. It raised its giant paws, unsheathing two sets of lethal claws. It gazed at Adwell and opened its mouth, the tip of its black tongue running around its thin lips in delighted antic-ipation.

Adwell had turned so pale I thought he might pass out. His hands clutched at the sheet on his bed and he stammered, 'Wh – wh – wh–' The big man couldn't even get a single comprehen-sible word out.

I allowed the monster to take another step forward. I was particularly proud of the fact that it didn't just look terrifying, it smelled terrifying too. The foul reek of rotting flesh filled Adwell's cell. Even I was finding it hard to breathe normally, and I knew it was nothing more than illusion.

Adwell's jaw worked as he continued to try and speak. Desperation was clawing at him now, his skin turning mottled and his pupils into mere pinpricks. He released his tight grip on the sheet and fumbled at his pillow instead. I watched with a curiosity that transformed into pleasure when he finally got hold of what he was looking for and pulled out the slender wand he'd stolen from me.

'Stay back!' he yelled, finding his voice. 'Stay the fuck back!'

I hastily spun a muffling spell to ensure that his cries wouldn't be heard by any of the other souls in this desperate place. He continued to screech, his wails growing more high pitched by the second. It didn't matter; no one would hear him now. When he seemed to realise this truth, he clutched at the wand with both hands and waved it threateningly at the red-eyed monster.

'Don't do it,' Adwell warned. 'Don't come a step closer.'

Naturally, the creature did just that. I nudged it with my wand, drew in a breath then swiped. Adwell threw his head back and screamed.

I walked forward, snatched the wand out of his grasp and called out to Jasper. 'Take off the invisibility spell. Let him see me.'

A tremor ran through my body as Jasper did as I asked. I spread out my arms, stepping up to the quivering monster and smiling down at Adwell. 'Hello, Art,' I cooed.

'You … you…' He swallowed. 'I knew it was you!'

I nodded. 'Aren't you the clever one? Yes. It's me.' I patted the beast on its massive shoulder. 'And I brought a friend.'

'I'm going to tell everyone! The whole world will know about you and what you are!'

'Uh-huh.' I regarded him for a long moment with pragmatic patience.

'I'll do it!' he warned again. 'Don't think I won't!'

I shrugged. 'Okay.'

Enraged by my insouciance, he lunged forward. He was braver than I'd expected but if he'd thought that my conjured creation was as insubstantial as the shadows around us, he was wrong. The monster snapped forward, its gnarled paw grabbing hold of Adwell's hand and squeezing it tight.

'Aaaaaaagh!'

I crouched down so that I was at eye level with him. 'You're very adept at screaming,' I said. 'That skill might serve you well in here.' I frowned slightly. 'If anyone cares enough to come running when you're attacked, of course.'

'You freak of nature bitch!' he snarled. 'You're supposed to grant wishes, not create nightmares.'

I tutted. 'Oh, Art. I am granting a wish. It's my wish that you suffer extraordinarily for everything that you have done.'

He reached for his pillow again and threw it at me. I didn't bother to dodge it and it smacked me in the face. 'Oh dear. You've done it now. Now my friend is going to get really angry.'

Adwell's eyes widened. 'What do you want? Why are you here? I'll give you the money. You can take it all!'

'I don't want your money.'

'Then what?' His voice shook. 'What do you want?'

'It's obvious, isn't it? I want you to tell the world that faery godmothers exist. I want you to broadcast it from the rooftops that magic abounds in this world. Tell everyone that a seven-foot monster appeared in your jail cell and threatened you. That it had red eyes and scary claws but,' I reached out and stroked it again, 'it was oh-so soft to the touch.'

'No one will believe me.'

'Huh.' I rocked back on my heels. 'You're right,' I said thoughtfully. 'They won't.' I tapped my mouth. 'Tell you what, then. Don't breathe a word of this. No more blog posts. No more internet whispers. *Nothing.* Say one word, write one word, and Cuddles here will pay you another visit. And,' I said, 'next time he won't be so friendly.'

To add emphasis, the furred monster dropped its head until it was merely inches from Adwell's face. Then it opened its jaws and roared.

Adwell recoiled, cowering with fear. 'I won't! I won't say anything!'

'For your sake I certainly hope not, Art. Personally, I'd prefer it if you did go back on your word. Rose Blairmont was my friend and you tried to have her killed. Not to mention the other atrocities you've committed in the past. If I had my way, you'd be hung, drawn and quartered. Nothing would please me more than watching you come to a very messy end.'

Adwell swallowed. 'I'll stay quiet. You can trust me.'

I raised an eyebrow. 'Trust a politician?'

'I won't tell anyone. I'll delete the blog. It might take me a couple of days – it's hard getting around the internet blocks in here – but I'll do it. I'll do it as soon as I can.'

'Twenty-four hours, that's all you're getting. Otherwise we'll be back.' I formed my thumb and forefinger into a gun and pointed it at him. 'Got that?'

'Yes. Yes.' He nodded vigorously. 'I've got it.'

'Good.' I twirled my wand and the monster vanished. 'Too-dle-pip, Art.' Then I spun on my heel and walked out.

Jasper's voice floated over to me. 'You enjoyed that, didn't you?'

I sighed. 'More than I should have. Still, I reckon it's done the trick. I've planted the seed that no one will believe in us, and put the fear of God into him about what will happen if he continues to spread the word. Last time we met, Art Adwell had a small army with him for back up. Now he's completely alone. I don't think we'll need to worry about him again.'

'Ethan will be pleased.'

'He will.' I drew in a breath. 'We need to meet the Director first thing tomorrow and make sure she's aware of all that's happened. This sort of thing can't be allowed to happen again.'

His response was quiet. 'I've already set it up.'

I'd have expected nothing less. 'Come on then,' I said. 'We've got enough time to grab a few hours' sleep.'

I wasn't sure if this counted as another win for Saffron Sawyer, faery godmother extraordinaire. I'd take it though. And I wouldn't fuck up like this ever again. From now on, I would follow every rule to the letter.

CHAPTER

FOURTEEN

Despite the continuing fizz in the air between Jasper and me, we were both so utterly knackered after the events of the day that the only thing either of us was capable of when we returned to his flat was sleep. With Vincent snoring on the sofa, we exchanged a glance of mutual understanding and departed to our separate rooms.

If I hadn't had work again in less than three hours, I might have chosen differently and, when I lay down on the bed with Pumpkin scooting away to the furthest possible corner of the room, I regretted my drowsy decision for all of three seconds. After that I was too deeply asleep to even think about it. So deeply asleep, in fact, that I didn't stir when my alarm went off.

'Saffrooooon. Oh, Saffrooooon.'

I slapped at the annoying buzzing in my ear and turned over, grabbing the pillow and stuffing it over my head.

'Mistress, slave owner, selfish hoarder of wishes...'

'Get lost,' I mumbled.

Vincent poked my shoulder. 'The Devil told me to wake you.'

'Five more minutes.'

Something snapped down on my big toe. The pain made me sit bolt upright. 'Fuck a puck!' I yelled. 'Did you just bite my damned toe?'

He grinned at me. 'Nope. That was your dog.'

Through the frizz of my hair, I followed Vincent's gaze. Pumpkin was sitting on the edge of bed, looking remarkably pleased with himself. 'The whole lot of you can burn in hell,' I mumbled. Then I flopped back down again.

'You can always pull a sickie,' Vincent suggested. 'I can forge a doctor's note for you and...'

I sat up again. Work. Right. Yes. I could do this. 'I'm getting up,' I grumbled. 'Faery godmothers do *not* pull sickies.'

'I bet they do.'

I sniffed. 'Not this one.'

Vincent crossed his legs. 'If you say so, my lady.'

'Don't call me that.'

He shrugged. 'What would you prefer I call you? Boss? Ruler of all that is holy?'

I raised an eyebrow. 'Are you suggesting that *you're* holy?'

'You have to admit I'm pretty angelic.'

I stared at him.

'Someone has to balance out the Devil. Where there is evil, there is also good.'

Appearing at the doorway, already dressed and looking as handsome as, well, the devil, Jasper frowned. 'My title is the Devil's Advocate. Not the Devil. As you already know.'

Vincent looked at me. 'Notice how he didn't argue the part about how he's evil.'

'I'm evil enough to throw you out of my home if you don't stop irritating me,' Jasper said darkly.

I was starting to get the feeling that this could go on all day. 'Out!' I ordered. 'I've got to get dressed.' I waved my hands at them both. 'Go on. Shoo!'

The binding was clearly still working its magic on Vincent. His legs propelled him out of the room as he continued to argue. 'What about the dog? Why does he get to stay? And why don't you have a day off? It won't kill you to take a break.'

Jasper grabbed Vincent's arm and yanked him out, closing the door behind them. I rolled my eyes and clambered out of bed. I'd not had nearly enough sleep. With any luck, some industrial-strength coffee would sort me out.

I dressed in my sharpest suit, glad that I'd had the foresight to bring it with me when I'd left my own flat. I was well aware that I had to face down the Director that morning. Jasper might have been kind and forgiving about my colossal fuck-up but somehow I doubted she'd be quite so delighted at yesterday's events, even if Art Adwell was now tucked away again and I had my old wand back.

My dark skirt and tailored jacket came with its own theme tune, which thumped dramatically in my head as I did up the buttons and tried to think of some way of calming my mess of curls. Shaving it all off would probably be the best option. I dug around in my washbag, crowing in delight when I found a scrunchie. I pulled my hair into the tightest bun I could manage then walked out, still with the imaginary music pumping away in my ears.

Vincent was hunched over a mug. When I approached, he gave me a quizzical look. 'Why are you walking so strangely?'

'"Ride of the Valkyries".'

'Huh?'

'Whenever I put this suit on, I hear "Ride of the Valkyries" in my head. It's an earworm that gets in there,' I tapped the side of my skull, 'and won't let go.'

He blinked a few times. 'Saffron,' he said slowly, 'are you completely crazy?'

I gestured at my clothes. 'Power dressing,' I explained. 'This outfit makes me feel powerful. "Ride of the Valkyries" is a powerful tune. When I wear this suit, I imagine I can hear it. It makes me feel ready for anything.'

'Uh-huh.' He gazed at me. 'I was right. You are crazy.'

Jasper strode out of his room, adjusting his cuffs. 'My song is "Another One Bites The Dust",' he said absently. 'I imagine I can hear it when I'm on my way to deal with a difficult situation.'

I gave Vincent a triumphant look but he just shook his head sadly. 'No wonder the two of you are destined to be together. You're both as nuts as each other.'

I started. Jasper smiled, a lazy grin that made my heart flip. 'Come on,' he said. 'It's time to go.'

Vincent hopped off his chair. 'I'm coming too!' he trilled.

I put my hands up. 'Whoa. No, you're not.'

'I'm your slave now. You can't get rid of me.'

'Yes,' I said firmly, 'I can.'

He pouted. 'But I can help you. I would be a very useful faery godmother's assistant.'

I thought about what Billy had said. If there was one way to ensure that everyone else in the office turned on me, it would be having a human servant trail around after me and jump to my every bidding. 'Absolutely no chance.'

'But I'm safe now!' he protested. 'I'm your slave so no one can worry that I'll spill all your little faery godmother secrets.'

'You're not my slave, Vincent. And you're not coming to my office.'

'But...'

I glared at him. I'd not had enough sleep for this crap. 'Fine,' I snapped. 'You can't come to the office but you can help me out.'

He beamed. 'Excellent! What can I do?'

I considered. 'You can keep an eye on my new client. He

works at a garage called Motor On in an industrial estate in Ipswich. Go there and see what he's up to. Do not speak to him. Do not let him see you. Just ... stake out the place.'

Vincent looked delighted. I hoped I wasn't going to regret this. He began humming to himself. I squinted. 'Is that "Itsy-Bitsy Teeny-Weeny Yellow Polka-Dot Bikini"?' I asked.

He grinned. 'I've decided it will be my power song!' He spread out his arms. 'Come on then. Magic me there!'

'You have to take the train.'

His face suddenly fell. 'But...'

I grabbed Pumpkin's lead and clipped it on then gave Jasper a meaningful look. Time to go. 'I'll come and find you there later. Bye, Vincent!'

THE LOBBY of the Office of Faery Godmothers was as sparkly and clean as usual. Mrs Jardine, in her normal position behind the front desk, had the same amused expression on her face as the day before.

'Good morning,' she said, smiling broadly at us both. 'Was it an early night again for you two?'

Unfortunately, at that particular point a yawn overtook me. I stifled it hastily. Frankly, it was a miracle that the receptionist managed not to burst out laughing. From her mirthful expression, it was a close-run thing.

'Morning, Miranda,' I said.

'Good morning, Miranda.' Jasper nodded.

We both signed in using our thumbprints and headed for the lift. I straightened my shoulders. I could take what was coming. The Director didn't scare me. Much.

'Da dum da dum da dah,' I hummed, letting the imaginary sound of 'Ride of the Valkyries' calm me down while I twisted my fingers together tightly and pretended that I was confident and capable and everything that an outstandingly gifted faery godmother should be.

Jasper took my hand and squeezed it. 'It'll be fine.'

'That's easy for you to say,' I muttered. I checked my watch and grimaced. Morning briefing was about to start. I'd hoped to get in earlier to prepare myself for my dressing down.

The lift doors slid open revealing the assembly of faery godmothers, all ready for the day's instructions. Every single eye in the place turned to Jasper and me. Some people looked amused, while some were pleased. I didn't fail to note, however, that several expressions were sour.

Raising my chin, I nodded a farewell to Jasper and hastily dropped Pumpkin off at my desk, along with my bag and my phone. Then I took up my position in the crowd next to Delilah. She nudged me with her elbow while Adeline, at the front, frowned at us both.

'Did you stay with him again?' Delilah waggled her eyebrows.

I nodded, remembering her earlier anxiety. 'Not because of the trolls. We've sorted them out. It was just a misunderstanding. I'm only staying with Jasper for a while longer because he's helping me with something else. Plus he's teaching me how to use magic without a wand,' I said. 'It's easier to crash at his place for the time being.'

'Oooh,' she teased. 'Look at you with the special treatment.'

I tutted. 'It's not special treatment.'

Alicia leaned across, joining in the conversation. 'Of course it's not. There are three days left of the audit. Why would Saffron be getting special treatment from the Devil's Advocate? Unless she's worried about what's going to happen when he submits his report, so she's making sure that she's safe. He won't fire his snuggle bunny, even if the rest of us get the boot.'

'It's not like that!' I protested, remembering what Billy had cautioned me about.

'Is there room in that bed for more of us?' she asked. 'I'm not beyond a threesome.'

I breathed out. Okay. This was just banter. Probably. That made a pleasant change, especially where Alicia was concerned.

Unfortunately not everyone got the memo. Philippa turned her head, her icy blue eyes meeting mine. 'Some of us are more professional than to allow our personal lives to leak into this office.'

Alright. That wasn't banter, that was pure bitchiness. I opened my mouth to snap at her but Figgy was already there. 'You mean like that time you slept with Rupert and then stalked him round the office leaving him love notes?' she asked, the picture of innocence.

'That didn't stop me from doing my job,' Philippa said, turning her glare onto Figgy, who blanched but squared her shoulders.

I raised both my chin and my voice. 'I'm the same as you, Philippa. And I take my job as seriously as you do. Besides, I think my results in this office speak for themselves. It's largely thanks to my efforts last month as leader of the taskforce that we now have relative peace with the trolls.'

'Who said we wanted peace with the trolls in the first place?' Philippa enquired. 'Those bastards abducted our friends and colleagues. Faery godmothers lost body parts because of those trolls. We shouldn't be aiming for peace with them – they deserve war for what they did to us.'

I counted to ten.

'And what about what we did to them?' Figgy asked pointedly, surprising me further.

'That was a long time ago,' she sniffed. 'And it was an accident.'

'Philippa…'

'The taskforce did a good job,' Delilah interrupted. 'We should be glad there's peace. We don't need more dead bodies on our hands. Everyone who was on that taskforce pulled their weight.'

'Are you suggesting that because I'm not shagging the Devil's Advocate and wasn't on the stupid taskforce that I don't pull my weight?' Philippa demanded. 'I have a hundred percent client satisfaction.'

'We all do,' I said quietly, looking for a way to defuse the high emotion that was continuing to build.

Philippa snorted. 'What about that client of yours who was killed? I don't imagine she's very satisfied in her cold, hard grave.'

My stomach clenched. That comment was uncalled for. My anger rose – and I didn't try to hide it.

'Are you going to tell on me?' Philippa taunted. 'Will you go running to the Devil's Advocate and get me into trouble?' She tossed her head, glancing at Jasper who was in deep discussion with Adeline. 'You think you're untouchable.'

Unbelievable.

'Oh, leave it out, Philippa,' Alicia sniped. 'You're like a broken record. Who really cares?'

'I care,' she said. 'The reputation of this office is vitally important. We are the best!'

I was getting tired of this. I didn't know where Philippa's attitude was coming from and why she was so worked up, but I'd had enough.

'I'm not sleeping with the Devil's Advocate.' Yet. I gave it hours, at best. 'And when I do,' I said, refusing to deny the prospect, 'it will have nothing to do my with my job and everything to do with the fact that he's kind, funny, intelligent, sexy and has the tightest arse this side of the Atlantic!'

I said that last part far louder than I'd intended. It didn't help that the Director had taken that moment to stride out of her office so everyone else had fallen silent. There wasn't a single faery godmother who didn't hear me. I felt my cheeks going bright red, although whether it was a result of embarrassment or my continued anger, I wasn't sure. I glanced over at Jasper, who was standing at the front. Although his face looked studiously blank, I noted the glint in his eyes.

The Director pretended not to have heard me. 'Good morning all,' she said. 'As I'm sure you know, only three days of the audit remain. We are all looking forward to the final report. I know how hard you've been working to maintain the standards we expect and I thank you for it.'

She paused and swept her imperious gaze across us all. 'I have heard rumours being passed around that the trolls are resuming hostilities. I can assure you that is not the case. We are all perfectly safe.'

There were some audible sighs of relief. I felt a wash of guilt that those rumours were my fault and dropped my head as the Director continued. 'Let's continue to focus on our clients and do the best that we can to improve their lives.'

Angela put up her hand. 'I would like to remind everyone,' she said, 'that it's team building today and you are all expected to attend. It will be a fantastic opportunity to cement the strong bonds that already exist between us.'

'Excellent.' The Director smiled. 'I'm sure you're all looking forward to it.'

Over to the right, another hand went up. I glanced over; it was Rupert. He cleared his throat nervously. 'I've been giving this matter a lot of thought,' he said loudly, 'and I've decided that now is the time to act. It's time that we started being more careful how we address each other. I've clarified the matter with Billy and I know that the rules say women are faery godmothers and men are faery godfathers. My problem is that we never use the term godfather. It's sexist and unfair. Everyone should be more careful. I'm not a mother. Neither is Martin. Or James. Or Thomas. Or...'

The Director interrupted him. 'Yes. Thank you for that, Rupert. As the rules say, please ensure that you use gender-specific terms when talking to your colleagues.' She smiled genially. 'We are faery godmothers!'

The chorus of answering voices responded. 'We are faery godmothers! We are faery godmothers!'

'We are faery godfathers!' Rupert yelled.

The Director sniffed. 'Saffron Sawyer,' she said. 'My office now.'

CHAPTER

FIFTEEN

As I followed the Director to her office, I spotted Adeline striking up conversation with Jasper again. I flicked suspicious eyes at the Director's back, wondering whether she'd told her to do that to keep him out of the way.

'What do you think that was all about?' she asked, as much to herself as to me once the door was closed and we were alone.

'Pardon?'

'Rupert. His faery godfather thing.' She looked baffled. 'He's never complained about it before.'

I twitched uncomfortably. 'I suppose he wants to make sure the rules are followed and that he's counted as one of the team, just like the rest of us.'

'Mmm. Next thing you know,' she said, 'he'll be demanding equal pay.'

I blinked at her.

'That was a joke.'

I forced a smile.

'Speaking of rules, however,' the Director continued, 'it's high time we had a candid conversation on the subject. I understand from the Devil's Advocate that there was an incident last night that you wish to discuss and that it involved rule break-ing. We both know that you've had problems with rules in the past, Saffron. I do hope this isn't another one of those incidents. I shouldn't have to remind you that you are still on probation.'

I licked my lips. 'I've not forgotten.'

'So?' she prompted.

I sighed then outlined what had happened with Art Adwell. As I spoke, the Director tapped her pencil on her desk. The tapping became more and more pronounced as I went on. When I reached the part where Adwell had advertised a reward of a million pounds in return for help in unlocking the magic in my old wand, she lifted up the pencil and snapped it in two.

'But it's okay now,' I said hastily. 'I visited him and used my powers of persuasion to ensure that he'll keep his mouth shut. I also retrieved my wand. There's nothing more to worry about.'

'So this is the reason why Ethan got in touch? This Adwell fellow?'

'Yes.'

'And it's thanks to your actions that memory magic no longer affects him?'

I could hardly deny it. 'Yes.'

The Director placed the two broken halves of her pencil on her desk. 'You cause me more problems and headaches than any other faery godmother in this office, Saffron.'

I tried to smile. 'But I solve more problems too.'

'Don't try and make light of this situation. Yes, your heroics have done us a good turn in the past, but you have to see how serious this is.'

I swallowed. 'It *was* serious but I've put a stop to it. Art Adwell won't bother us again.'

'Let us hope not.' Her eyes met mine. 'You've broken a lot of rules. If I can be candid, Saffron, I wonder whether you truly belong here. Your ... loyalty seems to lie elsewhere.'

My eyes widened. 'I'm loyal! I'm nothing but loyal!'

The Director continued to watch me. 'To this office?'

'Yes!'

'Hmm. We shall see about that. What troubles me is that, regardless of your achievements, I can't help wondering whether it is only the protection of the Devil's Advocate that ensures your continued employment.'

The panic I'd been feeling coalesced into something else and I stiffened. 'What?' I'd expect this sort of crap from colleagues like Philippa. To hear it from the Director herself was entirely different.

'I hear things,' she said. 'Don't think that I don't pay attention to what's going on in this office. If you were any other faery godmother, I am certain that the Devil's Advocate would have requested your termination by now. To allow a human to take your wand? And then to have that human drink a concoction that nullifies memory magic?' She shook her head. 'Can you imagine any other faery getting away with that sort of thing?'

'I ... uh ... I...'

She leaned forward. 'Tell me. Did the Devil's Advocate go with you to confront Adwell?'

'Yes, but...'

'He broke into a prison and encouraged you to terrorise a human?'

'Wait,' I said, 'it wasn't...'

'His soft spot for you is proving to be quite the weakness.' She suddenly smiled. 'Good work.'

I jerked. 'Pardon?'

The Director got to her feet and walked to her window, gazing out at the grey streets below. 'The man strides around here acting as if he owns this place. His job is an important one, to be sure. Faeries should be kept in check. But he doesn't appreciate the lineage and heritage of this office. We make considerable sacrifices in the pursuit of granting wishes. My faery godmothers work incredibly hard to achieve results. Others seem to think that what we do is easy but you know how difficult this job is.'

'Er...'

'The indignity of his presence here for all these weeks,' she murmured. 'It's almost too much to bear. Goodness knows what will end up in that final damned report of his. The man might have more magic than the rest of us, but that doesn't mean he understands how this office works. *My* faery godmothers do not need to be told how to act. And I do not need to be told how to run my office.'

I was flabbergasted. Until now, the Director had given little indication that she was vexed by Jasper's presence. She'd appeared to deal with the audit just like the rest of us, treating it as a necessary evil. We all knew there would be consequences when Jasper's report came out and that changes would have to be made as a result of his recommendations. But he was only seeking to make us better.

I stared at her stiff spine, realization dawning. The Director knew what some of those recommendations were going to be – and she wasn't happy about them.

She turned to face me, her features inscrutable. I swallowed, suddenly wary about what she would say next. She folded her hands together and fixed her gaze on mine. 'I assume he's told you *why* he possesses those magical abilities of his?'

'Uh...'

She laughed shortly. 'There aren't many faeries who can wield magic without a wand like he does. He probably thinks relying on a wand makes us weaker. But you and I,' she said, indicating both of us, 'know the truth of his particular brand of magic.'

I didn't have the faintest idea what she was alluding to. I

took a deep breath. I didn't want to be here. I had no problem with getting bawled out for what I'd done with Adwell but we'd gone far beyond that point. This was starting to feel like treason.

Stiffly, I stood up. 'I should get back to work now. I've got a lot to catch up on.'

'Sit down, Saffron!' the Director barked.

'I'm not comfortable with this conversation,' I said honestly. 'I'm going to...'

'He killed someone.'

I froze. 'What?'

The Director stepped round her desk, drawing closer to me. I couldn't make my feet work. I remained stock still and gaped at her like a damned guppy.

'No,' she said, 'he didn't tell you.' She laughed sharply. 'I should have realised that he'd hide his past. It's no wonder, when you think about it. Cold-blooded murder does tend to affect your reputation.' Her voice softened. 'But that's how it works. If you want to unlock the magic within yourself and push past the natural barriers that hold it back, that's what you have to do. You have to kill.'

My mouth felt painfully dry. Despite his stern demeanour, I knew that Jasper was a good person. He was sweet and kind, and he went out of his way to avoid hurting others. He wasn't a killer. The Director might have her own agenda but I knew Jasper. I knew he wouldn't have done what she was describing.

She smiled sweetly at my expression. 'Oh, Saffron,' she sighed. 'You're still so very young and so very naïve.' She turned and walked to a filing cabinet, sliding it open and plucking out a slim manila folder. She pushed it into my hands.

If I'd been thinking more clearly, I'd have stuck to my first instinct and walked out. Lack of sleep was making me confused, however, and my brain felt fuzzy. Almost zombie-like, I opened the folder and stared at the contents. Nausea rose up from the pit of my stomach.

I was made of stern stuff – after all, I'd been a dope faery. But garish, grisly photos of a very dead body were beyond me. Especially when those photos included a younger version of Jasper, his grim face and bloodied shirt and hands indicating in lurid technicolour exactly what had occurred.

'You see?' the Director said. 'The Devil's Advocate is no hero.'

I felt dizzy. I told myself that a picture might tell a thousand words but it didn't tell a whole story. It might have been self-defence. It might have been a justified death.

I set my jaw, wishing that the horror seeping through my veins could be quashed. Until I heard the truth from Jasper, I wouldn't jump to conclusions. But the photos still made me feel sick. I couldn't reconcile my knowledge of him with the brutality of the images.

I dropped the file onto her desk and raised my head. 'Why have you shown me these?' I asked, glad that my voice rang out crystal clear with no evidence of a shaky tremor.

'It's important you have all the facts, my dear.'

I wouldn't let her get away that easily. 'Why? Why is it so important?'

'Because,' she answered quietly, 'someone who's capable of such a terrible murder shouldn't be in a position to tell us what to do. This office has been successful for generations. My faery godmothers are at the very top of their game! And yet *he*,' she spat the word, 'wants to make changes. He wants to alter the way that we do things. He'll write his report and waltz out of here, then we'll have to deal with the fall-out for years to come. He doesn't understand what it's really like to be a faery godmother. Unless he's done this job like we have, Saffron, he can't possibly understand.'

I felt something inside me tighten. The Director was trying to manipulate me. I'd known for some time that she wasn't perfect but I hadn't expected anything from her on this scale. I had the sinking feeling that I knew exactly where she was going with her machinations and what she was going to say.

The Director continued. 'The offences you've committed involving this Adwell fellow are sackable. You know that and the Devil's Advocate knows it. You put this office in jeopardy.' She tutted loudly. 'Truthfully, you put *all* faeries, regardless of their job, in jeopardy. And the trolls, too. I can understand why Ethan is so concerned.'

'I'm not denying any of that.'

'Because you're a good faery, Saffron.' She reached out and took my hands. 'You want to do the best for this office. That's why I'm giving you this opportunity to make things right. You have to see that the Devil's Advocate can't possibly counsel us against things like nepotism then allow you to keep your job when you've done the things that you have. The man's a hypocrite of the worst kind. His hypocrisy benefits you at the moment, but that won't always be the case.' Her voice lowered. 'He won't always be here. But you could be. Where do you see yourself in five years' time?'

I pulled my hands away. 'What exactly are you asking me to do?' I said carefully.

'Saffron,' she said, 'there's no need to be so antagonistic! All I'm asking you to do is tell the truth. You told me you were loyal.'

I folded my arms. 'I *have* told the truth. I've left out no details.' I paused, gritting my teeth. 'And I *am* loyal.'

'You haven't told me if you've had sex with him.'

I couldn't believe she'd just said that. 'That's personal.'

'Because if you have had intimate relations with him,' she continued as if I hadn't spoken, 'one might construe it as sexual harassment on his part. After all,' she murmured, 'he's in a position of extreme power whereas you...' She lifted her eyebrows. 'Well, we all know about you.'

I could feel the blood roaring in my ears. 'He has not harassed me. Not in any way, shape or form.'

She pasted on a saccharine-sweet look of sympathy. 'You think that because of the way he's manipulated you. Deep down you know the truth.'

Yes, I did. And the truth was that every word spouting forth from the Director's mouth was bullshit.

'You know,' she purred, 'I noticed you had a little argument with Philippa this morning. I actually spoke to her before the morning briefing.' She smiled.

I was feeling more sick by the second. The Director had poured oily whisperings into Philippa's ear then wound her up and watched her go. 'I'm still the Director here, Saffron,' she told me. 'I've still got power. Lots of it.'

A long, heavy silence descended. I could feel the pressure weighing down between my shoulder blades. I'd expected many things from this meeting but I hadn't expected this.

'So,' I said eventually, 'let me see if I have this correctly. The carrot you're offering is that if I complain that the Devil's Advocate harassed me I get to keep my job and you stop turning my colleagues against me. And if I don't comply, the stick is that you'll sack me and make a complaint of nepotism against him.'

Jasper was supposed to be the embodiment of faery law. If he was seen to be twisting that law for his own ends, he'd lose all credibility. And probably his position, too.

'I think you're beginning to understand my position.' The Director leaned forward. 'I'm merely trying to protect my office, Saffron. That's all. I did tell you that I wouldn't let anyone threaten my faery godmothers.' She nodded at the folder. 'Don't forget that he's not the saint he pretends to be.'

There was a single harsh knock on the door. I jumped. Then it opened and Jasper stepped through. His green eyes scanned us both, narrowing slightly. 'I'm sorry I'm late,' he said. 'Adeline had an extremely urgent matter she wished to discuss with me.'

The Director smiled airily. 'Not to worry,' she said. 'Saffron has brought me up to speed with last night's events. I will consider what she has told me and make a decision as to how to proceed before the end of the week. Obviously, it's a serious matter.'

Jasper's face was set into a mask. 'We should discuss it between ourselves before any decisions are taken.'

'Mm-hmm.' She turned back to her desk, knocking the folder onto the floor. 'Oops.' The photos spilled across the carpet. She took a step back and gazed down at them. 'How clumsy of me.'

I looked at Jasper. His face had gone pure white. He stared at the photos, then at the Director, then at me. A moment later, he turned on his heel and stalked out.

The Director smiled primly. 'I'll give you two days, Saffron,' she said. 'Then I expect a proper answer.' She pursed her lips. 'I suggest that you do indeed have sex with the man. It will bolster your case.'

I clenched my fists. The woman was colder than I could ever have given her credit for. I couldn't even look at her any longer. I whirled round and ran after Jasper.

SIXTEEN

Jasper was nowhere in sight. I scanned the office, searching for him, then headed for his office. His door was open but he wasn't inside. A faint scent of cinnamon lingered in the air but the man himself had vanished.

I sucked on my bottom lip and tried to think logically. The Director was convinced that she held all the cards but, as long as I didn't rush into anything and make knee-jerk reactions, I was confident that I could find a way out of this for all of us. I had to speak to Jasper first. Desperately.

I stalked back into the main office. Figgy was sitting at her desk, cross-legged and humming. Her attention was fixed on an object in her hands, her brow furrowed as she gazed at it.

'Figgy.' I leaned over. 'Have you seen the Devil's Advocate?'

'Huh?' She blinked. 'Oh, he left. Big poof of smoke. He didn't look very happy.' She shrugged.

Fuck a puck. 'Did he say where he was going?'

'To me?' she looked astonished. 'No.'

I cursed again and turned to stomp off.

'Wait, Saffron,' Figgy called. 'Do you know how to work this?' She held up the object.

I stopped and squinted at it. 'It's an old-fashioned mobile phone. You have to flip it open.' I thumbed it upwards, revealing the small screen and keypad.

'Ohhh,' her face cleared. 'Thank you.' She tittered slightly. 'I'm so ditzy sometimes!'

'Figgy,' I asked slowly. 'How did you get this job?'

'Huh?' She was still staring at the old phone.

'How did you get this job?' I repeated.

'My dad got it for me,' she said absently. 'He thought I should make myself useful.'

I nodded and glanced round the room. Almost everyone here was probably a faery godmother because of their family connections. I couldn't work out whether the Director's attempts to dismiss the rampant nepotism that occurred under her watch by accusing Jasper of the same thing was genius or madness. Either way, it spelled serious trouble.

Desperate to speak to someone I could trust, I spotted Billy out of the corner of my eye. He understood far more about the goings-on in this office than any of the others. In Jasper's absence, he was the best person to talk to. I wheeled round in his direction. He'd help me find a way out of all this.

Keeping my head down to evade my colleagues and avoid getting dragged into any unnecessary conversation, I scuttled towards him. The man had eyes in the back of his head; he turned to scowl at me as I approached.

'Your beast,' he hissed, 'has peed all over the photocopier.'

He'd unwittingly provided me with the opening I needed. 'Oh dear,' I murmured. 'I'll help you clean it up. Where do you keep the mop?'

'I've already...'

'Billy,' I interrupted, adding an edge of steel to my voice, 'where do you keep the mop?'

He took another look at my face, his brows snapping together as he registered my unhappiness. 'This way.'

We headed towards the back of the office, skirting the corridor that led to the Adventus room.

'Saffron!' Rupert yelled from the portal. 'What do you think about a petition? To make everyone say godfather instead of godmother?'

I forced a smile and gave him a huge thumbs-up. Then I pushed Billy into his little store room and followed him in, closing the door behind us.

'Encouraging Rupert won't help anyone,' he frowned. 'He's got a real bee in his bonnet about this whole godfather thing. I'm all for parroting the rules but even I have limits. That idiot was suggesting that all the male faeries get together and go on strike to force the issue.'

Any other day that would have stirred a reaction, but today I had far bigger fish to fry. 'Rupert isn't my concern.'

'No,' he replied. 'But clearly something is. What's happened?'

I wasted no time. 'How do you feel about the Director?'

Billy stared at me. 'Saffron, I know you're ambitious but if you're thinking about trying to get her job...'

'Oh for goodness' sake, Billy! What do you think of her as a person? Because she's just tried to blackmail me so she can get Jasper off her back.'

His mouth dropped. 'Shit.'

'And then some. What can I do? There must be some sort of leverage I can use against her. I know from what happened with the abductions last month that she was angling to get hold of drugs. It was the reason she ended up being kidnapped with the others. If I threatened to tell other people...'

Billy held up his hands. 'Did she actually take any drugs?'

'I don't think so. The trolls nabbed her before she could.'

'And do you have any real proof that she was planning to take any drugs?'

'Not a signed affidavit,' I admitted. 'But I know she was.'

Billy shook his head. 'The Director is a canny woman. She'll have made moves to explain away that situation by now. All she had to do was drop a few hints that she was on the trail of the trolls, rather than on the trail of getting high, and she's in the clear.' He looked troubled. 'She's extremely powerful, Saffron. The only person who's probably stronger than her is the Devil's Advocate. And if she's trying to get him out of the way, she'll have planned her moves in advance. The Director doesn't gamble.'

'What can I do? I can't let her get away with this.'

Billy ran a hand over his bald head. 'I understand you have feelings for him, but the Devil's Advocate is very strong. I'm sure he can look after himself.'

'It's not that easy,' I said through gritted teeth.

'He's got magic coming out of his pores.'

'And do you know why that is?' I asked quietly.

Billy stared at me.

I thought about the other faeries Jasper had mentioned. 'Have you heard of a Yosei called Miseko Awahashi?'

'Of course. She's a very powerful Japanese faery. She's like the Devil's Advocate – she can use magic without a wand.'

'What about her history?' I pressed. 'Do you know anything about it? Or Jack Flanagan? What about him? Humbert Holstead? Carlos Sanchez?'

'I know Jack Flanagan,' Billy said. 'He's the Director of the Irish faery godmothers.'

I grabbed Billy's shoulders. 'This is important. Has he ever killed anyone?'

Billy recoiled. 'What?'

'Has Jack Flanagan ever killed anyone?'

His face dropped and he started to mumble. 'He was in prison for fifteen years. He shot someone – but he made amends. He's not the same person now. He wouldn't be the Irish Director if he was.'

An icy hand gripped my heart. I sat down heavily on a cardboard box, ignoring the fact that it sagged under my weight. 'And Jasper?' I asked dully. 'The Devil's Advocate? Has he ever killed anyone?'

'I don't…' Billy bit his lip. 'I don't know.' He met my eyes. 'Would you like me to find out?'

Yes. I sighed. 'No.' It was more important that Jasper told me himself rather than for me to go behind his back. I buried my face in my hands. 'How did this shit happen? How did I get here?'

The store room door opened. I looked up to see Adeline, framed by the light from behind her. The Director's stooge. How fabulous. 'Billy,' she said, 'go and make yourself useful.'

'I…'

Her voice hardened. 'Now.'

I stood up. I refused to hang around and listen to more blackmail crap; I'd had it with this place. I tried to push past Adeline and escape but she stood her ground.

'Stay there, Saffron.'

I clenched my jaw. 'You deliberately delayed Jasper. That was on the Director's orders, right? Do you know why? Do you know what she said me to in that office of hers?'

'I have an idea,' she replied.

'You're just as culpable as she is!'

'We do what we have to do in order to survive, Saffron.'

I put my hands on my hips. 'Do we?'

Adeline sighed. 'Have you seen any draft report details? Has the Devil's Advocate shown any of it to you?'

'No,' I answered instantly. 'And you know why? Because it

wouldn't have been professional for him to do so. *He's a professional.'*

She winced. 'The Director doing what she thinks is right. She's safeguarding the reputation of this office. She already feels that she's lost ground by apologising to the trolls for past wrongdoings. She already feels diminished – and cornered. The Devil's Advocate should have been prepared for this. He should have known she was going to fight back.'

'So it's his fault?' I asked disbelievingly.

She ran a hand through her hair. 'I don't know what she's said to you, Saffron, but I can imagine. If you fight her, it won't go well.'

I stared at her. 'You're scared. You're scared of the Director.'

She met my eyes. 'I always have been. Powerful people *are* scary.'

I thought about Jasper and the revelation that he'd probably committed murder. 'Not necessarily,' I whispered. 'What does she have on you?'

Adeline looked away. 'Enough.'

I grimaced. I knew that the Office of Faery Godmothers wasn't as virtuous as it pretended to be, but up until now I'd only scratched the surface. In the last hour my whole world had been turned on its head and I was still spinning. So much so that I was beginning to feel both hot and dizzy.

'Look, Saffron,' Adeline said. 'I like you and I think you're an asset to this office. I don't want to lose you. If you want to keep your position – or at least be in a position to fight for it – then you have to prove your worth. Hiding in a store cupboard isn't going to do it. Get out there and do the best by your clients. If you're doing your job properly, the Director hasn't got a leg to stand on.'

Both of us knew that wasn't true, but if I didn't do my job I'd only provide the Director with more ammunition. Goodness only knew when Jasper would return. Until I spoke to him, I couldn't do anything else. I *wouldn't* do anything else.

'Fine,' I said. 'I'll go and deal with my clients. If the Devil's Advocate does return, ask him to find me.'

She nodded. 'I can do that much.'

I breathed out. My chest felt painful and tight. Maybe this was nothing more than a bad dream. Perhaps visiting the prison and dealing with Art Adwell had unsettled me so much that I was now trapped in an horrific nightmare.

If only.

PUMPKIN WAGGED his tail in delight when we walked out of the Metafora room and onto the industrial estate. Animals are smarter than we give them credit for; I reckoned that he could sense the tension in the office and was thrilled to get out of there. Either that or he was hoping for more sprinting mechanics to chase.

I gulped in the fresh air, ignoring the faint reek of petrol that drifted over from the garage. Then I looked around for Vincent. He should have arrived by now but there was no sign of him. So much for my dedicated assistant.

I pressed the base of my palms into my temples. I had the beginnings of a stress headache that I knew would get worse as the day progressed. No prizes for guessing the source of that stress.

I grimaced. I still had a job to do and my client deserved my full attention, at least until I caught up with Jasper. I bit down the temptation to turn tail and head to Jasper's flat on the off-chance that he'd retreated there. Instead, I drew closer to the garage forecourt and peered in. It really was a busy place.

Spotting Eric – or rather Mark, as he wished to be called –

crouching down by the wheel of a Ford Escort that had seen better days, I walked towards him. Before I could get close, however, the unfriendly blond-haired man with the extravagant tattoos who I'd spoken to yesterday strode up and barred my approach.

'Can I help you?'

His words might have been polite but his expression certainly wasn't. Everything about his demeanour suggested that I should walk away now. That was the last thing I was in the mood for. Whatever machinations were going on back at the office, I was still great at my job – and I was damned well going to prove it to the world.

I fluttered my eyelashes in a bid to make myself look both feminine and weak. It amazes me how many men believe the two things go hand in hand. I'm just a girl, I projected at him. Cars are beyond me. I need manly help to survive.

'Oh yes,' I gasped, 'you certainly can. I'm so glad I found you. My phone is out of battery and I broke down a mile or two back. I tried to flag down other drivers but no one wanted to stop and help me. I started walking and then I saw this place. I'm *so* glad I found you.' I spoke with as much breathy emphasis as I could manage. If only the same idiocy would work on the Director.

The man's eyes didn't soften in the slightest. 'We're fully booked. I can give you the name of another garage.'

I swung my head round, checking the buildings along the street. 'Is it near here?' I asked hopefully, knowing full well that there were no other mechanics within a five-mile radius.

'It's on the other side of town.' He stuffed his hands in the pockets of overalls. 'They have a tow truck. You'll be fine.'

I blinked rapidly, allowing my eyes to fill with tears. Under normal circumstances I couldn't cry on demand, but today it was proving surprisingly easy. Even Pumpkin appeared to be affected, whining slightly and nudging my hand as if he cared.

'Okay,' I sniffed. A single tear rolled down my cheek. Surely that was enough to make him invite me into the garage for a cuppa?

'Good.' He turned away.

I cursed inwardly. I hadn't thought it would be this difficult. I'd have to try harder.

I looked down at my watch. 'My daughter will just have to wait on her own at the hospital, I guess.' I injected an appropriate tremor into my voice. 'She's undergoing kidney dialysis. It wouldn't be so bad if her father was around but...'

He faced me again. It was about time. 'I suppose we can check your car out and tow it to the other garage if it's going to be a big job.'

Bingo – though I had the feeling he'd agreed to help me in order to end the conversation rather than out of sympathy for my story. It didn't matter; as long as I got the opportunity to spirit Mark away so I could talk to him on his own, I'd be happy.

'Thank you!' I beamed through my tears and sprang forward to hug him. 'Thank you so much!'

He held up his hands to ward me off. It was just as well; there was an edge to this man that hinted at a vicious nastiness I didn't want to get too close to. 'It might take ten minutes or so before I can free someone up.'

'That's no problem!' I dropped my arms and walked into the garage before he changed his mind. 'Can I wait inside? It's so chilly out here.'

The man squinted at the sunlight but he could no longer argue since I was already inside. I hastily located a battered leather chair near the garage's office and sat down.

'I won't bother anyone,' I promised. 'I'll wait here until someone is free.'

He huffed and nodded, shuffling past me and walking into the office. He looked like he was already regretting his decision.

I breathed out. No matter what other crap was going on, I was still good at this. Now all I had to do was get Mark to talk to me again. The problem was that there were so many other mechanics around that I couldn't rely on luck alone to get him assigned to help me.

Leaning back so that I could gain a direct line of sight to the car Mark was working on, I slid out my wand and laid it on my lap. Then, starting with just a few minor tweaks, I flicked it surreptitiously towards the Ford Escort.

The exhaust, which had been trailing on the cement floor, reattached itself to the underside of the car. There were a few creaks as the various dents in the bodywork smoothed themselves out. A grizzled mechanic who happened to be passing glanced at the car, confusion on his oil-smeared face. I tweaked my wand again so that the magic halted. He shrugged and continued on his way.

Once the coast was clear, I swished my wand and raised the Ford's suspension. Mark, who was still crouched by one of the wheels, sat up straight and frowned. Magic spun round the tires, re-inflating them. Now all I had to do was turn my attention to the engine. By the time I was finished, this car would be better than the day it rolled off the assembly line. And my client would be free to escort me to my supposedly broken-down car.

Raising the tip of my wand, I concentrated, visualising the Escort's engine. If I just...

'Let me go!'

At the sound of the shriek, Pumpkin sprang to his feet and barked. I craned my neck, my heart sinking when I saw Vincent being manhandled towards me by two mechanics.

'I wasn't doing anything!' he protested. Then his head

turned and he caught sight of me, relief flooding his sallow features. 'Saf...'

I glared at him in warning. The last thing I needed was to have to start this rigmarole all over again because Vincent had got in my way.

He understood. From the twist of his mouth he wasn't happy about it, but at least he got the message. 'Safari!' he yelled. 'This place is a goddamned safari!'

I raised my eyes heavenward. That made no sense whatsoever.

Vincent twisted free of his captors, although he continued moving past me towards the exit. 'You're a lion. You're a crocodile.' He pointed at another man. 'And you're a monkey.' He threw back his head and laughed. 'Grease monkey! Get it? Get it?'

The door to the office banged open and the blond man stepped out to see what the ruckus was about. At the same time Mark stood up, wiping his hands nervously down his legs. Wariness flashed across his face and he stepped backwards.

'We caught this wanker poking around the back, Fox,' one of the mechanics said. His eyes flitted meaningfully to his boss. 'He was sniffing around the boxes by the spare carburettors.'

There was a faint stiffening in Fox's shoulders. A muscle jerked in his cheek and his right hand dropped. My eyes tracked the movement and I froze when I noted the bulge in the pocket of his overalls. It certainly wasn't there because he was happy to see me. What the hell was going on in this place?

'Let's take him outside for a little chat,' Fox said, his eyes flicking momentarily in my direction.

I was pretty certain that little chat wouldn't end well for Vincent. Thinking quickly, I tightened my grip on my wand and steeled myself. I bloody hoped this would work.

Pumpkin was the first to notice. The small dog sprang backwards, initially terrified. Then, from behind the relative safety of my feet, he started to bark again. The mechanics looked towards him.

I raised a shaky hand and pointed at the source of his anxiety. 'What is that?' I screamed. 'Is that a ... a ... snake?'

Everyone turned simultaneously, as if we were all starring in some cheesy pop video. For a single beat nobody moved then chaos broke out as all the mechanics sprinted away. To be fair, this was Ipswich and not the Amazon jungle – and it was a damned big snake. I was rather proud of myself: it was at least ten feet long, with a girth that was the stuff of nightmares. Its scarlet skin didn't help matters, either. I touched the edge of my wand and the snake snapped its jaws several times before slithering forward.

Fox, who had stayed where he was, took a step backwards. From behind his back, I gestured frantically at Vincent to escape. Wide-eyed, he remained frozen to the spot.

Cursing to myself, and aware that at any moment Fox was liable to pull out the gun from his pocket and start firing it either at Vincent or the snake or me, I tightened my hold on Pumpkin's lead and ran, motioning to Vincent to follow. This time he got the message and a split second later we were back outside, heading for freedom.

CHAPTER

SEVENTEEN

Every time I visited the garage, I ended up being forced to run out of it. I paced up and down. 'I had a plan,' I muttered. 'I was going to get my client out of there and speak to him on his own. Then I could have finally found out enough to grant his wish. You,' I paused long enough to jab my finger at Vincent's chest, 'ruined all of that. And you almost got yourself killed in the process. I'm certain that Fox fellow had a gun in his pocket.'

Instead of arguing with me, which frankly was what I wanted because I was more than ready for a fight and I didn't care who it was with, Vincent looked shaken.

'I've met a lot of dangerous blokes in my time and those mechanics definitely rank up there with the worst of them.' He exhaled. 'I can't believe there was a snake in that garage and that it appeared when it did.' He shook his head. 'Talk about a lucky break.'

I gave him a long look.

'Wait,' he said slowly. 'I was talking about a safari.' He thumped his chest. 'It was me. I made that snake appear because I was talking about animals! It must be some sort of magical osmosis. You're magic – and now I work for you I must be magic too.' He held up his hands to his face, wiggling his fingers. 'Abracadabra!'

Unbelievable. I rolled my eyes and paced harder, stomping up and down the deserted street. Pumpkin had the sense to scoot out of the danger zone but Vincent wasn't quite so smart. He wandered into my path and almost got knocked over. He huffed loudly. Then he paused, comprehension dawning on his face. 'Ohhhhh. You used your wand and conjured up that snake. It wasn't me.'

'Congratulations, genius,' I said, with enough sarcasm that even Vincent couldn't mistake my meaning.

'Wow.' He peered at me. 'What's happened to my sunny little Saffron? I know you didn't get much sleep last night but you're not usually this snarky.'

'I'm having a bad day,' I muttered.

'Well, you know what I think? You should turn that frown upside down!'

I folded my arms.

'When life gives you lemons, make lemonade!'

I glared at him.

'No?' He shrugged. 'How about when life gives you lemons, you freeze them and throw them at people instead?'

That was a bit better. 'Can I have some tequila and salt as well?'

Vincent pursed his lips. 'To drink or to throw?'

I considered. 'Does it matter?'

'I guess not.' He slung an arm round my shoulders. 'Feeling better now?'

'No.' I sniffed. 'What happened, anyway? What were you doing poking around the back of that garage? I told you to stake out the place, not lumber in and create bedlam.'

Vincent looked hurt. 'I wasn't deliberately trying to mess

things up for you. I was doing like you told me. I was too conspicuous out on the street and you ordered me not to let your client see me. I didn't know who he was and I couldn't take the risk that he'd notice me. I thought it would be smarter to head round the back and find somewhere to hide so I could watch what was going on.' He folded his arms. 'I'm telling you, Saffy, that place is dodgy as hell. Whoever your client is, he doesn't deserve any wishes whatsoever. Not if he works there.'

'Let me guess,' I said drily. 'I should use up his wish on you instead.'

'I didn't say that.' He paused. 'But it's not the worst idea in the world.'

I rolled my eyes. 'Yeah, yeah.' I stopped pacing. I was tired and freaked out by my chat with the Director and worried about Jasper and... Everything was getting on top of me. I breathed in. Focus, Saffron.

'What did you actually find back there?' I asked. 'Clearly there's something in those boxes that they didn't want you to see. In fact, they were prepared to put a bullet in you in case you'd peeked.'

Vincent gave an extravagant shrug. 'Fucked if I know. I assume it was car parts. Do you think it's something to do with your client?'

'I don't know – but I'm planning to find out. If that Fox bloke is so desperate to protect what's in those boxes, they're definitely worth investigating.' I tapped my mouth thoughtfully. 'The problem is that now they'll be guarding them more carefully.'

Vincent nodded. 'Because of the snake.' His eyes widened. 'It's not going to follow us, is it? I'm not much of a fan of cold-blooded creatures.'

'The snake's gone. It was nothing more than an illusion.'

'It looked pretty real to me.'

I smiled slightly. 'It was impressive, wasn't it? Fox is probably desperately ringing the RSPCA as we speak.'

'They'll remember the snake? Your memory magic doesn't cover it?'

'Nope.' I jabbed my finger at his chest. 'And it doesn't cover you either, so you have to keep well away.'

'What?' Vincent's eyes widened. 'What if they come after me? What if Fox tries to find me so he can finish what he started?'

'You'll be fine. He doesn't know who you are or where you live.'

'That's easy for you to say,' he grumbled. 'Anyway, if they're all on edge, how will you get back in? I've got to say, Saff, damsel in distress isn't a role that suits you.' He dipped his head and lowered his voice. 'You're kind of an ugly crier. Your face is still blotchy.'

'Gee,' I said sarcastically, 'thanks for that.'

'The truth hurts.'

I clicked my tongue. Whatever. 'Actually,' I said, 'there's something else I could try. Something far, far more effective.' I grinned. It wouldn't hurt to give it a shot.

Vincent took a step back. 'You have a scary look on your face.'

Good. I could do with some of that right now. 'Don't fuck with the faery godmother,' I told him, 'or the faery godmother will fuck right back with you.'

WE FOUND a quiet corner next to the field which had so entertained Pumpkin the day before and ducked behind a cluster of sick-looking trees. If there were any crazed mechanics out for blood and searching the industrial estate, I didn't see them.

'If you can make yourself invisible,' Vincent said, his expression more puppy dog than Pumpkin's, 'why don't you do it more often? Just think of the fun you could have. And the power!' He licked his lips salaciously. I tried not to wonder what delights were currently running through his imagination. That would definitely lead to madness.

'I can't make myself invisible,' I said absently, rolling up my sleeves and pondering the best way to proceed. 'Or at least I've not been able to before now. It's magic that very few faeries have at their disposal. But Jasper can do it. I reckon that if I practise a bit first, I might manage it too.'

Vincent looked me up and down. 'Far be it for me to comment on your faery skills,' he said, 'but is it possible that you're over-reaching?'

'Where there's a will, there's a way.'

'I'm simply saying that I know a little about what it's like to have delusions of grandeur.' He still sounded dubious. 'There was one time when I reckoned I could take over the distribution of all the amphetamines in Colchester. There's a big market, you see, and I had an excellent supply chain. At least, I did have an excellent supply chain until the manufacturer sampled a little too much of his own product. And then there were a few gangs from Liverpool and Manchester who weren't too happy about what I was attempting.' He paled at the memory. 'It didn't go well for me.'

I wrinkled my nose. 'I'm not running drugs and I'm not trying anything illegal. I'm just stretching my abilities and learning from the best.'

'Have you ever tried it before?'

'At school once or twice.'

'And did you turn invisible then?'

'Nope. But my mate Harry managed to make his big toe transparent.'

Unsurprisingly, Vincent was unimpressed.

'Look,' I said, 'I'll try this first. If it doesn't work, I'll go back to the garage and present myself as a snake wrangler.' I glanced down at Pumpkin. 'I've lost one client to a bullet. I won't risk the same thing happening again. Whatever is going on in that garage, it's clear that Mark Smith's employer is up to no good.' I set my jaw. 'I will find out exactly what's in those damned boxes.'

Vincent held up his hands, palms facing outwards in surrender. 'It's your funeral.'

Dismissing his concern, I slid out my wand. Using magic successfully is often about self-belief and inner confidence. All I had to do was concentrate.

I swished my wand experimentally a few times. Both Vincent and Pumpkin backed away. I paid them no attention. I had this. Squeezing my eyes shut and holding my breath, I tensed my stomach muscles. Then I went for it. Go invisibility, go!

I opened one eye and looked down. I remained just as solidly visible as before. Gritting my teeth, I tried again. In theory it shouldn't be that hard. When Jasper had done it for the both of us, his hand movements had been barely perceptible.

I created an image of myself in my mind's eye before blanking it out, limb by limb. Then I twirled my wand once more.

'Saff,' Vincent whispered, 'I can see your bones.'

Startled out of my concentration, I looked down at my body again. Fuck a puck. He was right. Panic zipped through me. My flesh was actually translucent. What if someone saw me like this? I felt more naked and exposed than if I'd stripped off my clothes and streaked down Colchester's high street.

I'd transformed myself into a monster, a garish skeleton more suited to a graveyard than a faery kingdom. Vincent was correct; I'd been over-ambitious. Yet again, I'd made a decision that was stupid and rash and would have far-reaching consequences that I couldn't yet envisage.

I was finding it hard to breathe and my body tingled all over. What was I going to do? How was I going to fix this? What about…?

'Saffron? Are you still there?'

I checked myself again. This time I was so shocked that I almost fell over. 'It worked.' I stared at myself just in case I was imagining it. 'It bloody worked.'

Pumpkin darted forward, his body quivering and nose twitching. He collided with my legs and fell backwards before picking himself up again, his head swinging from side to side. He could still smell me – but he couldn't see me. He whined then sat back, his head tilting upwards. A moment later he started to howl, a keening sound that filled the air.

'Pumpkin!' I reached for him. 'You have to be quiet! We can't draw attention to ourselves! We're still too close to the garage.'

He stopped mid-howl as my fingers brushed against his fur. He snapped his teeth. I jumped back.

'That dog is not happy,' Vincent observed. He bent down and picked up Pumpkin before stretching out one hand and poking me. 'Is that really you? Can I still touch you?'

I flung out my hands and cupped his face. Vincent jumped and pulled away. 'That's seriously freaky.' He touched his cheek and looked around. 'Where are you exactly?'

I beamed. 'I'm here! I did it, Vincent. I actually did it.'

I spun round, still marvelling at myself. I wasn't sure how

I'd achieved it. I'd been overtaken by panic, unable to think straight and then ... something had clicked. It was amazing. I crowed in delight. Super Saffron, that was me. Finally something was going right and I had to take full advantage of my good luck.

'I'm going in, Vincent. You and Pumpkin take the train and go back to Jasper's place. If he's there, call me.' I paused. 'And tell him to stay there and that I want to speak to him as soon as possible. And don't let him leave till I return. And tell him that things at the office are much worse than I'd realised, and I don't care what he's done before but we need to think about what's coming next. And that I still don't want to be friends with him. And that he can't trust the Director. And that I don't care about the photos. Well, I do care, but I'm learning not to jump to conclusions. And tell him that...'

'Saffron,' Vincent broke in. 'I realise I'm your slave and I'm supposed to do your bidding, but I'm not sure I can remember all that. Whatever's going on between you two and has put you in this weird mood is probably a matter for the two of you alone. Shouldn't you wait and talk to him yourself?'

I exhaled. For once Vincent was speaking sense. 'Yeah. Alright.' I thought again. 'Just call me if he's there. I'll meet him at the flat as soon as I can. Otherwise I'll head back to the office and hopefully I'll see him there. This garage business won't take long.'

Vincent nodded agreement and I took off, running back in the direction of the garage. The only indication that I was moving were the tiny clouds forming on the ground where my feet hit the dust. I picked up speed until, mere minutes later, I was back in front of Motor On. I had this in the bag.

As far as I could tell, most of the mechanics were still too afraid to re-enter the garage forecourt. They were milling around outside, their eyes darting to and fro as they searched for any sign of the snake. I'd probably gone too far by involving so many of them in the same magic, and the evidence of the chaos I'd caused was right in front of my eyes, but I'd had to act quickly and there'd been little choice.

I edged round the men and headed inside. Fox was standing in the centre, a grim look on his face.

One of the mechanics who'd had hold of Vincent strode up to him. 'I can't see it anywhere. We should call someone. Get a professional to check the area. If that snake is coiled up under a car…'

'We can't call anyone. You know that. We can't involve others. Nobody is allowed in here unless we're sure they can keep their mouths shut.'

'If we move the boxes out before they get here, it should be okay.'

Fox rounded on the man. 'And put them where exactly? Do you want them in your house? Around your children?'

The mechanic's face fell. 'No,' he said quietly. 'But we can't let that snake slither around in here. It'll be worse for us in the long run if it ends up attacking someone.'

Their sinister conversation wasn't exactly heartening. I started to tiptoe past them. I definitely needed to find out what they were hiding. Unfortunately, my steps weren't as silent as I hoped and Fox's head snapped round. He stared right at me. His hand went to his pocket again, fingering his weapon.

I froze, barely daring to breathe. Could he see me? Was the invisibility wearing off?

'Jumping at bleeding shadows now,' he muttered to himself.

I sagged in relief and continued. Invisibility didn't equal invincibility – I still had to be bloody careful.

Picking my way around the downed tools and streaks of oil, I skirted various cars in different states of repair and made a beeline for the rear of the garage. I ignored the door on the right-hand side, which I already knew led outside, and veered left. When I spotted a stack of black crates in the far corner, I knew I'd found what I was looking for.

I went towards them, stopping every so often to check that no one else was around. When I finally reached the stack, anticipation thudded through me. I flipped open the lid of the top box and peered inside.

At first my brain couldn't compute the contents, and the collection of black metal confused me. Were they just car parts? I reached in, pulled out the nearest object and squinted at it. Then I realised what I was holding and dropped it with an involuntary squeak. Not car parts but gun parts. Lots of gun parts.

I backed away until my spine was pressed against the wall. I'd known this place was dodgy; I'd known it was probably a front for something far less legal than car repairs. But the last thing I'd expected was gun running. The lethal potential of those boxes scant feet away from me was chilling.

I also had to face the very real possibility that Mark Smith, my client, had not only fluently and effectively lied about turning over a new leaf but was progressing from accidental murder to wide-scale terrorism. And I was supposed to be his damned faery godmother helping him to achieve his life goals.

CHAPTER

EIGHTEEN

What I wanted to do was invoke the Metafora magic and return to the office. I was starting to feel like I was playing a dangerous game of whack-a-mole, with life-threatening problems rearing their heads every time I took a breath. Just as I solved one issue, another one sprang up in its place. I was teetering on the edge of an abyss; one wrong step and I'd plunge into the depths of an unforgiving and utterly chaotic hell.

It was clear that I couldn't run back to Jasper and confront him with the Director's machinations, not until I'd dealt with the very real threat of the guns. The prospect of mass casualties trumped the politics of the Office of Faery Godmothers. There was no choice but to stay right here and see this through.

Calling the police was the sensible option. I fumbled down my invisible self, wondering which pocket I'd left my phone in. An anonymous mention of guns would bring them running. It might not bode well for Mark Smith, especially given his past history, but I didn't have much choice when lives were possibly at stake.

I cursed. Fuck a puck. After the stress and confusion of my

meeting with the Director, I'd left my phone on my desk at the office. I wouldn't be making any calls, not unless I could sneak into Fox's hideaway and use his phone. In theory that wouldn't be particularly hard. Nodding to myself, I moved right – just as Fox and his sidekick came into view.

'Check under there,' Fox ordered, pointing to the underbelly of a car awaiting attention. 'It might have slithered there to hide.'

The other mechanic swallowed, obviously unenthusiastic about the prospect of getting down onto the floor when there was a gigantic snake somewhere in the vicinity. But he did as he was asked and dropped down to check for any signs of snakey action. As he did so, Fox stared at the stack of gun boxes, his eyes narrowing when he noted that the lid from the top one had been removed.

'Barry,' he said slowly, 'that wee fucker who was poking his nose around here...'

'Yeah?' grunted the mechanic, twisting his head to check the other side of the floor.

'Did he open the crates?'

'Not as far as I'm aware.'

A muscle ticked in Fox's jaw. 'Did anyone else open the crates?'

'No.' Barry got to his feet and brushed himself down. 'No snake here.' His gaze landed on the open box and his face tightened with dismay. 'Oh shit.' He darted forward, inches from me, and peered inside. 'Nothing's been taken. It's all still here.'

Fox sucked on his teeth and turned, examining the area around him. Yet again, his hand went to his pocket; this time, I saw the handle of a pistol as he half-pulled it out. 'No one's here now.' He paused. 'But someone was. That ... thing was a diversion to get everyone out of the building. While we were running around like a bunch of schoolgirls, someone was back here messing with our product.' His fingers curled tighter round the gun. 'We had one of them and we let him escape.' He pulled out the gun and pointed it at his employee. Even the Director's managerial style had nothing on this guy. '*You* let them escape.'

Barry began to stutter. 'It wasn't me, boss! It wasn't my fault!'

'I can't afford fuck-ups, Barry.' Then before I could think, let alone act, Fox pulled the trigger.

Barry didn't have time to look surprised. His body flew backwards with the force of the shot, slamming into a shelving unit before crumpling to the floor. While I clamped my hand over my mouth and gazed in horror, there was the sound of booted feet running in our direction.

'You found it!' a grey-whiskered man called. 'Well done, boss!' His face was wreathed in smiles. Then he rounded the corner with three others directly behind him and saw not the corpse of a snake but the corpse of a man. A man he'd been working alongside just minutes before. His mouth dropped open. 'Wh – wh – what?'

The other mechanics skidded to a halt, staring down with white faces.

'We don't have time for fuck-ups.' Fox gestured at the whiskered mechanic. 'Get this cleaned up.' He looked at the others. 'We're moving our schedule forward. We need to transport the product out of here in the next hour. It's all hands on deck. Split it up between the vehicles and drive them out.'

A thin guy, who had a hard, vicious edge to his features that belied his slight and unimposing frame, stepped forward. 'We can't. We don't have enough people.'

'There's twenty men out on that floor.'

'And,' the man argued, 'only seven of them know what's going on here.'

Fox waved the gun. 'They're all ex-cons, I made sure of that.

No matter how stupid they are, they know this place isn't squeaky clean. It's high time they were all promoted anyway.' His eyes hardened. 'Unless one of them has been blabbing and that's why we've had problems back here.'

'Blabbing? To the coppers?'

'No. We'd all be in handcuffs if that was the case.' Fox's lip curled. 'It must be another gang trying to muscle in on our turf. Before more of them show up, we're getting this shit out of here. Got that?'

All four of them nodded.

'What about the snake?' asked the whiskered guy.

Fox pointed the gun at him. No. Oh no. Not again. 'Well,' he drawled, 'that comes down to who you're more afraid of. Some animal,' he bared his teeth, 'or me.'

'We'll forget about the snake,' Whiskers said hastily. 'It's probably gone by now.'

'Wise choice,' Fox said. He glared at them all. 'Well? What are you waiting for? Get moving!'

He stalked off. I stayed where I was, frozen to the spot, while the men started muttering to themselves.

'Deal with Barry first,' one of them said. 'Then the others. There's some plastic sheeting we can use to get him out of the way. Put him in one of the car boots for now. The green Audi is big enough.'

They nodded and moved. A distant part of my brain reverberated with questions. Was the worst thing that none of them was particularly surprised by what had happened to their work colleague? Or was the worst thing that he'd died because I'd not put the lid back on the gun box?

I shivered, even though I felt feverishly hot. I was supposed to be on the path to being the best faery godmother in the world. Instead, all I had to show was a catalogue of fuck-ups. I wasn't getting better at my job as I went along, I was getting worse. Lethally so.

My grip tightened on my wand. Dwelling on my failings wouldn't help anyone, least of all Mark Smith. I was still in a position to do something and be of use. I was still a damned faery godmother.

I avoided looking at Barry's dead body and tried to think. Pulsating blood was thumping through my ears, making it diffi-cult to concentrate. I gritted my teeth. There was a strange metallic taste in my mouth. I shook out my hair. Enough, Saffron. Do your damned job.

This was obviously a distribution centre for illegal weapons. These guns were about to be delivered to criminal hot spots up and down the country. By stumbling across the enterprise – and putting a stop to it – I'd be helping far more people than my client.

Fox had said that all his mechanics were ex-cons. That was why he'd hired Mark without worrying about his past, and why the young mechanic had bolted when he thought I was the police. Fox employed men who had already drifted to the wrong side of society, men who would turn a blind eye to organised criminal activity or join in and help out. Hell, he employed men who were willing to turn a blind eye to murder. Maybe Mark Smith had been right: maybe you could never escape your past no matter how hard you tried.

I stood up straighter. The heat I'd felt inside me was now more like a burn, spreading through my veins and piercing my insides. It gave me the resolve I needed. Screw it. Fox was the bastard around here – deal with him and this whole operation would tumble down like a house of cards.

I gazed at the gun crates then I flicked my wand. Magic swirled round them, spinning in the air and growing in power before delving inside to render every single weapon part useless. Get all the gun experts you want, I thought grimly; none of these will ever be assembled into guns that can take another life. I nodded as the metal components clanked and clattered. It was a start – but I wasn't done yet. Not by a long shot.

I drew in a breath then turned my wand on myself, removing the invisibility spell. There was a quiet whooshing sound and again it felt as if my very skin was being turned inside out. Goosebumps prickled along my arms and legs but I paid them scant attention. I strode in the direction of Fox's office, almost colliding with the four men who were returning with some sheeting for Barry's body.

'What the...?'

I flicked my wand at the group and they crumpled. I blinked, startled by the ease with which I'd conjured up magic to put them out of commission. That had never happened before. Then I shrugged; as long as they weren't in a position to stop me, what did it matter? The mechanics weren't dead, they were merely sleeping.

What did you call a group of mechanics anyway? A troupe? A gaggle? A murder? A hysterical giggle bubbled from my lips and threatened to overwhelm me. I quashed it. Fox. I had to deal with Fox.

Moving faster now, I sped across the garage floor. A few men were still hovering by the entrance, clearly nervous of the snake. I spotted Mark Smith amongst them and the kid who'd run from me the other day. They were going to get their chance to start afresh – I wasn't going to let Fox ruin it for them. I ignored them, and the other braver ones who headed in my direction to stop me. Let them try. Let them fucking try.

No one did. Whether it was my grim determination or the crazed look in my eyes, I didn't know. Either way, those who'd started towards me hesitated and fell back. Maybe some part of their subconscious selves registered the magic crackling around me and decided to keep out of my way. I didn't look at them. I had bigger fish to fry.

Apparently sensing a disturbance, Fox flung open the door to his office and walked out, a mobile phone glued to his ear. When he caught sight of me, his eyes narrowed. 'I'll have to call you back,' he muttered. He put the phone away and glared at me. 'Who are you? What do you want?'

I smiled nastily. 'You.'

Fox wasted no time and drew out his damned gun again. 'I'm not having the greatest day, girly,' he snarled. 'So get the fuck out of my garage before I lay you out for good.'

I tipped the edge of my wand and a swirl of magic caught the gun's muzzle, wrapping round it like a noose. I tightened it and yanked, snatching the weapon away from him. It flew through the air then clattered onto the cement floor to my right.

'What was that?' I enquired.

Fox's nostrils flared. He stared at his empty hands then at me. I shrugged and gave him my best disarming smile. He roared, clearly still unable to grasp how much power I possessed and how far I was prepared to go.

He started down the steps and I flicked my wand again, taking his feet out from under him. He landed on his back and I winced theatrically on his behalf.

'Ouch,' I said. 'That must have hurt.'

Fox groaned. I advanced towards him, wand raised.

'Who the fuck are you?' he moaned.

'I'm Saffron Sawyer,' I told him. 'I'm a faery godmother.' I paused. 'Not yours, though. You don't deserve one.' I prepared to wave my wand one last time. The bastard would get what was coming to him.

'Saffron.' A familiar voice penetrated through the roar of blood in my ears.

I glanced over. 'Hey, Ethan,' I said. 'Still following me then?'

'Melissa was,' he said quietly. 'She saw what was going on and called me.'

'Has her eye healed yet?' I asked politely, as if I were merely enquiring about the weather.

'It's improving.'

I considered this. 'Good,' I said finally. Out of the corner of my eye, I noted Fox stirring and trying to get back to his feet. I focused on him once more. He wasn't getting away that easily.

'Saffron,' Ethan said again. 'Enough now.'

I shook my head. 'I don't think so.'

He walked up and placed a hand on my arm. 'You're snapping.'

I frowned. 'No.'

'You are. Your magic is threatening to overwhelm you. You have to back down.'

'I don't think I'm going to do that, Ethan.'

'Saffron, you have to.'

'I...'

There was a cough from behind. 'Don't make a mistake you'll have to live with for the rest of your life.'

I glanced round. 'Eric Maker,' I said softly.

He paled. 'My name is Mark.'

I raised my shoulders. 'Whatever.' I turned back to Fox. Ready or not, here I come.

'Don't do it,' Mark said.

Ethan's grip on my arm tightened. 'He's right.'

'Calm down, dear,' I whispered. I looked at Ethan. 'That's what you're telling me, right? Funny that a troll, of all people, is telling me to sort my head out and stop being rash.' I laughed.

'Not just any troll either. The head of the trolls. The one who instigated a terror campaign against faery godmothers.'

'It was more complicated than that and you know it. Sort yourself out, Saffron. You're better than this.'

'That's not what you said the last time we met,' I said faintly.

'I was angry then.'

'I'm angry now.'

He smiled at me. 'No, you're not. This is what happens. It happened to us, to all the trolls after most of our kind were killed. It's why we can use magic now without the need for a booster tool like your wands. The magic inside us snapped and took over. It's happening to you.'

I pursed my lips. Nah. 'The Director said you had to kill someone for that to happen. I've not killed anyone.' I smiled at Fox. 'Yet.'

'The Director's wrong. Snapping might lead you to kill someone, but it's not what causes your magic to break out and overwhelm you. Trauma does that.'

He didn't know what he was talking about. 'I've known lots of traumatised faeries. They haven't snapped. Honestly, you don't have to worry – I'm fully in control. Maybe you ought to take up meditation or something, Ethan. It'd be good for you.'

Fox moaned slightly. I lifted my wand. Groin first, I decided. That would hurt the most.

'Saffron,' Ethan persisted, 'what would the Devil's Advocate say if he were here? What would Jasper tell you?'

A vision of Jasper's piercing green eyes flashed in front of me.

I looked from Ethan to Fox and then to the fear-pinched faces of the watching mechanics. What was I doing? This wasn't me: I wanted to help people, not kill them. I gasped suddenly, my stomach cramping. I doubled over, feeling like I'd been punched. Ethan was right, I was acting like a mad thing.

From the steps, Fox grunted. He got to his feet, his head down, before barrelling at full speed towards the fallen gun. I straightened, my wrist twisting as I directed my wand towards him again, but before I could do anything Ethan thrust out his hand, palm first. Fox faltered and collapsed to the ground once again.

The troll strolled over, stepping over him and picking up the weapon. Then he turned back to me and eyed me for a moment. I drew in a shuddering breath and nodded. He passed the gun to me.

'This is your scene. I don't care what you do with the humans,' he said quietly. 'But I'm starting to think that our fates are intertwined, Saffron, whether we like it or not.' He tilted his head, considering. 'Strange as it might seem that I am looking after the interests of a faery godmother, I did promise you that you wouldn't be harmed by a troll. I guess that extends to not looking the other way when you put yourself in danger and could harm yourself. What happened, anyway? Did someone close to you die suddenly? Did you kill someone? Is that why?'

I swallowed and started to shiver. A mad surge of emotion had taken control of me temporarily and only through Ethan's intervention had I managed to bring my real self back again. This wasn't *Invasion of the Bodysnatchers,* though. In the end, the only person I could truly blame for my moment of madness was myself.

'I think it's been an accumulation of events.' Once I'd said it aloud, I knew I was right. It had started with Rose – my clients weren't supposed to die on me. Jasper's presence had mitigated the revelation of my epic mistake with Art Adwell and the after-effects of my face-off with Finch and Melissa, but the Director's nastiness had turned my world on its head.

Making myself invisible should have been the big clue. I could never have done that if I hadn't already been close to the edge. Barry's murder right in front of my eyes had been the final straw. My inability to rationalize it had sent me over that edge.

I thought of my determination to wield magic like Jasper. Maybe a small, subconscious part of me had willed this to happen. What an idiot. I didn't deserve to be a faery godmother.

Ethan smiled sympathetically. 'I've read old manuscripts that say it can happen that way. Don't feel too bad about yourself.'

I tucked the gun into my waistband, together with my wand. My fingers were still shaking but I felt calmer. Clearer. 'What now?' I whispered.

He stepped back. 'That's up to you. You're past the worst now, so I will take my leave and you can decide.' He paused. 'Tell that dog who worries about you so much that we're even now.'

I frowned but, before I could say anything else, Ethan had gone.

'Where did he go?' one of the mechanics asked. 'Where the fuck did that guy go? He vanished into thin air.'

I looked round. They were all staring at the spot where Ethan had been. As I watched, however, I could see the memory magic worming its way into their brains. Their baffled expressions faded; their memory of his existence dissipated just as quickly as their memory of me would do after I left. I should never have tried to bypass the system. It was there for good reasons.

'Who are you?' Mark asked. 'Who are you really?'

The last wispy shreds of fogged lunacy cleared from my mind. 'I'm Saffron Sawyer,' I said. 'I'm your faery godmother.'

The cluster of mechanics gaped at me. They'd seen what had happened to Fox. As long as I remained here, they would remember the magic that had spun its web in front of their eyes. Despite that, they couldn't believe what I told them. They couldn't appreciate that truth was usually far stranger than fiction.

Mark touched his chest. '*My* faery godmother?'

'Yes. You made a wish.' I struggled to recall the contents of his file. 'It was your birthday,' I said. 'You blew out the candles on your cake and made a wish that brought you to my attention. It's my job to improve your lot and make your life better.' I gestured at Fox's unmoving body. 'I wasn't expecting your circumstances to be quite so complicated but,' I struggled to find the words, 'everyone's different.'

The young man who'd run from me on the first day seemed more willing to accept my words than his older work colleagues. 'Do we all have faery godmothers?' he asked. 'Do I have a faery godmother?' His eyes were wide and shining. It would be a shame to burst his bubble.

'You all have the potential to be assigned a faery godmother,' I said carefully. I licked my lips. 'Anyway,' I continued, 'I suspect that I've got to the bottom of your desires, Mark. Everything about your life has been about turning over a new leaf and starting afresh. Your employer was getting in the way of that, but I think we've solved that problem. I recommend that you boost your status in the eyes of the law and call the police. Along with Fox, there are some ... things round the back that they should know about.' That was putting it mildly.

Mark's lips moved. He was mumbling something but I couldn't quite make it out.

'Pardon?'

His skin flushed and he glanced round, aware that everyone was watching him. 'Thank you.

'It's what I'm here for.' I tilted my head. 'I'm sorry things got a little crazy.'

'A *little* crazy?'

I allowed myself a ghost of a smile. 'Don't worry,' I told him. 'You won't remember any of it.' I could feel the tug of the Metafora magic as it started to pull me away. 'The next few days will be weird for you,' I said, 'but things will settle down. You'll get your shot at a new life.'

The mechanics' faces were growing transparent. As the familiar whoosh sounded, one of them nudged the kid. 'Do you think she's talking about the cake you nicked?' he asked. 'The one that said...'

And then the transportation spell did what it was supposed to and I was gone.

CHAPTER

NINETEEN

My feet were dragging. I pushed the Metafora door open with such force that it recoiled back towards me, smacking my forehead. I let out a soft pained oomph and looked round.

The place was deserted. I checked my watch, frowning. Where the hell was everyone? They should all still be here. It was only early afternoon and there was no chance that they'd all traipsed out on client visits.

I stared into the empty corners of the room. I could really do with a hug, preferably from Billy. Or maybe Delilah. Hell, at this stage I'd take one from Rupert. That was a true measure of how shaky I was feeling.

I touched my wand, my fingers brushing against its smooth tip. I never thought I'd be grateful that I had to rely on it in order to perform strong feats of magic, but I now understood what it took to discard such a reliance, I was relieved. I determined not to be like that.

Jasper's face flashed into my mind, and the photos the Director had shown me. He was powerful and strong and he had magical skills I could only dream of – and my heart ached for him. I'd have to find him as soon as possible. Now more than ever, I felt like I understood him – and what those grim, bloody photos had alluded to. I needed to speak to him. And to listen, if he'd let me.

I heaved myself over to my desk. The absence of any other faeries troubled me. Where had everyone gone? Had something disastrous happened? Then I spotted the collection of chairs in a circle in the centre of the room where morning briefings were usually held and realization dawned. Of course. Today was Team Building Tuesday. They must have started here before decamping to somewhere with more space.

I doubted Angela would be impressed that I was missing yet another of her initiatives, even if we were on better terms these days. It didn't mean that I wanted to find her and the others, though. The last thing in the world that I wanted right now was to stand up and tell two truths and one lie, or make bridges out of matchsticks.

Rubbing the growing bump above my left eyebrow, I sat down at my desk. My phone was sitting where I'd left it, in my bag in front of my computer screen. I picked it up and glanced at it. Five missed calls – one from Vincent and the rest from Jasper. I bit my lip and pressed the button to listen to my voicemail, fumbling with the handset in the process and dropping it. Muttering a vexed curse, I bent down to retrieve it as a door opened and two familiar voices floated through.

'What you fail to understand, Adeline,' the Director said, 'is that my job is not just to maintain the efficient running of this office but also to ensure that its heritage and history remain undamaged. Anyone who meddles with that does so at their peril. We're not the tooth faeries. I'm not going to permit a purge of my faeries. Not unless I'm the one who starts it. Neither will I accept that man's ridiculous recommendations that we move with the times. We have excellent success rates. There's simply no need for his interference.'

I stiffened then crouched down further to stay out of sight. Eavesdropping wasn't my usual sort of sneaky manoeuvre, but this opportunity had fallen into my lap. Perhaps I'd learn something helpful.

For a long moment, Adeline didn't say anything and I started to think she'd been struck dumb. Then she cleared her throat. 'Maybe we should take some of his recommendations on board.'

The Director's derisive snort left no doubt as to her opinion. 'Don't be so stupid! He told me, amongst other things, that he was planning to make us change our recruitment policy so we hired more faery-godmother wannabes like Saffron Sawyer. What a horrific notion! We hire the crème de la crème for a reason – because we *are* the crème de la crème. We can't permit any dirty little faery to wander in and take up a position here. We're supposed to be the best. I won't allow us to be anything else.'

'Saffron has done a lot of good for this office,' Adeline hedged. 'The way she worked to stop the trolls and help bring about peace...'

'A temporary peace,' the Director interrupted. 'How long before those bastards go back to their old ways? I give it less than a month. We'd have done far better to simply root them out and exterminate them. It's the only way to be sure that my faery godmothers remain safe. Don't forget they kidnapped me. Me! And they took one of my fingers in the process. Saffron Sawyer and that fool of a Devil's Advocate think we should forget that and pretend it doesn't matter. But those trolls have made me look weak on more than one occasion – and I can tell you, Adeline, that the last thing I am is weak.'

I swallowed at the bitterness in her tone. The Director had

given herself away; no matter how much she protested about wanting to protect her faery godmothers and the sanctity of this office, she hated the fact that she'd been made to look like anything other than an iron-willed hero. At my suggestion, Jasper had persuaded her to make a formal apology to the trolls for what had happened to them as a result of a faery godmother wish that went wrong. Now I wondered if that had been the spark that had sent her down this terrible road.

'You're stronger than any other faery in the country,' Adeline said hastily. 'And better than all the trolls. But maybe we should think about this a little more.'

The Director continued as if Adeline hadn't spoken. 'Can you imagine having more faery godmothers like Saffron Sawyer? She swans around, taking initiative where none is required and causing havoc everywhere she goes. She already has Billy eating out of her hand. I had him exactly where I wanted him – I've been cultivating him for years – then she sweeps him away right under my watch! The others are beginning to like her far too much as well. No.' She clicked her tongue. 'She's getting far too big for her britches. She needs to be put back in her place. The last thing we need are others like her.'

'But,' Adeline said nervously, 'won't she go running to the Devil's Advocate and tell him what you said to her? Won't she tell him that you want her to accuse him of harassment?'

'This is why I'm in charge and you're not, Adeline,' the Director said. 'You're incapable of grasping the full picture. I'm counting on the fact that Saffron will already be blabbing everything to him. She's as besotted by him as he is by her. She'll run off at the mouth and he will have no choice but to remove me from my position.'

'You want her to tell him? You want him to sack you?' Disbelief coloured Adeline's tone.

This time, there was a smile in the Director's voice. 'I want him to try. The irony is that it would never have worked *without* Saffron Sawyer. Her presence – and the Devil's Advocate's feelings for her – have made my plan all but foolproof. He'll try to have me fired and, in return, I'll point out that his soft spot for her means that he jumps to her bidding. That she has utterly compromised his position and therefore his integrity cannot be assured. She's made no secret of her ambition. It won't take much to get the other faery departments to believe that he is prepping her to take my place. She's even living with him right now, for goodness' sake! All the evidence is there. And in case that's not enough, her failings will become very public in a day or two. Just wait and see. In one fell swoop I shall rid myself of both Saffron Sawyer and the Devil's Advocate. When they fall, they will fall hard. Then this office will remain independent and,' she added in a satisfied voice, 'mine.'

'Director,' Adeline said, 'far be it from me to disagree with you but perhaps this isn't the best course of action. Perhaps it would be better to discuss the Devil's Advocate's report with him and come to a compromise.'

'I'm done compromising. And if you continue to gainsay me, I shall have no choice but to publicise your past mistakes too. None of us is perfect, Adeline, but some of us are less perfect than others.'

Adeline's answer was quiet. 'Yes, Director.'

'Good,' she said briskly. 'I'm glad we understand each other. Now, come with me. I want to examine the Adventus Room.'

Their footsteps – and their voices – drifted away. I squeezed my eyes shut and hugged my knees tightly against my chest. Fuck. A. Puck.

~

I DIDN'T KNOW what to do. After several long minutes staring into space, I slowly got up from my hunched position under my desk and sat down on the chair. It creaked under my weight but I paid no attention. Now what?

I reached out and picked up a paperweight, hefting it in my hands, then I raised it to throw it into the glass wall of the meeting room. A moment later I dropped my hand and returned it to its original position. I'd already come close to losing my sanity today; I wouldn't let the Director's conniving actions send me over the edge.

Breathe, Saffron. Focus. There was a way out of this. There had to be something I could do that would beat the Director at her own game. It would come to me if I thought hard enough.

Just then my phone rang, startling me out of my reverie. I stared at it, unseeing, before realising it was Jasper who was calling. Part of me didn't want to answer but I knew I had to.

Reluctantly, I pressed the green button. 'Hey,' I said softly into the receiver.

'Hi.' His voice was gruff. 'I've been trying to reach you.'

I smoothed my hands down my thighs. 'I was with a client,' I told him. 'I left my phone in the office.'

'Uh-huh.' I could tell that he didn't believe me. 'Are you back in the office now?'

'Yes.'

'Can we meet? Somewhere else? I'm sorry I walked out on you. I think you deserve an explanation and I'd prefer you heard it from me rather than from the Director.'

Too late, I thought sadly. 'Sure,' I said. My voice sounded distant even to my own ears. Maybe I wasn't really here at all. 'Name the place.'

'The café on Nero Street?'

I nodded. 'I can be there in fifteen minutes.'

'I'll see you then. And,' he drew in a breath, 'Saffron, I want you to know that...' His voice trailed off.

'Know what?'

'Never mind. I'll tell you when I see you.' He hung up.

I dropped my hand, the phone still in it, then I got decisively to my feet and picked up my bag. I put the phone inside, followed by my wand. I also slid Fox's gun from my waistband as I had a brief vision of myself holding it at the Director's head. That wasn't the way to handle things and it would cause far more problems than it would solve – but it was still tempting.

I sighed and checked the safety was on before shoving the gun into my bag's side pocket. I couldn't leave it lying around the office; if it were discovered, it would only serve as further evidence for the Director to advertise my devious, malicious nature. I grimaced. I'd find a way to get rid of it properly later. Jasper was my priority now.

CHAPTER

TWENTY

He was sitting at a small table in the corner of the café. When I walked in the door, he glanced up, his emerald eyes flaring with a flash of optimism. He quickly shuttered his emotions, however, and got to his feet. 'Here,' he said, pulling out the chair opposite. 'Have a seat.'

I nodded. 'Thank you,' I said. I sat down awkwardly while he ordered me a cup of tea before returning.

'Where's Pumpkin?' he asked.

'With Vincent. The pair of them went back to your flat to see if you were there.'

Jasper's mouth tightened fractionally. 'I went for a walk to clear my head. I was somewhat ... taken aback by the photos.'

Him and me both. 'Me too,' I said in a small voice.

'I don't know how the Director got hold of them.' His expression hardened. 'Although I think I know why.'

Jasper wasn't stupid – far from it – but I doubted that he knew just how far the Director was prepared to go to safeguard her own interests. 'Did you kill someone, Jasper?'

He didn't blink or miss a beat. 'Yes.'

I closed my eyes briefly. 'Tell me,' I said. 'Tell me what happened.'

He inhaled deeply. 'It's why I'm here.' He pulled his chair in closer. 'You saw the photo of my sister at my flat.'

'Anna.'

'Yes.' His eyes took on a distant focus. 'Anna. She was a few years older than me. We weren't alike in the slightest. She was the life and soul of every party, with a wide group of friends. There wasn't anyone she met that she couldn't charm. Anyone else would have ignored a grubby little brother who scowled if someone smiled at him and who preferred to hide in his bedroom instead of experiencing the world. Anna didn't. She had infinite patience. She'd coax me out and drag me with her to all sorts of places. We had so much fun together.'

He sighed. 'When she laughed, which was often, she made you want to laugh with her. Even now,' he said quietly, 'it still hurts to think about what she might have become. She could have done anything.'

The waitress appeared and placed the tea in front of me. I poured in a splash of milk and took a tiny sip, although the drink was hot enough to burn my tongue. My mouth was painfully dry. I knew what was coming next, not the painful details but the outline. I placed the cup carefully back onto the saucer as Jasper continued.

'One night when I was sixteen, she walked home after dinner with some of her friends. It wasn't far. She should have been safe.' He shrugged, both baffled and depressed by the vagaries of life. 'It was less than a half a mile. I walked it myself afterwards, over and over again. Even if she'd been dawdling, it shouldn't have taken her more than fifteen minutes to get home. But that was more than enough time.'

He pulled back, his voice growing less emotional and more matter-of-fact. In a flash, I understood why: the only way to cope with this was to distance himself from the details. And to distance himself from me.

'He hit her over the head and knocked her unconscious. Then he hit her again. She had her wand but it didn't help because she had no chance to use it. When I hunted him down afterwards, he said that he didn't mean to kill her. He'd only wanted her purse and she'd fallen badly. I never found out if that was true or not. I didn't give him the chance to tell me.'

'You snapped,' I said quietly. 'You snapped and you found him and you killed him.'

His eyes met mine. 'I did.'

'That's why you don't need a wand to use magic. You broke the barriers that kept your magic in place. And once they'd gone, you couldn't put them back again.'

Jasper didn't disagree. 'I have blood on my hands, Saffron. And the fact that I can do this,' he held up his hand and clicked his fingers, causing a tiny earthquake to ripple through the small café, shake the walls, spill my tea and make the waitress squeak with fear, 'is a constant reminder of what I've done.'

'You were sixteen, Jasper. You were still a child. Your emotions overwhelmed you and your magic took over. That's not your fault.'

'Yes, it is.' He didn't look away. 'It's my fault and I should have been jailed for it. Instead I was given this job. Vincent is right, you know. This job might have saved me, but I'm not the Devil's Advocate. I'm the Devil.'

'No.' I shook my head. 'You're not.' I didn't reach out for his hands although I was desperate to hold him. I'd been right; Jasper was so much more vulnerable than anyone realised. That was why I had to walk such a fine line now.

'What I did wasn't an accident, Saffron. It was brutal and deliberate. I could have told you before,' he said, in a strangled whisper. 'You wanted to learn to use magic like me, and that was the perfect opening to reveal the truth about myself.' A spasm of self-hatred crossed his face. 'But I didn't tell you, did I? I just pretended to teach you.'

He might not have told me the truth but he'd dangled it in front of me. Jasper had given me the names of other faeries who were like him. A little more investigation into who they were, and I'd have worked it out for myself without the Director's intervention. Jasper knew that I was so determined to be like him that I'd eventually have looked closely at those five faeries' backgrounds. I'd have got there sooner or later. Deep down, he'd wanted me to do just that.

'I was given the job of Devil's Advocate with the proviso that I never break the law again. This job saved me from myself and I believe I'm good at what I do. But I imagine,' he said with a harsh laugh, 'that you think it's crazy that I sit in judgment of others when I'm the one who should be judged.'

Actually, that was why he was so perfect for the role. He could hold himself at a distance because he'd been doing it his entire life. He understood the depths we were all capable of and the bitter consequences of our own actions. It was why he'd understood that forgiving the trolls for their misdeeds was the only way forward. There were always two sides to a story and he knew when redemption was possible –and when it wasn't. Jasper's magic was merely a secondary bonus to his role as Devil's Advocate.

The truth about who he was didn't make me think less of him; it made me understand him better. That was why I had no choice but to protect him. He'd already said his job had saved him; now it was my turn.

'You're a good man, Jasper. I know you feel guilty for what you've done and you probably always will.'

My tone made his gaze sharpen. 'I sense a but.'

I swallowed. My heart felt as if it were breaking in two. 'But it's a lot for me to deal with. I think it's best if I go to my own home tonight.'

His jaw clenched. The worst part was that he wasn't surprised; he'd been expecting it. 'You want us to be friends again.'

I licked my lips. 'Yes.' At least until I could find a way to put an end to the Director's manipulations.

Associating with me was putting him in danger. He loved his job as much as I loved mine and, since his sister had died, he'd poured his entire being into being the Devil's Advocate. If he stuck with me, he'd lose everything he'd worked for. And I was damned if I was going to let that happen.

He got to his feet, his knees banging against the table top and knocking over my cup. We both ignored it. 'I understand,' he bit out. 'Thank you for taking the time to meet with me and listen.'

Regret and guilt flooded through me. 'Jasper, wait, let's...'

'I'll see you in the office tomorrow, Saffron,' he said. He whirled round, his back stiff. A moment later he was gone.

I STAYED in the café until long after my tea had gone cold. Despite my best intentions, there remained a massive, selfish part of me that wanted to run after Jasper and tell him the truth. That I'd come close to snapping too – and for far worse reasons than he had. That I would help him face his demons because I was beginning to realise that I loved him. That I would never hold his past against him. But I also worried that stepping back from our relationship wouldn't be enough to save him.

Eventually, the waitress wandered over. 'It's closing time soon,' she said, with a pointed look at my cup. 'Are you done?'

'Yes. Sorry. I didn't mean to keep you waiting.' I pushed my cup towards her and gathered up my things.

'That's alright, duckie. You've had a fight with your boyfriend. You looked like you needed time to think.'

'He wasn't my boyfriend,' I said sadly. 'Though I wish he was. We were at a point where we understood and accepted each other. I'd finally broken through all his defences and seen through the façade he puts up to the world to keep himself safe.'

'Ah,' she clucked wisely. 'That doesn't happen very often. Not with men. They like you to see things as they want them to be, not how they really are. Deep down, they're all frightened little boys.'

'We're all frightened little girls too,' I murmured.

I sighed and pushed my hair out of my eyes. She was right: we all spent our lives pretending to be more than we were. The Director pretended, even to herself, that her primary focus was the well-being of her faery godmothers. I pretended, even to myself, that I had the potential to be the best faery godmother in the world. Billy pretended he cared about rules. Alicia pretended she believed she was better than everyone else. We all did it, humans as well as faeries. For goodness' sake, Eric Maker pretended he was Mark Smith. He put up more of a façade than the rest of us.

Then I paused. 'Shit,' I said aloud.

'Are you okay?'

'Yeah.' I nodded. I got up to my feet. 'Thank you for letting me sit for so long. I've got to go.'

The waitress nodded and smiled. 'Go get your man.'

I sprinted to the office, waving at Mrs Jardine as I entered through the front door.

'Have you been playing hooky, Saffron?' she enquired.

'Nope.' I jogged past her, then I halted and turned round. 'Nothing's going on between Jasper and I.'

'Of course it's not.'

I gritted my teeth. I needed her to believe me. I needed everyone to believe me. 'It's true,' I said. 'He doesn't want anything to do with me any more. I've been dumped.' I grimaced. 'Not that we were ever really together, but you know what I mean. He hates my guts. Despises me. I'm like a piece of shit on the bottom of his shoe.'

She gazed at me as if I were mad. 'I find that very hard to believe.'

'It's true. I'm not going to deny that I feel horrible about it, Miranda,' I said honestly. 'The bottom of my world has caved in. But I was never going to be good enough for him. I'm just Saffron Sawyer and he's the Devil's Advocate.'

'Hmm.' Mrs Jardine didn't look convinced but it was a start. As long as word reached the Director's ears before she put any more plans into action, it didn't matter what the receptionist thought. I nodded and continued on my way.

My stomach lurched when the lift doors opened. I wasn't sure I had the steel inside me to face Jasper again. I was likely to collapse at his feet and tell him I'd made a terrible mistake – and that wouldn't help him at all.

I carefully scanned the room, filled now with faery godmothers, then edged out. There didn't appear to be any sign of him and suddenly I was as disappointed as I was relieved. Then I saw the Director, standing in the doorway of her office and frowning at me. I forced a smile in her direction, even though it killed me to do so, before ducking my head and scurrying to my desk.

'How did you get out of Team Building Tuesday?' Delilah hissed before I'd had a chance to sit down.

'I had a complicated client.'

Delilah rolled her eyes. 'Saffron, you always have complicated clients.'

I couldn't argue with that. 'Yeah,' I said. 'I do.' A single unbidden tear rolled down my cheek, taking me by surprise. I hastily dashed it away.

'Saffron!' Delilah looked alarmed. 'What's happened? What did your client do?'

'Nothing. It's nothing.' I clenched my jaw. I didn't want to take advantage of my very real tears but I didn't have any choice. 'It's over between Jasper and me. Not that it ever really began. It was all my fault and now he hates me.'

'What?' Her mouth dropped open. 'What did you do?'

I shook my head, willing myself not to break down entirely. 'I can't tell you the details. I'm too ashamed. But he doesn't want me, Delilah. Not now.'

'Oh my goodness.' She reached out to draw me into a hug.

I resisted. Physical contact would tip me over. 'I'm sorry, Delilah. I have work to do. It'll keep my mind off everything else. Do you mind?'

She pulled back. 'Of course. Of course.' She gazed at me with concern. 'Are you going to be okay?'

Eventually. My bottom lip quivered. Even though I needed Delilah to believe me and to tell everyone that Jasper and I were done, I wasn't faking how I felt. I drew in a ragged breath, unable to look at her any longer, then I turned to my computer and switched it on. I wanted to go home, crawl under my duvet and hide but I couldn't. I was still a professional with a job to do, whether I liked it or not.

Struggling to keep my emotions under control, I accessed every social media account connected to Motor On that I could find. There were already numerous posts from the last hour asking about the sudden massive police presence at the garage. I ignored them and scanned through the older posts. It didn't take long. I already knew Mark Smith's date of birth, so it wasn't hard to find his birthday celebrations. I found the photo I needed and enlarged it, then stared hard.

Mark grinned out at me. Three other mechanics who I recognised were with him. One of them was pointing down at the birthday cake and laughing. *Happy Ninetieth Birthday, Nan!* I cursed. His wish had been nothing to do with concerns about his new identity or worries about his employer. The truth had been staring me in the face all along and I'd been too blinkered to see it.

I checked my watch and strode to the Metafora room. This wouldn't take long.

TWENTY-ONE

This wasn't my first time in a police station – far from it. But it was the first time I'd seen so many mechanics in a police station. I magicked myself up an appropriate suit and waved at the desk sergeant to let me through to the interview rooms.

'Saffron Sawyer,' I said. 'I'm here from Scotland Yard to check on the Motor On investigation.'

He blinked at me. 'That was fast. We only called your lot thirty minutes ago.'

'I was already in the vicinity.' I held up a non-existent badge, tweaking my wand to ensure the policeman's suspicions weren't aroused. He peered at it and nodded, buzzing me in.

It looked like all hands were on deck. I doubted there were usually this many police on duty at any one time. I ducked my head into the staffroom for a moment to check the lay of the land. The television was on in the background with images of an overly enthusiastic reporter beaming out to the world from outside the Motor On garage. Fortunately the sound was off, although the reporter's animated expression and dramatic gestures left little to the imagination.

'Five in hospital with unexplained injuries,' a policewoman was saying, shaking her head, 'one of whom appears to be the mastermind of the operation. A cache of guns, one dead body, and a bunch of grease monkeys with criminal records as long as my arm. This is a mess.'

'So far,' a uniformed copper interjected, 'most of the mechanics are denying knowledge of the guns. Every man we've spoken to is saying they were unaware of what was going on under their noses.'

'I find that hard to believe. It's obvious the garage was nothing more than a front.'

'Yeah,' he said, 'but those mechanics are also the ones who called us in. They wanted jobs and they were prepared to pretend, even to themselves, that everything was kosher in order to keep those jobs. They'd probably have been drawn into the rest of the business eventually but, right now, the evidence suggests they're telling the truth.'

'They don't have jobs now, do they?'

I grimaced and made a mental note to sort out that little detail as soon as I got back to my desk. It wouldn't take much to send a community-minded investor or two in the right direction.

The good news was that it looked like Mark Smith and the others were going to be cleared of any wrongdoing. I stepped into the corridor again, glancing up and down before spotting the room I needed. I nodded decisively and headed there, grabbing an unattended clipboard with a few sheets attached along the way.

Mark Smith was alone, slumped over the desk with his head in his arms. He looked up when I marched in.

'Good afternoon,' I said briskly. 'I'm Sergeant Sawyer. I'm here to discuss your statement in a little more detail.'

'I've already told you lot everything. I haven't done

anything wrong,' he enunciated clearly. 'Not this time. I know I've got a record, and I know I've not always been a perfect member of society, but what was going inside that garage was nothing to do with me. I changed my name for a reason. I'm trying to be a better person.'

I took the seat opposite him and gave him a long look. 'Mmm. Let's talk about that record, shall we? You attacked an innocent man. Why exactly was that?'

'It was my fault. I lost my temper and punched him. I know I shouldn't have done it and I've learned to curb my anger since then.' He sounded as if he was reciting a well-worn tale.

I leaned forward. 'Why did you lose your temper?'

Mark looked away. 'It doesn't matter why. I shouldn't have done it.'

I watched him for a moment. He was refusing to meet my eyes. 'If you say so, Mr Smith. Let's discuss Motor On.' Very deliberately, I placed the clipboard in front of him and jabbed the centre of it. 'We took this from Mr Fox's office. It says here that you were paid a large sum of money to help with a special project. What exactly was that special project?'

Mark stared down at the clipboard and the long list of cleaning duties for the police station that was supposed to be ticked off every morning. 'It's a lie! I wasn't doing any special projects for Fox! I fix cars, that's all!' His voice quavered with panic. 'Check my bank account. There's no money in there. I haven't done anything wrong.'

I sighed and pulled the clipboard towards me. To be an effective faery godmother and do the best by your clients, you really have to pay attention and see the whole person. Mark Smith's problems might well have been related to his dodgy employment. He might well have almost been drawn unwittingly into a far greater criminal enterprise than he'd have wanted. But that wasn't why he'd made a wish.

I thought of the car magazines he'd held up as a barrier between us and the way he'd flinched when I'd casually suggested his daughter might be dyslexic. Then there was the book which Pumpkin had found in his garden, and the birthday cake that didn't have his name iced on it.

'The man you punched,' I said quietly, 'he was teasing you. He was making fun of you because you can't read.'

Mark's pupils flared and his cheeks flushed red. 'So?' he said angrily. 'So what if I can't read? I'm a mechanic. I don't need to read!'

'I bet you wish you could though, right?'

His head dropped. 'More than anything.'

I sighed. 'I'm sorry that I didn't see that before.' No doubt his lack of literacy had proved as much of a stumbling block in finding a job as his criminal record. I could solve that.

I took out my wand and reached across, feeling the power surge through my fingertips, then I tapped his head lightly.

He jumped as if struck by an electric shock. 'What are you doing? What was that?'

I pushed the clipboard towards him. 'Tell me about the special project,' I said, tapping on the cleaning rota again.

'I just told you I can't read,' he spat. 'Why are you...?' he stared at the sheet. 'Emptying the bins? Scrubbing the...?' His nose wrinkled. 'What?'

I gave him a half smile. 'Your wish is granted.' I stood up and walked to the door. Mark Smith's mouth fell open. He was still staring down at the clipboard. 'Put bleach in the toilets,' he said. A huge grin spread across his face. 'This says I have to put bleach in the toilets!'

'Yes,' I said. 'It does.' I opened the door and walked out.

Rather than feeling elated that I'd finally got to the bottom of Mark Smith's true desires, I simply felt tired. This had been one of the longest days of my adult life and, much as I'd have liked to celebrate achieving success for my client, the weight of the day's events pressed heavily on my shoulders. The last thing I wanted was to head back to the office but I had no choice. I had to confront the Director once and for all.

Jasper was safe now. But that didn't mean I was finished.

I walked down the busy police corridor and past the front desk, all the while running through what I was going to say to the Director. I was so absorbed in my thoughts that at first I didn't hear the desk sergeant speaking to me.

'I heard it from my cousin. She works with you guys in London and she told me about it. I don't believe it's true. I thought the case against him was watertight, but she said they'd found a key piece of information that exonerates him and he's already been released.'

I slowly turned as his words filtered through. 'Pardon?'

He tapped the side of his nose. 'It's supposed to be kept hush-hush until tomorrow, right? So he can get out before the tabloid scrum gets going and the Crown Prosecution Service has time to sort out the press conference. Don't worry, I won't tell anyone. I thought, with you being from Scotland Yard and all that, you'd be able to confirm that it's happening.' He whistled under his breath. 'I mean, I thought things were going crazy here but that'll be nothing compared to what will happen when the news about *him* hits.'

All of a sudden I had a very bad feeling. 'Who are you talking about?'

The desk sergeant visibly brightened. 'So it's not true?'

I took another step towards him. 'Who,' I repeated through gritted teeth, 'are you talking about?'

He blinked at me. 'Art Adwell, of course. My cousin says he's innocent.'

Blood roared in my ears and knees almost gave way. 'She

said it,' I whispered. 'She said that in a day or two my failings would become public. She's done this.'

The desk sergeant frowned. 'Eh?'

I closed my eyes. The Director was prepared to stop at nothing to get Jasper and me out of the way. Heaven help us.

I HALF-RAN, half-stumbled through the office, scrolling through the news on my phone at the same time. There was nothing yet; assuming the desk sergeant was right – and I had no reason to think otherwise – Adwell had already been released but there was a news embargo until the morning when a press conference would be held.

I might have come across the information by accident but there was no doubt in my mind who was responsible. There was no evidence to suggest Adwell's innocence so the only way this could be happening was by magic – and of the most nefarious kind.

I'd set the events involving Art Adwell into motion and I was obviously going to be blamed for them. And because Jasper had got himself involved, he'd be fingered as a culprit too. Adwell would proclaim the existence of faery godmothers to all and sundry; even if the world at large didn't believe him, there would be considerable damage.

The Director was putting all of us at risk simply to avoid the contents of Jasper's damned report. What she couldn't know was that I'd had advance warning. I still had a chance to fix things.

'Saffron!' Rupert stepped into my path, barring my way. He thrust a glossy leaflet into my hands and beamed proudly. 'Take a look at this. It's my campaign for fairer treatment of faery godfathers. I've outlined an eight-step approach. First of all—'

'Oh for fuck's sake, Rupert!' I exploded. 'Enough already!'

Obviously taken by surprise, Rupert rocked back on his heels. Other heads turned, gazing at us curiously.

'But you're the one who pointed out the injustice of this in the first place. I thought you'd be pleased. It's time to stamp out sexism in the workplace.' He raised his fist in a gesture of power then, when he noted my expression, slowly lowered it.

'Sexism in the workplace? Rupert, you're the biggest culprit.'

'I...' He blinked. 'I...' He lifted his chin. 'No, I'm not.'

'You're sleazy beyond belief. You spend most of your day making us feel uncomfortable with your pointed comments and leery suggestions. Yeah, you probably should be called godfathers instead of godmothers, but you know what? You also should have been given your final warning and tossed out on your ear long ago because of your repeated harassment of the rest of us. What you do is swept under the carpet because you come from a supposedly good family. But if your family is that good, you'd have been brought up to treat women with more respect!'

'There's nothing wrong with a little bit of flirting...'

I thrust the leaflet back at him. 'Get. Out. Of. My. Way.'

'Saff...'

I shoved him to the side, ignoring the gasps from the watching faery godmothers. I didn't have time for Rupert; I didn't have time for anything other than dealing with Art Adwell. I stormed forward, a plan already forming in my mind. Then another shadow fell in front of me.

'What do you think you're doing, Saffron?'

I looked up into Jasper's furious, glittering green eyes. 'You mean with Rupert?'

'I mean with me,' he bit out in a low voice. He took a step

towards me. 'You're waltzing round the office, telling everyone that I hate you.'

I stared at him, my tongue suddenly cleaving to the roof of my mouth.

'What kind of game are you playing? I thought that you didn't play games. I respected what you said in the café, but you and I both know that I don't hate you. If this is about making you look good…'

I had to do it; I didn't want to, but I had to do it. If I could goad Jasper into publicly dismissing me, his fate would no longer be tangled up with mine. It was going to be horrible. But it would be worth it.

'Oh come on, Jasper,' I said lightly. 'You know I want to be the best damned faery godmother in the world. Everything I do is about looking good.'

Disbelief flashed across his face. 'What?'

'We both know I'm not really cut out for this job and that I keep making too many mistakes to succeed as a faery godmother. But I won't let go of what I have here without a fight. I'll do whatever it takes to look good, whether that's nearly killing a man this afternoon because I felt like it, or pretending that I like you so that I can keep my job.'

I swept an arm around the room but kept my voice quiet. I didn't want the others overhearing this part. 'All this? It's just a game. If that includes spreading a few tall tales about you, that's the way it's got to be. It's not personal. But this is a game I will win, one way or another, which is why I had to drop you this afternoon. I don't want my reputation tainted. I've already had to work too damned hard for it.'

The rage in Jasper's green eyes made me step backwards. No wonder he commanded such a fearsome reputation; when he decided he wanted to intimidate, he was an unstoppable force.

For the first time, a trickle of doubt about my hastily conceived plan seeped into my veins.

'You're right,' he ground out. 'You're not cut out to be a faery godmother.'

Although the wide eyes of the entire office were on us, I wasn't convinced that anyone had heard him. I needed every single faery to be in no doubt about his words, otherwise all this would be for nothing.

'What was that?' I asked, keeping my tone as light and irritating as possible.

'I said,' he repeated, raising his voice, 'you're not cut out to be a faery godmother.'

There was a round of audible gasps from my co-workers. Good.

'Well,' I sniffed, this time speaking more loudly to ensure everyone got my message, 'it's just as well that my job status has nothing to do with you. It's the Director who hires and fires around here, not you. Devil's Advocate or not, *she's* my boss. *She's* responsible for my actions. You have no say.'

For the briefest moment his eyes narrowed and I detected a hint of suspicion in his face. Had I overplayed my hand? I swallowed. If he hadn't already been feeling so hurt, he'd have seen right through me from the start.

I couldn't allow that to happen. I wondered whether to push him further, even though the thought terrified me.

He crossed his arms over his broad chest and his expression shuttered. 'Get out of my sight.'

I forced back the hot ball of tears forming in my chest. This was what I'd wanted so I had no right to cry about it. 'As you wish.' I spun on my heel, heading for the lift. I had to get out of there.

CHAPTER

TWENTY-TWO

Even though I'd engineered the whole argument, the ache in my chest and the sickness in my stomach were altogether real. I ran past Mrs Jardine, aware that her lips were moving and she was saying something to me, her brow etched with concern. I couldn't hear her. My ears were still there and everything remained in working order, but there was a strange disconnect between my consciousness and my reality.

It wasn't until I burst outside and felt the cold, pelting rain on my face that the sane corner of my mind kicked in. No matter how much it hurt and how much my soul ached, I'd achieved what I wanted with Jasper. But this wasn't over yet. Far from it.

I reached into my bag, my fingers brushing against the cold metal of the gun. Shivering, I ignored it and took out my phone. 'Vincent,' I said, as soon as he picked up. 'I need you to pack up all my things, bring Pumpkin and meet me in front of the train station.'

'Is that it? No hello? No how are you?'

'I'm on a clock. I don't have time for niceties, Vincent. I need you to do as I've asked.'

'The Devil isn't here. I tried calling you to tell you but you didn't pick up.'

'I know,' I said, my heart twisting. 'I saw him in the office. And he's not the Devil.'

'I watched the news earlier,' he burbled on. 'You really did a number on that garage.'

I gritted my teeth. 'Vincent...'

'I know, I know,' he said. 'Get your stuff. Take the dog. Meet you at the train station. I heard you the first time. It's not like I can refuse, is it? I'm your slave. I have to do what you say.'

I passed a hand over my forehead. 'Please, Vincent.'

He must have heard the tension in my voice because he stopped complaining. 'I'll be there,' he said. 'Just...' He faltered.

Dread flashed through me. Oh no. What now? 'Tell me.'

'I'm not sure about Pumpkin,' Vincent said. 'The wee guy's not doing very well.'

My stomach lurched again. 'What do you mean?' I demanded. 'What's wrong with him?'

'He's curled up in a corner of the sofa – won't eat, won't move, won't do anything.'

'Is he in pain?'

'I don't think so, Saffy,' Vincent sighed. 'But he ain't right.'

Worry knotted my intestines. There had to be an emergency vet somewhere nearby; I'd have to send Vincent there and alter my plans. Everything was happening at once. Pumpkin needed me and I wasn't there for him.

The pain in my chest increased. I couldn't cry, though; I didn't have time for tears. 'Vincent, put the phone up to his ear.'

'Saff,' he said, 'you do know that Pumpkin's a dog, right?' However he was already doing as I'd asked and his voice was growing more distant.

I exhaled. 'Pumpkin,' I said, into the receiver. 'I'm sorry that you're not...' I heard a bark. It was short and to the point but it also sounded oddly ... joyful. 'Pumpkin?' I asked, crossing my fingers tightly.

'Well, that's weird.' Vincent spoke into the phone again. 'As soon as he heard you, he jumped up. He's actually wagging his tail. Maybe he does like you after all.'

I gulped in a breath, listening in as he spoke to the dog. 'Pumpkin, were you pining? Were you upset that Saffron had gone?'

I heard another bark that was unmistakably Pumpkin. Thank Fae. More tears pricked at the back of my eyes.

'We'll see you at the station in twenty minutes!' Vincent said. 'Come on, Pumpkin, let's vamoose!' He hung up before I could say anything else.

I stared at the phone. I was tempted to call him and tell him to take Pumpkin to the vet's anyway – the last thing I wanted was to take any chances. But it had sounded like the wee bastard was alright. He'd damn well better be, I thought grimly. I needed Pumpkin, more than I was willing to admit.

I wiped the rain from my stinging eyes and made one more call. I didn't want to, but I wasn't convinced I had any other remaining options.

Ethan answered immediately. 'Saffron Sawyer,' he said. 'Is there a problem? Are you still snapping?'

I took a deep breath. 'Yes, there's a problem. No, I'm not snapping.'

'Let me guess,' he said flatly. 'Art Adwell.' Ethan was no fool.

'I'm afraid so,' I replied.

His voice darkened. 'Just because I helped you today doesn't mean anything has changed with our agreement about that man. You said you would solve the issue. By my watch there are only forty-one hours remaining to do so.'

'I will solve the issue, Ethan,' I said, glad that I sounded calm and confident at least to my own ears. 'But we need to change the time limit.'

'You're pushing your luck, Saffron. I'm not giving you more time. Three days is more than enough time to deal with one human. You're the one who kept telling me that I was worrying about nothing. I appreciate that you've had other things on your mind, but you are not the only faery godmother in the country. If you can't deal with Adwell then get help from your colleagues. There are plenty of them.'

'I can't get help from them,' I said baldly. Not now the Director had made her move. 'And I don't want more time, I want less.'

For probably the first time, I'd completely confused the troll leader. 'Huh?'

I inhaled. 'If I don't ring and tell you that I've dealt with Adwell for good,' I glanced at my watch, 'by nine o'clock tomorrow morning, then assume that I've failed. You'll have to move fast and take care of him yourself.'

'Saffron,' he said, 'what's going on?'

'It's not worth getting into. Just … don't trust the Director. And be wary of anyone from the Office of Faery Godmothers.'

He let out a mild snort. 'You don't have to tell *me* that.' He paused. 'What about the Devil's Advocate?'

'Never mind him,' I said briskly. 'Nine o'clock tomorrow, Ethan. Be ready to move if you've not heard from me.'

I heard him sigh. 'Are you drowning, Saffron?'

'Not yet.' The water was right up to my head, though.

'Do you want my help? Because I can offer it if…'

'No.' I swallowed. I couldn't involve the trolls except as a last resort. Not only would their methods involve blood and brutality, it would be better for them in the long run if they kept their hands clean. It would be better for us as well. I didn't want to give them ammunition to use against the faery godmothers; the peace between us was still too fragile.

'This is my responsibility. I created this mess and I have to clean it up. I need you to be there as emergency back-up in case my plan doesn't work.'

'We'll be ready.'

I glanced round. If Melissa – or indeed any other trolls – was tailing me, then she was doing a damned good job. I'd not spotted so much as a whisker from any of them. I didn't want to give the Director any reason to accuse the trolls of further conspiracy against us, however. At this point, there was no telling what she was capable of. 'Do you still have people watching me?'

'I do.'

'Call them off. I'll text you Adwell's address once I've got it. It's better for you all if you're not nearby unless you need to be.'

'Saffron, what is going on?'

'Thanks, Ethan!' I said in an overly bright voice. 'I'll speak to you before 9am.' I hoped. I hung up before he could ask my any more questions. A moment later, I sprinted for the train station.

I arrived a few minutes before Vincent and Pumpkin. The little dog started straining at his lead as soon as he saw me and I felt a surge of delight. Maybe not everything in my life had gone to shit.

Then he broke free, darted up and bit my hand. 'Ouch!' I jumped back. 'What the hell, Pumpkin?'

He lunged for me again. 'Stop it!' I grabbed his lead and glared at him. He bared his teeth but at least he backed away.

Vincent ambled up and shrugged. 'Don't look at me,' he said. 'That dog's actions are a mystery to me.'

I gazed at Pumpkin. 'I'm here,' I said to him. 'You don't have to worry.'

'I'm not worried,' Vincent retorted.

I frowned at him. 'Maybe you should be.'

'Why? What's going on?'

I pointed behind me to the station. 'We're going to find Art Adwell.'

'I thought he was in jail.'

'Not any more.'

'But...'

'I'll explain along the way. He's got a residence in London and I'm betting that's where he'll be.' I set my mouth into a firm line. 'Let's go.'

By the time we reached the expensive, leafy suburb where I hoped Adwell was holed up, evening was well under way. The sky had darkened to a deep indigo and the air had turned distinctly chilly. Vincent, Pumpkin and I walked down to number sixty-three, then we stood back and examined the building from the opposite side of the street.

Vincent whistled. 'Must be nice to have money and be able to afford a place like this. Just how rich is he?'

'Rich enough to offer a million pounds to anyone who could help him expose the faery godmothers,' I said grimly. Unfortunately the Director's motivation went far beyond money. She was all about ideology; that was what made her so dangerous.

'Are you sure you don't want me to do anything else?' Vincent asked.

I shook my head. 'All you have to do is stay out of his reach and film everything he says. Don't let him see that you're recording him until I tell you otherwise.' Under normal circumstances, memory magic would include technology such as cameras but memory magic no longer affected Adwell. I was banking on it not affecting any technology in his vicinity, though I couldn't be sure.

'Is this going to work?'

I drew in a breath. 'We're on a wing and a prayer. But you know what? No matter how much I've messed up, I'm still a damned good faery godmother.'

'Does that make Pumpkin and me damned good sidekicks?'

I considered briefly. 'Nah,' I said finally. 'You're the *best* sidekicks.'

Vincent puffed out his chest and even Pumpkin looked rather pleased with himself.

I crossed my fingers tightly and prayed that Adwell was in the house. Then I crossed the street with my team right behind me.

There were two ways we could play this. One was to go in all guns blazing; the other was to try the softly-softly approach. After what had happened at the garage, I'd decided that being a proverbial bull in a china shop was definitely my preferred style. This wasn't about checking the lay of the land or subtly pulling strings behind the scenes, this was a problem that needed to be tackled head on.

With that in mind, when I reached Adwell's front door I raised my wand and used magic to force it open. I added a blast and a puff of smoke for effect. The door burst open and the three of us strode across the threshold.

Pumpkin scented Adwell almost immediately. Starting with a few low-key growls, he quickly progressed to a series of vicious, angry barks. In the narrow hallway the sound reverberated off the walls and echoed around the house.

Two figures, no doubt already alerted by the noise of the door crashing open, appeared at the top of the stairs. Neither was the man I was looking for. I thought grimly that it hadn't taken Adwell long to draw his team of square-jawed, broad-shouldered goons back around him. Honestly, they were such caricatures of muscle men that it was a wonder they didn't get better gigs. Maybe they enjoyed working for a murderous politician. And I already knew that Adwell paid well.

The first man, whose black moustache made him look like the perfect villain even if I hadn't already known what he was, had his gun out. I wondered whether he'd bought it via the same dodgy supply network that Motor On had been part of. Such weapons were pretty much illegal in this country; it wasn't as if you could wander into the nearest supermarket and pick one up along with your milk and your cookies.

Moustache Man didn't shoot, of course. With Adwell only hours out of prison, the last thing he'd need was a shoot-out in his own home. It didn't mean the goon wouldn't put a bullet in my skull if he thought it was necessary, but I had a bit of wiggle room before that happened.

'Who are you?' he demanded.

I gave him my most brilliant smile. 'I'm Saffron Sawyer,' I said. 'I'm here to see your boss.'

Pumpkin took that moment to pull free from his lead and tear up the stairs as fast as his little legs would carry him. I flicked my wand upwards, ready to use as much magic as necessary to deter the two men from shooting at my little dog. Both their faces twisted, however; they might not have hesitated to kill me but they had no desire to kill a dog, even one as obviously unfriendly as Pumpkin.

Fortunately he ignored them both. Paws skidding on the tiled floor, he continued searching for his quarry. I nodded, satisfied. There was no longer any doubt that Art Adwell was in residence.

'Pumpkin,' I called softly. 'Here.'

For the first time ever, he listened. The skittering of claws stopped halfway up the next flight of stairs and he abandoned his crazed barking in favour of a small whine. I didn't have to repeat myself; somehow I knew that the dog and I had finally reached an understanding and he'd do as I commanded.

A second later he flew back down again, landing by my side. The entire operation had taken less than a minute, but it had thrown the muscle-bound goons off balance.

And it had alerted my quarry to my presence. 'Tell Saffron Sawyer,' a familiar, chilling voice called, 'to come on up.'

I turned and glanced at Vincent. His face was pale and he looked completely terrified but determination was etched onto his features. He gave me a nod.

I breathed out. He was here of his own free will. We all were.

I curtsied prettily in the direction of the two men then, as if I were fresh out of a Swiss finishing school, I sashayed up the stairs. 'Hello, boys,' I murmured.

They both gave me identical glares. 'Fourth floor,' the second man said. 'First door on the right.'

'Thank you.' I smiled again and continued on my way. Pumpkin snapped at the ankles of the nearest man and he shied away. I gave an amused laugh; nothing about this was fun but I could pretend I was enjoying myself. Pumpkin certainly seemed to be.

We pushed on upwards past an array of dull-looking paintings, most of which depicted hunting scenes. Art Adwell probably liked to imagine himself as a red-coated hunter astride a noble steed with his pack of baying hounds at his heels. Nothing could have been further from the truth.

The door to the drawing room was already open. I could tell from the way Pumpkin's entire body quivered that Adwell was inside. 'We've got this,' I told him softly.

'I fucking hope so,' Vincent muttered.

I reached back and squeezed his arm. 'Camera?'

He waved his hand at me, his phone primed and ready. 'Yep.'

'Start filming now.' Then I lifted up my chin and walked in.

Adwell was seated in a large armchair next to a fireplace. Dustsheets still covered several pieces of furniture but there was no denying the grandeur of the room. Despite the jailhouse pallor, he looked relaxed, his legs crossed and a glass of what looked like brandy in his right hand. The only thing missing was a fluffy white cat.

'Ms Sawyer,' he drawled. 'How good of you to join us.' He smiled and took a sip of his drink.

'Hey, Saffron!'

I swivelled slowly on my heel. Figgy, who looked delighted to see me, was standing next to an old teak sideboard.

CHAPTER

TWENTY-THREE

After everything else, I should have expected something like this – but I hadn't. My mouth dropped open and I gaped at her. 'F–Figgy,' I said faintly. 'What are you doing here?'

She smiled happily at me. 'Helping Mr Adwell, of course. He's had a terribly tough time of it.'

'Yes,' Adwell drawled. He placed his glass on a side table and stood up, walked over to Figgy and put an arm around her shoulders. 'It's been very traumatic. But thanks to darling Figs here, things are already starting to improve.'

Vincent nudged me. 'Is that...?'

'Yes,' I bit out. 'She's a faery godmother like me.' I met Figgy's eyes. 'You're not here for the reward then?' I asked.

'Reward?' She gave me a blank shrug. 'No. What reward?'

Adwell smiled smarmily and winked.

'Never mind,' I muttered.

'Did the Devil's Advocate send you here too?' Figgy asked brightly.

I took a step backwards. 'You're here because...' I shook my head in disbelief. '*Jasper* told you to come?'

My expression made her falter slightly. 'Uh, yes?' she said. Suddenly she didn't seem sure.

'He sounds like quite the chap,' Adwell burbled.

I ignored him.

'Saff,' Vincent whispered. 'Should I still be filming this?'

I swallowed. I thought I'd covered every eventuality, but the idea that Jasper was betraying us all hadn't figured in any of my plans. It didn't make sense. He simply wasn't like that.

I nodded at Vincent and focused on Figgy. 'What did he say exactly?' I asked. 'What did the Devil's Advocate say to you?'

She scratched her head. 'He didn't actually *say* anything. He left me a note and that old phone I showed you. Told me to use it to contact Mr Adwell, then get him out of prison and help him settle back into normal life.'

A note. I ran a hand through my hair. Of course it was a bloody note. There was no doubt in my mind that Jasper knew nothing about it. This was all down to the Director. She wouldn't have wanted to take the risk of getting her own hands dirty with Adwell, so sending someone in her place made sense. The fact that she was willing to sacrifice a loyal faery godmother to her ridiculous plan stunned me – but by seeking to pin the blame on Jasper maybe she thought it was a sacrifice she could still avoid.

'Do you have this note with you?'

Figgy looked surprised. 'It's on my desk.'

Somehow I doubted that it was still there. Even the best forgery wouldn't fool faery eyes for long; it wouldn't have occurred to Figgy to question it – but others would. As long as she made it out of here, however, and told everyone that she'd helped Adwell on Jasper's instructions, it didn't matter. She was completely guileless, the perfect fall guy.

I glanced at Adwell, wondering whether he knew the truth about his new situation. He just grinned at me.

Apparently deciding that there had been far too much discussion and not enough biting, Pumpkin lunged for Adwell. This time I kept his lead wrapped round my wrist. There were suddenly too many unknowns to turn the dog loose.

Figgy gave my dog a confused look. 'Why is Pumpkin so upset?' She looked at me. 'What did you do to him?'

Unbelievable. 'Nothing,' I said through gritted teeth.

Adwell pointed, realisation lighting his eyes. 'I know that dog. That stinky mutt.' His lip curled. 'Damn thing should have been put to sleep long ago.'

I curled my hands into fists and Pumpkin growled. Even Figgy looked upset.

'Saffy,' Vincent murmured, 'do something about this poor excuse for a human being before I do.'

'I'm getting to it.' I straightened my back. 'Figgy, the note you were sent is fake. This man,' I found it hard to look Adwell in the face, 'does not deserve a faery godmother.'

'But the Devil's Advocate—'

'Jasper wouldn't have sent you here. I guarantee it.' Aware that there was a harsh, pained tone to my voice, I tried to soften my words. 'You remember the client I had. Rose? The one who died in the office?'

Figgy's face twisted into a snarl. It didn't suit her but it was a measure of how deep her feelings ran. 'The one the evil bastard trolls killed?'

'They're not evil.'

'But...'

I held up my hands. I wasn't going to get into an argument. Not right now. 'This man was trying to kill Rose too. He's killed others. He's a bad, bad man.'

'I'm not bad in the slightest,' Adwell declared. 'I'm the victim of a shocking injustice.'

'Yeah, yeah.' I kept my gaze trained on Figgy. 'He wants to expose us. He wants to tell the world about faery godmothers.'

'My goodness!' Adwell put his hands to his cheeks in mock horror. 'I wouldn't do such a thing!'

'But Saffron,' Figgy objected, 'he can't do that. The memory magic will stop him.' She gave me a kindly look. 'I know you're still quite new and you don't understand how everything works yet, but he won't remember us once we've gone. He won't be able to tell anyone.'

I had to keep myself under control. 'He's not affected by memory magic.'

She blinked. 'What? But that's not possible.'

'Unfortunately it is.' I drew in a breath. 'Look, Figgy, just trust me on this. He's not a genuine client and you've been fooled into coming here. The man you're helping is a cold-blooded murderer.'

Figgy's eyes flicked from me to Adwell and back again. 'Maybe I should go and speak to the Director,' she began.

'No!'

She jumped.

'Don't do that, Figgy. You can't trust her.'

'Of course you can,' Adwell interrupted. 'She's a wonderful woman. Call her,' he urged. 'You can use my phone if you like.'

I knew it; I knew he and the Director would come to some sort of arrangement. They were both snakes. But surely, although their interests converged for the moment, they realised that they couldn't trust each other?

'Who can you trust, Figgy?' Adwell asked, echoing my thoughts. 'The poor human client with no magical powers who's been the victim of a miscarriage of justice and who is telling you to call your boss? Or the faery who burst in here unannounced and is telling you that you can't trust your boss?

And who is pursuing a crazy vendetta against me because I didn't get on with her last client?'

Figgy's face was pale. She pulled out her phone and hit a button. 'I'll speak to the Director,' she said. 'I'll get this cleared up.'

I could already hear the phone ringing. Fuck a puck. If the Director knew I was here and aware of her plan, all hell would break loose. Figgy would believe whatever the Director told her. I couldn't let her make that call.

I lifted my wand. The jolt of magic that flew from it curled round the phone's base and snatched it out of Figgy's hand. It went skidding across the room.

'Saffron!' she gasped, horrified that I would do such a thing.

'You see?' Adwell murmured. 'She's untrustworthy. She's evil.' He leaned in towards her. 'She's not a real faery godmother.'

Figgy pulled her wand out and brandished it towards me. 'I'm sorry, Saffron,' she said. Then she zapped me.

I did my best to defend myself, raising my own wand and trying to create a shield to ward off the worst of the blow, but the force of Figgy's magic still slammed into me and knocked me backwards. I collided with Vincent, who was still standing behind me and filming the action. 'Get out of here,' I said to him, through tears of pain. I thrust the lead at him 'Take Pumpkin and go.'

Vincent spun round to run; Pumpkin refused point blank to go, however. The little dog snarled, first at Adwell then at Figgy. 'Don't be a hero, Pumpkin,' I muttered. 'Go with Vincent.'

Figgy twisted her wand once again and blasted me.

My knees buckled and I collapsed to the floor, retching. I knew I had to fight back but I didn't want to hurt her. None of this was her fault – she was only doing what she thought was right.

I jerked my hand, sending out enough magic to swipe Figgy's feet from under her and bring her crashing down to the floor with me. She slashed at me, the tip of her wand striking my cheek. The searing pain was like nothing I'd ever felt before. Sticky thick blood spurted out.

'Wow,' Adwell said, his voice hovering somewhere over me. 'Is that your actual cheek bone I can see through all that blood?'

'I don't want to hurt you,' Figgy told me. 'But I will. I don't know why you're doing this, Saffron, but it's wrong. Just stop,' she pleaded.

I tightened my grip on my wand and rolled to the side. I was targeting the wrong person. No matter what Figgy threw at me, I had to let her do it. As long as I stopped Adwell, I'd worry about the rest later. I hadn't been planning on hurting him but that didn't mean that I wouldn't.

Pumpkin leapt towards me until he was in front of my body, acting as a tiny barrier between me and the others. Figgy lifted her wand, clearly desperate to attempt another shot, but she liked the little dog. She didn't want to hurt him too. 'Call him off, Saffron,' she said. 'Call the dog off.'

I reached round and angled my wand towards Adwell. I just needed him to sidestep to the left and I'd have him. Once he was down, I'd worry about Figgy.

'I can't, Figgy. I need you to listen to me. I know that you want to call the Director, and I know it seems stupid that I won't let you. But she's working against us, not for us. You have to believe me.'

Figgy raised her wand and Pumpkin snapped his jaws. She sighed. 'I'm sorry, Pumpkin,' she said. 'I don't want to do this.'

Fear for the dog zipped through me. I abandoned my attempt to get at Adwell and swung my wand towards Figgy again. 'Don't you dare,' I said. 'Don't you dare hurt him.'

'Then call him off!' she yelled, her voice vibrating with tension.

I squinted. I had to take Figgy out, there was no longer any choice. 'Okay,' I said. 'Okay. But he doesn't always do as I ask. You know that. He has a mind of his own.'

I shifted my weight slightly to the left. I had a clear view of her carotid artery; if I could send enough magic in that direction, I might be able to knock her out without doing her any real damage. It wouldn't be easy: too much magic and I'd kill her; too little and she'd probably kill me.

'Forget the dog,' Adwell snapped. 'Get rid of it and deal with this bitch once and for all. She's trying to stop you from doing your job, Figgy! She'll kill me, given half a chance. She's a complete lunatic!'

I blotted out Adwell's voice as best as I could. Figgy, however, turned towards him. There. There it was. I held my breath, preparing to flick the tip of my wand. I could do this.

Then pain exploded in my head. A second later, I blacked out.

I COULDN'T HAVE BEEN out for long. When I came round, my eyes blinking against the harsh light, something was tightening against my wrists. I was upright in a chair and being tied to it so I couldn't move.

Frantically looking round, I searched for Pumpkin. His lead was wrapped round the leg of a heavy-looking chair and he wasn't moving. I gasped, then Figgy's face swam into view. She looked teary and apologetic – but also very determined.

'Pumpkin will be fine. It's just a bit of magic to keep him calm.'

He didn't look calm to me, he looked bloody comatose, but

I trusted Figgy not to have actually hurt him. I nodded slightly while she continued to gaze at me. My head was throbbing and I was fairly certain that my nose was broken. But I had to remain focused. Everything depended on what happened next.

'Why are you doing this, Saffron? I don't understand.'

I blinked at her and tried to speak. 'Guuuuh.'

My eyes dropped and I realised she was holding her wand while mine lay forlornly on the table. It didn't mean I was entirely defenceless but things weren't looking good.

'You stupid mare,' Vincent bellowed from the corner of the room where he was being held by the two men who'd been on the stairwell. 'Saffron is on your side! That fucking politician is the one you need to worry about!'

One of the men kicked him. A shock of pain smashed into my knee and I gasped. So that was why I'd been knocked out – one of them had hit Vincent and I'd suffered the results. My dread grew. This could be bad for all of us.

Figgy frowned, clearly confused. It was Adwell, of all people, who seemed to understand what was happening. He walked over to Vincent, drew back his fist then slammed it into his stomach.

Vincent's answering yell was a good attempt but ultimately unconvincing. I bit my tongue and tried not to cry out, but I couldn't prevent the spasm of pain that twisted my face.

Adwell saw it. 'Well, well, well,' he murmured. He raised an eyebrow at Figgy. 'How do I get me some of that magic? A slave proxy who'll absorb pain for me? I could definitely do with some of that kind of love.'

Figgy, who was clearly disturbed by Adwell's continued violence, stared at me wide-eyed. 'You've bound a human to you, Saffron? That's ... that's...' She shook her head. 'Awful,' she finished. 'That poor man.'

'He agreed to it! He couldn't be bound to me otherwise, Figgy! It was for a good reason!'

'She's right,' Vincent said. 'Nothing was done to me without my permission. Stop being a dippy girl and open your eyes to what's really going on here.'

'The pair of you need to shut the fuck up.' Adwell raised his fist again and smiled at me. 'This,' he grunted, 'is for that damned monster.' This time he connected with the side of Vincent's head and dots of bright light flashed in front of my eyes. Fuck a puck. That bloody hurt.

'Stop that!' Figgy said. 'Stop hitting him! It's not necessary.'

I wheezed, turning my head to the side and spitting a gob of blood onto the floor. 'You see?' I whispered. 'He's not a good man, Figgy.'

Doubt was appearing on her face. I knew that she wanted to believe me. I had to persuade her that I was speaking the truth. A few more nasty hits from Adwell would do it – assuming I could tolerate them without passing out for good.

Unfortunately Adwell seemed to realise that he was on shaky ground with his own faery godmother. He snorted and stalked over to me, then he scooped up my bag and rummaged through it. When his expression turned gleeful, I knew what he'd found. It wouldn't help my cause in the slightest.

'Now explain to me,' he purred, 'why a faery godmother would carry one of these?' He picked out Fox's gun between his thumb and forefinger and gave Figgy a questioning look.

She took a step back, shock etched into her every feature. 'A gun? Saffron, why do you have a gun?'

Any inch of control I had was slipping away. I clenched my fists in desperation. 'It's to do with my last client, Figgy. I only have it because I'm going to dispose of it properly...'

Adwell threw back his head and laughed. 'A likely story. You have a rogue faery godmother on your hands, Figgy. One who's prepared to kill. You need to get rid of her now.' He pointed the gun at me, thumbing the safety as he did so. 'If you don't,' he said, 'I will.'

I steeled myself, drawing up as much energy as I could from the pit of my stomach. I might not have my wand but I could still call on my inherent magic. I'd probably only manage one burst, but I'd do it if I had to.

Then Figgy surprised me. She twisted her wand and plucked the gun out of Adwell's slimy grasp and into her own. The two men holding Vincent reached for their weapons. Without a second glance at them, she jerked her wand once more. Their guns fell to the floor with a clatter whilst Figgy pulled back her shoulders and glared.

'I don't know what's going on here,' she said, with more energy than I'd ever seen before. 'What I do know is that nobody is making another move unless I say so. And I'm not saying anything until I've spoken to the fucking Director.'

As if on cue Figgy's phone, which was still lying on the floor in the corner of the room, started to ring. I shook my head vehemently. 'No, Figgy. The Director is part of this. You can't talk to her – it will only make things worse.'

'Shut up, Saffron,' she spat. She strode towards the still-ringing phone.

'Yeah, Saffron,' Adwell sneered. 'Shut up.'

'Don't tell her to shut up!' Vincent yelled, pulling at his captors in a bid to get away.

Adwell tutted. 'Take that man downstairs for now,' he ordered. 'He's starting to get on my nerves.'

The men nodded. They actually looked relieved that they could leave. In unison, they bent down for their guns.

'Leave them,' Figgy ordered.

They exchanged glances then, without a murmur, they yanked Vincent away and disappeared out of the room.

'Adwell's going to a press conference tomorrow morning,' I said, struggling to get her to understand. 'He's planning to tell everyone that faery godmothers exist! This man is the enemy and the Director is helping him! She's using him as an excuse to avoid Jasper's report. She's using you for the same reason. Figgy...'

She turned her head and flicked her wand at me, using magic to seal my lips. I swallowed down my panic. Now there was only one course of action left to me. I'd blow this room apart if I had to, even if it meant I took all of us with it.

'As if anyone would believe me that faery godmothers and trolls exist,' Adwell said. 'It beggars belief.'

I pulled on the threads of my magic, binding them together. I'd only get one chance and I had to make it count.

Figgy's phone stopped ringing. Rather than reach for it, she stopped about a metre away from it and slowly turned towards Adwell. 'What did you say?' she asked.

'No one would believe me about faery godmothers or trolls. It's more evidence that your colleague here is lying to you.'

She tilted her head. 'How do you know about the trolls?'

Adwell's features froze for a moment. 'You must have mentioned them.'

'No.' Her brow wrinkled. 'I did not.' She looked at me. 'You knew Saffron's name as well. Before she got here, you knew who she was. Memory magic really doesn't work on you.'

I nodded vigorously. She was getting it. The facts were filtering through and Figgy was beginning to understand.

'Oh for heaven's sake.' Adwell rolled his eyes. 'Does it matter? What I'm doing here is with the full blessing of your boss. What do you call her? The Director?' He waved his hand dismissively. 'She knows about all of this. Phone her and double-check if you need to – but don't forget you're *my* faery godmother. You have to do what I tell you.'

'No. I don't.' Figgy looked at me, clear-eyed. This was a side of her I'd never seen before. 'There is someone else besides the Director I can call for help.' She picked up her phone and gazed at the screen, her eyes screwed up with concentration. When she found the number she wanted, she nodded. 'I should have done this at the start.'

Adwell leaned down and grabbed my wand from the table where Figgy had left it. He swished it experimentally a few times. 'So how does this work?' he asked. 'I tried incredibly hard to get the other wand to do something but nothing ever happened.'

Figgy ignored him. 'Devil's Advocate?' she said into the phone. I squeezed my eyes shut in dismay. I'd tried so hard to keep him away from all this. 'Listen, I'm sorry to call at this hour but I need your help.'

Adwell moved towards her. There was something in the expression that alarmed me. I could feel the magic inside me burning a hole. It was ready to escape – and so was I. On a count of three, two...

Adwell raised the wand and thrust it forward, straight into Figgy's jugular. Her eyes widened and she started to collapse.

'So that's how these wand things work,' he said as Figgy fell on the floor in front of him. 'I told you to call your boss,' he told her, sounding rather sad. The light had already leaked out of Figgy's eyes. 'I have a deal with her and I don't want you to mess it up.'

CHAPTER

TWENTY-FOUR

Magic exploded out of me. Within an instant, every window in the room shattered, half of the furniture splintered and collapsed, and the walls heaved and cracked as the plasterwork split. The bindings holding me in place snapped and Pumpkin sprang to his feet, his barking louder than ever.

Adwell was knocked off his feet – but so was I. I found myself lying flat on the floor, my face pressed against the tassels of an expensive rug. I felt sick and dizzy, and my limbs were so heavy that I wasn't sure I'd ever move again.

There were shouts from the men downstairs, then the sounds of booted feet. The pair of them burst in, gawping at the scene of devastation in front of them.

There was a groan from Adwell. He lifted his head, a trickle of blood running from his temple. I squinted and realised he'd slammed against the teak sideboard when he'd fallen. His eyes were glassy with pain but he managed to wave at his men.

I tried desperately to move, to lift my arm or leg, but I was too weak. The magic had taken too much out of me. And now it was three against one – or two against three if you counted the belligerent Jack Russell, who was standing in front of my body and guarding it. Helpful as that was, I still couldn't move. I was about as capable of defending myself as a soggy, washed-up jellyfish.

'She's dead,' Moustache Man said, nodding at Figgy.

Adwell grunted at them again and started to struggle to his feet.

'The windows have all gone,' the other heavy noted. He pursed his lips.

'Get her,' Adwell gasped, pulling himself into a sitting position and pointing a trembling finger at me. 'Get her.'

Pumpkin growled and bared his teeth. I could feel my skin tingling all over and my fingertips were beginning to twitch, but I still didn't have the strength for anything more than breathing. Even that was a struggle.

'You know what?' Moustache Man said.

'What?'

I coughed and spluttered, looking away from the two of them. My mouth was filling up with a seemingly endless supply of blood. Figgy's dead eyes stared at me accusingly from half a dozen metres away.

Pumpkin nudged my hand and whined softly before turning to face the men again.

'Ain't no amount of money worth this.' Moustache Man reached down and picked up both guns, pocketing one and handing the other to his mate.

There was a beat of silence. Then, 'Amen,' his pal said.

I lifted my gaze towards them. They were already heading out of the door. Bought loyalty, I realised; it would only carry a person so far. It was unlike the loyalty that the Director engendered in the Office of the Faery Godmothers, where we all fell into line and believed in her as a leader. Well, I amended to myself, not all of us, not any more. At the end of the day, the loyalty she demanded was as misplaced as the so-called loyalty that Art Adwell paid for.

'Traitors,' Adwell hissed. 'Fucking traitors.' He staggered to his feet. 'If you want a job done properly, you have to do it yourself.'

He fumbled around. I knew what he was searching for, I just didn't have it in me to stop him.

'Looking for something?' drawled a familiar voice from the door. 'This, perhaps?'

I could barely make out the blurry figure of Vincent, holding a gun in his right hand.

'You,' Adwell snarled. 'Who the fuck are you, anyway?'

'I'm the sidekick,' Vincent replied. 'And you don't mess with the sidekick. Isn't that right, Pumpkin?'

Next to me, Pumpkin lifted his head and howled, a low keening sound that filled the room. A moment later Vincent pulled the trigger.

Nothing happened. Pumpkin fell silent while both Adwell and I stared, albeit from very different positions. Then the ex-politician threw back his head and laughed. 'So much for that.'

Figgy, I realised. While the rest of us had been arguing and panicking and freaking out, she'd magically rendered the gun useless. My eyes stung with the renewed threat of tears. She'd maintained a level head under desperate circumstances. She'd deserved a better ending than this one. Far better.

Vincent dropped the gun and shrugged. 'I don't need a gun anyway. Not for this.' He put his head down and, without pausing any longer, barrelled towards Adwell.

The politician roared and ran forward to meet him. Both men collided, fists flying. Adwell landed a punch on Vincent's shoulder but I was the one who absorbed the pain, of course. Vincent returned the blow with a kick. Then he grabbed Adwell's hair and yanked hard.

'Pumpkin,' I whispered. I stretched out one hand and brushed my fingertips against his smooth side. 'Wand. Get my wand.'

Pumpkin turned and looked at me. Adwell's elbow slammed into the base of Vincent's spine and I cried out from the sharp pain.

'Pumpkin,' I tried again, 'please.' The dog gave my nose a tiny lick before trotting off and disappearing from view.

Adwell had pulled back from the fight. Chest heaving, he raised his fists. 'You don't have to do this. You can walk away.' He stared at Vincent. 'I'll give you money. I'll give you whatever you want. A million pounds. Two million pounds. Name your price.'

A huge grin spread across Vincent's face. 'How about some new teeth?'

Adwell nodded his head furiously. 'Yes! You can have the works! I'll give you the best teeth in the world. Whiter than white. I promise. Just walk away now.'

Vincent scratched his chin. 'Hmm. Unfortunately,' he said, still smiling, 'I'm not your sidekick. I'm with her.'

Adwell snarled and reached for a broken chair, raising it towards Vincent like a weapon. It didn't seem to affect Vincent, who continued to advance and push him back step by step.

'Where are you gonna go?' Vincent taunted. 'There's nothing behind you but air.'

The wind whipping in through the broken window ruffled Adwell's hair. He paid it no attention and jabbed the chair, snagging the front of Vincent's shirt. All of a sudden he looked delighted and I spotted his fingers tighten as he prepared to shove the sharp wooden edges into Vincent's chest. I tried to call out a warning but Vincent already knew. He reached and took hold of the chair, yanking it out of Adwell's hands in one swift movement and throwing it to the side.

Adwell lunged forward, grabbing Vincent's throat and squeezing hard – just as Pumpkin dropped my wand in front of me.

'Good,' I gasped, 'dog.'

Pumpkin wagged his tail. I licked my lips and touched the wand's gnarled wooden tip, angling it before flicking it. Tendrils of snaky magic pulled at Adwell's shoulders, hauling him backwards. His hands remained around Vincent's throat.

I held my breath but Pumpkin already knew what to do. He launched himself forward, his sharp teeth sinking into Adwell's ankle. The pain made him release his grip on Vincent, while the magic gave a final surge and tugged at his body.

The politician had time to gape, his mouth falling open almost comically while Pumpkin opened his jaw and leapt backwards out of the way. Then Adwell disappeared out of the window. Two seconds later, there was a loud thud.

I felt it. God help me, but I felt it. Heat flickered inside me, burning a hole through my stomach and my chest. It was as if my entire body had become a bonfire that was spontaneously combusting. My skin sizzled. I heaved in breath but I couldn't contain the burning sensation; it was leeching at my pores, desperate to get out.

There was a blinding flash of light. Me, I thought dully, as I squeezed my eyes shut to shield my vision. That came from me.

'Fucking hell!' Vincent shrieked, a high-pitched sound that seemed to burst through my eardrums. Then he was next to me, his hands grabbing my arms as he tried to haul me upwards. 'A bomb,' he said breathlessly. 'That was a damn bomb! We have to get out of here. We have to...'

I opened my eyes and gazed at him blearily. 'It was me,' I croaked.

'What?'

'I'm the bomb.' I stared down at my hands. Was it my imagination or were sparks of magic dancing from my fingertips? 'I *was* the bomb, anyway.' The heat inside me had already dissipated, leaving little more than a warm glow like the soft embers of a dying fire.

I allowed Vincent to help me up. I wobbled slightly but I kept my balance. Then, out of a vague, detached curiosity, I lifted one hand and directed it towards one of the fallen chairs. It jiggled then rose, hovering in the air before I released it. It settled upright on the floor again with barely a whisper.

Vincent swallowed. 'You didn't use your wand.'

'No.' I wouldn't need to use a wand ever again. I could feel the crackle of power beneath my skin. It was there, ready to be called on whenever I needed it. So this was what it was like to be Jasper. I shook my head in sober, unhappy shock.

'Thank you, Vincent. And Pumpkin.' I licked my cracked lips. 'Without you two...'

'We're the best damn sidekicks in the world,' Vincent said.

'You are.' I managed to smile down at the little dog. 'Both of you.' I heaved a breath and looked at Figgy's body. Pain wrenched at me as I stumbled over towards her. I had all this magic now, waiting to be used; surely there was something I could do.

I fell onto my knees next to her and started murmuring to myself, running my hands over her. All I needed was a pulse, it didn't matter how faint.

'Saffron,' Vincent said, 'she's gone. Unless you have power of life and death then...'

'I don't.' I pulled away, unable to stop my tears. 'She did nothing wrong. She was following orders and she didn't know. This isn't her fault, it's mine. It's all mine. I started this when I let Art Adwell take the gingko biloba. She's dead because of me.'

Vincent's voice was grim. 'You didn't send her here. You didn't fill her head with lies.'

Something inside me hardened. No, that was the Director. A surge of bitter hatred assailed me. I was culpable for Figgy's death but I wasn't the only one who was responsible. 'She'll pay for this,' I vowed to Figgy's lifeless body. 'Both of us will.'

Pumpkin growled from the other side of the room. A second later, the air started to hum.

'Saff,' Vincent whispered. 'Is that you? Are you doing that?'

I turned and saw sparks of red light in the centre of the room. Pumpkin skittered towards us while I frowned stupidly, my brain still sluggish. Then I realised what was about to happen and stiffened. Fuck a puck.

'Jasper,' I said. 'He's almost here.'

The red sparks were growing brighter by the second.

Vincent's mouth fell open and he looked around. 'Wh– what? How?'

'Figgy called him. He must have tracked her here.'

The sparks were vanishing and in their place were trails of light red smoke. We had seconds at best.

'That's a good thing, right?'

'No.' I shook my head. 'Yes. I don't know.' I made a decision, unsure if it was the right one. 'Hold onto me,' I instructed. 'Don't make a sound and don't let go.'

Vincent's hand gripped my forearm and he gazed at me mutely. I grabbed Pumpkin and held him to my chest. The dog gave me a wide-eyed stare but thankfully didn't resist. I allowed the magic to pour out of me. As the red smoke grew thicker, our bodies disappeared. The three of us backed away into a far corner and, a moment later, Jasper himself appeared.

His expression was both grim and wary. There was a weariness about him that I'd never seen before. I almost abandoned the invisibility magic and ran towards him, but something held me back. Cold logic, perhaps, or maybe fear of his condemnation.

As the smoke cleared he turned, his sharp emerald eyes taking in the scene. As soon as he saw Figgy, he strode over and knelt by her side. Vincent's hand tightened on my arm.

'Goddamnit,' Jasper muttered. He stood up. 'Goddamnit!' He grabbed a chair and threw it against the wall, where it splintered with a loud crack. Then he walked over to the nearest window and peered out, staring down at what could only have been Adwell's corpse. He passed a hand in front of his eyes and took out his phone. I could already hear sirens approaching.

Jasper didn't waste time on greetings. 'Invoke the Metafora magic and get here now,' he said. 'It's an emergency.' He bit out the address and hung up. I held my breath. There was only one person he could have called and when she got here I had no idea what she was going to do – or whether I'd be able to hold myself back.

The Director wasted no time. Less than a minute after Jasper vanished out of the door, presumably to check the rest of the building, she appeared – albeit with considerably less drama than he had. My body tightened as I tried to stay calm but I couldn't stop the fury throbbing through me.

The expression on her face when she arrived suggested that she already had an inkling her plan had gone wrong. When she saw the state of the room – and Figgy's body – her skin paled and she let out a cry of dismay. 'No,' she whispered. 'This wasn't supposed to happen. It shouldn't have been like this.'

There was a creak on the floorboards and Jasper returned. 'The rest of the building is empty,' he declared grimly. 'We don't have long before the police and paramedics arrive. We need to move Figgy and get out of here.'

The Director got shakily to her feet, her movements jerky. 'This is unbelievable.'

Jasper nodded. 'On the surface, it appears that she was working with Adwell, perhaps to get hold of the money he was offering. Something went wrong and he killed her. Before she died, she must have used magic to defend herself. That magic sent him flying out of the window and onto the street below.' His jaw tightened. 'But I suspect there might be a great deal more to it than that.'

Something flickered in the Director's face. I could see it; I could see her calculating thoughts as she tried to work out how to proceed. She was going into full damage-limitation mode. With Adwell's and Figgy's deaths, her plan to attach the blame to Jasper and me wouldn't work; there would be too many unanswered questions. Now she was focusing on how to protect herself instead.

'No,' she said. 'I think that's exactly what happened. The foolish, foolish girl.'

My hold on Pumpkin tightened. He was as good as gold, somehow recognising the importance of staying quiet, and merely nipped at my arm in gentle warning. I loosened my grip. If only I could quell my murderous thoughts with the same ease.

'The problems this is likely to cause in the office will be unprecedented,' the Director said. 'We've never had to deal with anything remotely like this before. I wonder how many of poor Figgy's bad choices are related to anxiety concerning your audit.'

A spasm of irritation flashed in Jasper's eyes. 'I don't see what the audit has to do with anything.'

'All the same,' the Director continued smoothly, 'I do think it's best if you delay the publication of your report. Once we break the news of what has happened to my faery godmothers, they will have more than enough to deal with.'

Alarm shot through me; a further delay would allow the Director more time to come up with an alternative plan. Fortunately, Jasper was smarter than that. 'Actually,' he said stiffly, 'this gives me all the more reason to release my findings and my recommendations as soon as possible.'

'Recommendations?' The Director's dismay was making her give away too many of her true feelings. 'As if we have any choice about implementing them,' she spat.

Something subtle altered in Jasper's physique. He stared down at the Director and I shivered. 'It's interesting,' he murmured, 'that when faced with the brutal killing of one your own, your main concern is my report. If anything, the events that have occurred here prove there is even greater need for it than before. You have created a culture where your faery godmothers and godfathers are running scared. Your last recruit was sent to deal with clients without any real training or any understanding of the rules and regulations...'

She rolled her eyes. 'Saffron Sawyer,' she hissed. 'I might have known you'd bring her into this sooner or later. Until her arrival, we had none of these problems.'

'Bullshit. She was brought in to help you deal with your problems. Against my better judgment, I might add.'

Her face contorted. 'You have no understanding of what it's like to be a faery godmother!'

He regarded her implacably. 'Sadly, Director, neither do you. The Office of Faery Godmothers needs to change. And believe me, it *will* change, whether you like it or not. Figgy's death demands it. Frankly, if it wouldn't cause even more trauma amongst your faeries, I would include your removal as part of my recommendations. I strongly suggest that you consider your position. It might be time to start planning for your retirement.'

He turned away and marched over to Figgy's body, picking her up with surprising gentleness and cradling her against his chest. Then, without a backward glance at the Director, he spun his magic and they both disappeared.

The Director remained where she was for a long moment,

her fists clenching and unclenching and her expression tight. I wished I knew what was going on inside her head. As far as I could see, her only remaining hope was that her attempts to blackmail me would prove fruitful. No chance: if that was the case, she'd already lost.

Eventually, when the sounds of the police entering the building filtered up, the Director sighed heavily and invoked the necessary magic to disappear. Once she'd gone, my shoulders sagged.

'Saffron,' Vincent whispered, 'what do we do now?'

'We leave,' I told him. 'There are no barriers to my magic now. I can transport us away. You don't have to worry.'

'What about everything else? What about that woman? Your boss is vicious.'

'Yeah,' I said sadly. 'She is.' I glanced at the spot where Figgy had fallen; there was no longer any evidence that she'd ever been here. The police would label Adwell's death as suicide and the world would move on. Sooner or later, it always did.

'I'm sorry, Figgy,' I whispered.

It was time to go.

CHAPTER
TWENTY-FIVE

Pumpkin and I took shelter from the driving rain on one of the wide doorsteps not far from the office. Despite my best efforts to keep both of us dry, my hair was plastered to my face and drips were sliding down the back of my neck and edging their way down my spine.

Every minute or so, Pumpkin shook himself and splattered me with more droplets. I'd long since given up trying to avoid his showery efforts; there had come a point where I was so drenched that a little more water didn't make any difference. It was irritating that my socks and shoes were squelchy but I supposed that I should be grateful my feet didn't feel cold. I'd take every silver lining I could and hug it hard. I needed something to maintain my sanity.

Kneeling down, I looked Pumpkin in the eyes. His tail was drooping between his legs and his ears, which were normally pricked up and alert, were flat against his head. 'Hey,' I said softly.

His chocolate-brown eyes gazed into mine and he let out a tiny whine.

'I'm not going anywhere,' I told him. 'I get it now. I get that you've been too afraid to let me get close. You lost Rose and that hurt. It hurt more than anything else in the world, and you were too frightened to get close in case the same thing happened to me.'

Pumpkin's tail thumped once, splashing into a puddle. Neither of us paid it any attention.

'I'm not going anywhere,' I said. 'You hear me? You and I are in this for the long haul. No matter what happens, I won't abandon you. We're going to stick together. All we've got is each other.'

Pumpkin blinked once. I nodded and, very gently, reached out and stroked the top of his head. The little dog didn't shy away; instead he inched forward until his body was leaning against mine. Emboldened, I wrapped my arms around him and squeezed. Pumpkin raised his head and gave my nose a delicate lick.

'I love you too, you daft mutt,' I whispered. I swallowed and glanced round at the office building less than fifty metres away. 'It's now or never, buddy. Let's face the music.'

I ignored the fact that it wasn't 'Ride of the Valkyries' pounding through my skull but instead the more muted and sombre tones of Barber's 'Adagio For Strings' and stood up. Pumpkin nudged my leg and I smiled. 'We've got this.'

He wagged his tail. Then we crossed the street and made a beeline for the office entrance.

Mrs Jardine was standing just inside the door, rather than sitting in her usual spot behind her desk. 'Good morning, Saffron.'

I inclined my head. 'Good morning, Miranda.'

'You're dripping all over my floor.'

I drew out my wand and gazed at it. Then I sniffed and put it away again, lifting my left hand and waving it at both

Pumpkin and myself. Warm air gusted round us, drying everything in an instant.

Mrs Jardine drew in a sharp breath before looking at me with sorrowful eyes. 'Don't tell them,' she said quietly. 'Don't tell them you can do that.' She turned and walked to her desk, her heels clicking.

I followed her, reaching for the book and pressing my thumbprint to register my presence. Behind us, the door opened again. I heard Pumpkin growl and looked up.

Alicia shook her umbrella and walked slowly towards us. She was bare-faced for the first time since I'd known her, and she was wearing old tracksuit bottoms and an over-sized sweatshirt. Her usually gleaming blonde hair was dull and limp.

'Nobody will blame you if you take a few days off,' I said. 'Figgy was your friend. We all know that. Everyone will understand if you're not here.'

Alicia drew herself up, steel in her gaze. She was still in there; she was grieving but, deep down, she was the same Alicia she'd always been. She'd get through this. All of us would.

'We're short-handed now,' she said. 'And the Office of Faery Godmothers doesn't stop its work for any reason. My clients need me.' She paused. 'Figgy was my friend,' she said in a clear voice, 'but she also betrayed us. I will mourn her but I won't let her death change who I am.'

I lifted my chin. 'I don't think Figgy betrayed anyone. One day, when the truth is revealed, I think you'll find that she was a better faery than any of us. She wouldn't have gone to Art Adwell to take a bribe. She had no need to. She wasn't like that.'

In a small voice, Alicia replied, 'That's exactly what I keep thinking.'

I leaned over to hug her but Alicia held up her hands to ward me off, her expression switching without warning to imperious haughtiness. 'What do you think you're doing?' she asked. 'I'm a Beauchamp. Beauchamps are above public displays of affection.' She tossed her head and glared at me but I couldn't fail to note the faint quiver in her bottom lip.

I immediately stepped back. I understood entirely. She was barely holding it together. It had clearly taken every ounce of will Alicia possessed – and she possessed it in spades – to come into work this morning. Sympathy of any kind would break her. Alicia needed to allow herself to cry – but it had to be on her terms. We were all part of the same team, but we were individuals as well, with our own facades to maintain and fuck-ups to fret over.

'If you ever need to talk, Alicia,' I said, 'I'll always be here.'

'Ugh.' She wrinkled her nose. 'I can't imagine why I'd talk to *you.*'

I smiled slightly and turned towards the lift, Pumpkin by my side. I was already pressing the button to call it down when I heard Alicia whisper, 'Thank you, Saffron.'

I paused long enough to let her know that I'd heard her, then I stepped into the lift without looking back.

Almost all of the faery godmothers were already present, although nobody appeared to be working. Most of them were milling around in small clusters, talking to each other in hushed tones. A few were at their desks but, as far as I could tell, they were merely sitting quietly and contemplating matters.

There was a wide gap around Figgy's desk, as if nobody dared to go near it for fear of being tainted. I couldn't stop myself staring at it. An empty coffee cup sat to one side with the cold dregs of her final drink still inside it. A brightly patterned scarf hung over the back of her chair, waiting for her to return, scoop it up and wind it round her neck.

'Saffron?'

I blinked up at Delilah, who had approached without me even realising.

'Are you alright?'

I nodded. 'I am. How about you? Are you alright?'

'Of course.' She smiled briskly. 'We are faery godmothers, Saffron.'

I didn't respond.

Billy appeared from the far end of the office carrying a cardboard box in his arms. He walked slowly towards Figgy's desk and, as he drew close, every head in the place turned towards him. He didn't falter, despite the weight of everyone's eyes; he simply put the box down and started carefully filling it with her things.

I held up my head and strode over to join him. I picked up Figgy's scarf and folded it while Billy peeled off her stickers from the edge of her computer screen.

'She was a good faery godmother,' I said quietly.

Billy's answer was gruff. 'She could have ruined everything. Not just for this office but for all faeries.'

I held my gaze. 'It wasn't her fault.'

He didn't say anything. I placed Figgy's scarf in the box and turned away. There were other matters to take care of.

Angela beckoned to me from the doorway of the HR office. She was holding a piece of paper in her hands. 'In the case of events such as these,' she said quietly, 'there are procedures that need to be followed. You will have a formal debriefing, conducted by the Director herself. You will also be required to sign this.'

I squinted at it. 'What is it?'

'It's a liability thing,' she said dismissively. 'It's to ensure that the events of the last day or two go no further. You were involved with Art Adwell from the beginning, even if you had nothing to do with what happened afterwards.'

It was on the tip of my tongue to reveal everything - but I had no proof. Until I did, I couldn't make a move; the Director had too much power and any allegations I made would fall on deaf ears. Things wouldn't always be that way, though. I'd made Figgy a promise and I was determined to keep it.

'You mean you're going to sweep what's happened under the carpet so that it's never spoken of again?'

'There are lessons that can be learnt,' Angela said, not meeting my eyes. 'But essentially, yes. That's what is going to happen. It's the Director's preference. If you can just sign...'

I twisted round and walked away.

'Saffron!' Angela called.

I ignored her and kept moving.

Pumpkin knew exactly where I was heading. He tugged on his lead, all but dragging me there. The door was open and I could still smell a touch of cinnamon spice. Of course, there was no sign of Jasper and all his belongings had been packed up into a box, painfully similar to the one on Figgy's desk.

I glanced inside it. Then I reached into my pocket and pulled out the little dandelion I'd grabbed from St Clement's Park on my way to work. I laid it on top of the stacked books inside the box, feeling my heart twist painfully.

'Saffron?' Adeline questioned from the door. 'Are you ready? The Director would like to speak to you now.'

I gazed at the lonely dandelion for another moment before straightening my shoulders. 'Yes,' I said. 'I'm ready.'

I walked back through the office. This time Pumpkin was in no hurry and, instead of him yanking me forward, I practically had to drag him. In the end I bent down and scooped him up into my arms. He gave me another small lick as Rupert wandered towards us, a bright red badge pinned to his suit which proclaimed that we should all 'Beat Sexism Now'. I smiled slightly at him but I didn't stop.

'Before you go in,' Adeline said, 'I think you should know that she doesn't always have your best interests at heart. I know it might be hard to hear but, please, Saffron, don't trust her.'

I understood what it cost Adeline to admit that the Director wasn't the epitome of all that was good and beautiful about the faery godmothers. I gave her a small smile. 'Thank you.' Then I bowed and continued on my way.

The Director's office door was open and I could see her sitting behind her desk, reading through some paperwork. I didn't knock or cough or say anything; I simply walked in, deposited Pumpkin on the floor and waited.

She didn't look up or acknowledge me. This was a power trip and she wanted to force me to acknowledge that she was in charge. Right now that meant I had to cool my heels while she pretended to work. I didn't let it bother me; I was far beyond that.

After what felt like several minutes, the Director put down the papers and looked up. 'Ah, Saffron, I'm glad you're here. Close the door, please.'

I didn't move a muscle. She raised an eyebrow and reached for her wand, which was nestled in a custom-built holder. If I wasn't mistaken, the decoration on the holder's exterior was ivory. Figured. She lifted the wand up and flicked the tip of it, a breath of magic extending towards the door so that it closed itself. I remained exactly where I was, without betraying so much as a hint of a twitch.

'The events of last night have been tragic indeed,' she murmured. 'Who would have thought that Figgy of all people would end up being a traitor? I always thought the girl had nothing more than candy floss between her ears. Instead it appears she was some sort of Mata Hari.'

She sighed. 'Anyway, all's well that ends well. We now have a more open dialogue with the trolls. I spoke to Ethan on the phone this morning, so you'll be pleased to know that you are no longer the sole conduit between our two races. He is satisfied that the Adwell threat has been neutralised and that we are taking steps to ensure this sort of thing does not happen again. Everyone makes mistakes and he has acknowledged that. In the end, the Office of Faery Godmothers has triumphed. As it always does and always will.'

I felt a breath of relief that Ethan had done as I'd asked. I hadn't been sure that he would and he'd been confused when I'd called him after I left Adwell's home. Regardless of what happened with the Director, I couldn't let the trolls march into the shadows again. It was even possible that they could affect this office positively in the future.

The Director gazed at me over her glasses. 'Now as to the other matter. I assume you have made a decision? I know that you must be stunned by Figgy's passing and the manner of her betrayal, but time is ticking. We can delay no longer. The Devil's Advocate will release his report very shortly and appropriate action must be taken before that happens. My faery godmothers have been through enough – they don't need the stress of his recommendations to worry about as well. Let's nip it in the bud and put a stop to his plans. I know you'll do the right thing, Saffron.'

'I will do the right thing.' My voice was louder than I intended and the Director winced slightly.

'So you will make a public accusation of harassment immediately?'

'No,' I said. 'I won't. Because it's not true.'

The Director's face whitened. If I didn't play along, she had nowhere left to go. She would have to accept Jasper's report, no matter what it entailed. Whether she knew it or not, I'd won the battle. But I hadn't won the war.

'I suggest you reconsider.'

'I don't think I will.' I waited to see if she would threaten me further. There was something oddly diminished about her, as if Figgy's death had laid bare all her failings. She couldn't pretend any longer that all she cared about was the well-being of her team.

'I'm very disappointed to hear that,' she bit out. 'You could have had a great future here.'

I shrugged. 'I guess we'll never know.' Before she could speak again and fire me, I reached into the pocket where the dandelion had been and drew out an envelope. 'The Devil's Advocate stated publicly yesterday morning that he believed I should leave this job. You can't bring accusations of nepotism against someone who loudly proclaimed that I shouldn't be here. Equally,' I continued, 'you can't sack me if I've already resigned.'

I dropped the envelope onto her desk, pulled off my lanyard and tossed it on top. Then I pulled out my wand and, without a moment's pause, added it to the pile.

The Director kept her eyes trained on mine. 'Nobody,' she said, 'has ever resigned from this office. This is the Office of Faery Godmothers. We are the crème de la crème. If you resign, you'll never get another job. Anywhere. I'll see to that.'

'You do what you have to do,' I said quietly. 'And I'll do what I have to.'

Just you wait and see, I promised silently. Sooner or later I'd see her burn in hell for what she'd done.

'You're making a massive mistake.'

'No,' I told her. 'I don't think I am. I'm not cut out to be a faery godmother. I thought I was going to be the best but all I do is mess things up. People have died because of my actions. It's better for everyone if I'm not here.' I glanced down. 'Ready to go, Pumpkin?'

He got up off his haunches and regarded me seriously. Then he cocked his leg against the Director's desk. She hissed.

I raised my shoulders. 'My dog does what he has to do as well.' I gave him a nod of approval and we walked out.

I didn't bother clearing out my desk; there was nothing in it that I needed or cared about. I didn't bother saying farewell to any of my colleagues, although Alicia stood up and watched me as I marched towards the lift. I wouldn't make a scene. This office had already had more than enough drama to last a lifetime.

Mrs Jardine stared at me as I exited the lift and strolled past her, whistling. I opened the front door and walked out of the building. The rain had finally stopped its incessant pouring and the skies were starting to clear. Towards the end of the street, a sliver of golden sunshine was emerging.

I glanced back at the Office of Faery Godmothers. It had been fun while it lasted.

This wasn't the end of the story, however. After all, I wasn't dead yet. I'd ensure the Director got her comeuppance. It wouldn't happen today – but it would happen.

About the Author

After teaching English literature in the UK, Japan and Malaysia, Helen Harper left behind the world of education following the worldwide success of her Blood Destiny series of books. She is a professional member of the Alliance of Independent Authors and writes full time, thanking her lucky stars every day that's she lucky enough to do so!

Helen has always been a book lover, devouring science fiction and fantasy tales when she was a child growing up in Scotland.

She currently lives in Edinburgh with far too many cats – not to mention the dragons, fairies, demons, wizards and vampires that seem to keep appearing from nowhere.